The Syllabus of Errors

Or

Twelve Stories of Obsession, Loss and Getting In A State

ASHLEY STOKES

Dear Tom
Hope you enjoy The Syllabus

Best wishes
Ashley

UNTHANK

First published in 2013
By Unthank Books
www.unthankbooks.com

Printed in England by Lightning Source, Milton Keynes

A CIP record for this book is available from the British Library

Any resemblance to persons fictional or real who are living, dead or
undead is purely coincidental.

ISBN 978-0-9564223-9-2

Cover design by Jenny Swindells

CONTENTS

Introduction
– David Rose –

Lovers of *mitteleuropa* period fiction, or of contemporary fiction, or - ideally - both, will love this book. It's Joseph Roth meets Roberto Bolaño, and it is simply wonderful.

Actually, not so simply. And the comparisons are not hyperbole; I choose them with care.

Roth, writing through the Twenties and early Thirties, wrote exhaustively in his fiction of the slow build-up to the collapse of the Austro-Hungarian Empire and its civilization in the First World War. It wasn't a case of being overtaken by History - he used the material for its premonitory parallels with the build-up to the Second; the hysteria of *fin-de-siècle* Vienna ("the laboratory for the scientific study of apocalypse" according to Karl Kraus) foreshadowing the violence of Weimar Berlin and the greater collapse of European civilization.

Stokes now shunts the parallel a stage further: Weimar Berlin, Fascist Rome paralleling present-day London. Many of the stories in *The Syllabus Of Errors* end violently, on the streets of London as much as of Berlin. Fanciful?

George Steiner, in *In Bluebeard's Castle*, described the First War as a willed breaking of the tensions of the enervating ennui of a generation of peace after the Napoleonic era, breeding a "nostalgia for disaster". Mainland Britain has now had a generation (65+ years) of peace. Maybe the riots, gang war, street knifings, flirtation with terrorism are a similar snapping of tension.

In the first story, *Island Gardens*, the central character, an English teacher teaching in Berlin, now back in London, cruising around Piccadilly Circus in search of his Russian girlfriend, an ex-pupil in Berlin, remembers explaining to her that German had as many words for *anxiety* as English does for *horrible people*. We are beginning, perhaps to need them in English. *Ahnen* in particular, which is what he is feeling - a vague, unspecified dread.

In another story, *Tomorrow Belongs To Me*, a history teacher goes to the fancy-dress party of his Head of Department disguised as *M*, the Peter Lorre character in the Fritz Lang film. An unknown girl dressed as Sally Bowles, "not the one from Cabaret, the original, in the book", recognizes his disguise, and the need it disguises, the only one to do so. They slink off from the party together to enact a scene from a movie of their own.

So maybe we should add Isherwood's name to the other two? But Isherwood spent his life as a tourist. The characters in Stokes, all of them, are exiles, exiles from their own lives, trying to reconnect by their search for roots, precedents.

So we are back to Roth, the supreme writer of exile; and to Bolaño, the modern equivalent, his twin themes being exile and violence, and the links between them.

Like Bolaño, Stokes dares his readers to follow him. In one story set wholly in Weimar Berlin, *The Prettiest Girl In Berlin*, an ex-soldier, mentally and physically maimed, prosthetically-transformed, wanders the streets, winding through the bloody shoot-outs between Communist Spartacists and Right-wing *Freikorps* in search of a pre-war love. It takes huge risks of obscurity but they are entirely justified; we share the bewilderment of the soldier to the end. It's an immensely powerful story, a George Grosz painting come to life, to music by Hanns Eisler.

Another, set in pre-Fascist Rome, involves a mural artist and Mussolini supporter so vividly drawn I wondered if he were modelled on the Fascist propagandist artist Mario Sironi, but the links are tenuous, and besides, the character, Dario Inchesa, is too strongly delineated from within for it to matter.

These are a series of linked, overlapping stories, but the links function subliminally. Motifs recur: a metal jaw, for example, transmuted from literality to figure of speech; characters appear as extras in a story, then reappear as leading actors in their own, many of them teachers - of English, History or Art - many with an interest, professional or personal, in Hitler Studies.

But in the last story there is the teasing possibility that there is a stronger link binding them together, as the product of the imagination of its narrator, yet another Hitler Studies academic whose teenage interest in the subject was fuelled by a friendship with a (possible) ex-Nazi.

This, though, is not a reductive "explanation" of the book: the preceding stories are just too powerful, too closely imagined, too fictionally autonomous to be reduced to a "Usual Suspects"-type unravelling. It is, rather, yet another layer of significance.

And this story brings us back again to Bolaño, whose funniest, most inventive book, *Nazi Literature In The Americas, The Syllabus Of Errors* invokes, perhaps confronts. Stokes more than stands up to the comparison.

There's a verve and crackling wit throughout, sharp observation and pinpoint characterization lacing the eloquence of loss. There is brilliantly witty dialogue, but there not just for its wit but to reveal depths of the characters, dimensions of their predicaments. And a wonderfully wide range of cultural allusion.

But it's the eloquence that lingers when you finish the book. In the story *Abyssinia*, Mellis, an Art Historian facing redundancy describes his first encounter with a soul-mate, Caitlin, whom he later loses to the university's philistine Human Resources manager. It's in a small provincial art gallery displaying an installation, *The Archive Of Water*.

That installation - normally an art form Mellis despises - touches him as it touches Caitlin. It consists in a series of glass tubes containing meltwater from Greenlandic glaciers, some tubes clouded, some sparklingly pure, but in all of them, the "waters are like memory" with "the vanishing point elsewhere".

This functions as a perfect description of this book.

Island Gardens

At the railings the boy with the case was still mauling the red headed girl in the red baseball cap. This time Grant noticed her knuckles. They stood out like the spine of a fish as she gripped the boy's cheek. His arm was stuffed up her green vest top and when his elbow jerked the hem of the vest lifted. Each time Grant walked by the vest had ridden up a little higher. At this rate it would be over her face by the time he next came round. He laughed at this. He had to laugh at something and turned back to face Eros once more.

The steps were flush with girls: girls in mini-dresses, girls who fanned themselves with thick magazines and others who stared at the sky as if something there stared back. There were plenty of the girls with Oompa-Loompa spray-on tans and boyfriends slathered with brand names. At the language school in Berlin where he taught Grant called these proliferating trans-global types the Loomparettes and the Adverts. It felt peculiar not to have their attention now, Mr Woods, the English teacher with his word games and conversational exercises and what V called his so English English. He was starting to sweat so paused in the shade of the statue. Still no sign of V.

She should have been here three-quarters of an hour ago, but she'd never visited London before and the sheer density of the crowds funnelling through the West End disorientated even him. In sixteen years he'd come back to England only for funerals and on those occasions spent no time in London. The city appeared transformed and disrupted. The Far Eastern futurist style of the new, high-rise buildings unnerved him, as did the strange North American atmosphere at street level. Every second shop was now a coffee shop and every coffee shop was the same coffee shop. He might easily lose his bearings, so a perfectly understandable problem could be delaying V. Her map-reading skills may have let her down. There was overcrowding on the 'U-train' as she called it, or she'd left her mobile somewhere, or deleted his number by mistake or misunderstood the arrangement. He had called her five times already and left two voicemails.

A feeling congealed in his gut. The Germans have a word for this feeling. They call it *ahnen*: a sensation that something is wrong without knowledge of its cause. The Germans have as many words for anxiety as the English have for horrible people. When he'd once explained this to V she'd giggled so much she spilt great splashes of red wine on his floor.

He found a space on the lowest step between a Loomparette and her Advert. V liked these words as well. She said she enjoyed learning all of the silly names he gave to things and people. It thrilled him that she liked the way he spoke and what he did for a living and didn't like his oldest friend Alex call him an 'underpaid lingo gypsy'. Since arriving back in London, four days ago now, he had missed that sense in Berlin that he was creating a private language with V. Kicking around in Alex's spare flat this morning, waiting for the time when he could leave for their rendezvous on the steps, he admitted to himself that the shilly-shallying was over.

At the railings the long thin case slithered from the boy's shoulder. It dangled from his elbow, twirling as he now put both his hands up inside the green vest. Her spiny knuckles flexed as she massaged the seat of his tracksuit bottoms. The strap then slipped over the boy's elbow towards his wrist. The end of the case clunked on the pavement.

Grant wondered what was in the case. Maybe a collapsible snooker cue. The boy did not look like a snooker player, though he might be a pool player. Maybe earlier he'd fleeced some ageing hotshot and was celebrating here with Knuckles, his beguiling muse. They were existentialists. They went from town to town and lived in cheap hotels with names like Zodiac Heights or The Magic Mountain. They would head out straight from the statue of love at the heart of the city to where the desert meets the ocean and the breakers roll like satin on the ancient sands. Or perhaps they had simply hooked up in a pool hall. Her eyes swam into view in the glass front of a vending machine. He bought her a *Twix* and it was life without compromise thereafter. Maybe he'd wagered his soul for her hand in a green-baize showdown with a locksmith called Flinty 'The Octopus' Ray.

He'd not been inside a pool hall since he'd last lived in London. After they graduated he shared an unheated flat with Alex for six months. During that summer, before Alex became the sort of bloke he is now, with two properties in London and a holiday home in Umbria, the trader, bespoke-suit and bonus-flush Alex who Grant imagined was at this moment high up in one of those Far Eastern futurist buildings but wishing he was down here in the Circus waiting for a Russian girl with a beautiful name and beautiful

4

eyes and a lovely turn of phrase, and despite being from Berkhampstead and educated at Oundle public school and Churchill College, Cambridge and whose father was Britain's ambassador to Indonesia Alex decided to make his living by trouncing the peasants at pool. He wasted his days in a spider hole of a venue behind London Bridge station that went by the name of the *4Play*. To reach the required standard, he said, all he needed to do was crack the jargon and spit like a player. Vicariously Grant discovered that a pool hall has a food chain of 'algae', 'guppies', 'fish' and 'sharks', that there were 'ghost balls', and 'bait shots' and something called 'riding the nine', that a ball with a bit of spin was an 'English'. Eventually Alex gave up the gig, man, because he'd been trousered by too many handcuff artists with names like The Cockman or Double Geegees. Meanwhile, Grant decided to do something useful with his talents and decamped to St Petersburg to teach English to newly liberated surgeons and electrical engineers. He thought of Alex trying to put a bit of "English' on a white ball and laughed quietly to himself despite the crushingly heavy sensation hardening in the pit of his stomach. When he became aware of someone standing in front of him the sensation started to lift.

The vest girl wore at least three silverish rings on each of her fingers that rode up against the knuckles. Grant couldn't tell how old she was. The cap was pulled over her eyes. The boy was late-teens at most, shaven-headed and seemed to have far too many plates and ridges in his skull. His tracksuit bottoms, a stylish white affair with navy blue piping had a great mass of unravelling cotton spilling out from one of the pockets.

'You well bate, blood,' said the boy, separating his fingers and stabbing his thumb upwards.

'Pardon?' said Grant. As he stood up it crossed his mind that back in Alex's unforgiving pool hall world this one's opening shot would have been a 'Reverse English'.

'You want a piece you step up, standard?' said the Reverse English.

'Standard what?' said Grant. 'Standard lamp? Standard Oil? The Standard Model of Particle Physics?'

'You done now, blood, I's banking.'

'I think there's been a misunderstanding here,' said Grant. 'I think there's something that you need to have a quiet think about, so I'm going to walk away to let you do that.'

He checked around for V and then strode briskly towards Leicester Square. He would cross by the Angus Steak House and track back to the steps. The Reverses would move off. They would go for a Happy Meal or get horny again and make a baby called Tupac or Fing. A brood of black cabs made a buzzing sound as he waited at the crossing for the lights to change. Then the heat of the day seemed to press down on him. He wished he'd punched the exhibitionist little twat's lights out. Something came back to him. Being fourteen, fifteen. Kids like the Reverse English rolling their shoulders across a pedestrianized area after the bad film had ended. Their bones and baseball caps and the low-voltage slappers they impressed.

By the time he actually made it to the other side of the road he'd told himself that this language was a dead language. He was nearly forty years old. He did not live there any more. He did not even live here. He knew that any sort of altercation always fired him up. In the moment he did the adult thing, but afterwards wished he'd acted with certainty and force. He paused under some arches and asked himself what Alex would have done. Alex would have threatened to sue them. He would have shouted in their faces that he lives in Blackheath and is a yellow belt in karate. Grant sniggered and was about to wander back to the steps when he noticed something oblong and slender poking up from behind the people filing across the zebra: the Reverse English's cue case.

He tried to walk away towards Eros. The pavement was clotted with people. If he waited for them to clear the Reverses would catch up with him. The back of his neck was hot with sweat as he darted into the entranceway of a mall. Shops on either side stretched towards an escalator housed in a giant transparent tube. He wanted to use shop windows to check behind him for the Reverses but the viral coffee bars, day-glo sweet shops and tourist-tat merchants were all open-fronted. It was as bad as the mall under Alexanderplatz U-Bahn where you can buy fish and chips in a baguette. On the escalator, halfway up the tube, he looked back. There they were, the Reverses jogging towards the first of the gliding, glimmering slats.

At the top he found himself in some sort of amusement arcade. There were rows of fruit machines and games machines and grabbers and sirens. Several Euro dance-anthems combined to sound like the incessant clinking of chains or money-belts. He hurried along an aisle of flashing machines where Advert Dads helped their kids put money into slots. Ducking behind a pillar, he watched the Reverses emerge at the escalator and start to scan around. Knuckles then followed the Reverse English into a chamber of lights and disco on the other side. Grant stayed hidden. This was stupid, ridiculous. He was Mister Woods and nearly forty. He'd lived in Berlin for two years and had lived in Russia and Finland and Sweden and Spain and he shouldn't be making this easy for bullies or letting them think this was a reasonable way to behave. He was supposed to be a teacher, an example. He counted to ten and then skulked back to the escalator. He didn't see them, so he assumed they couldn't see him.

He checked over his shoulder as he walked back towards Piccadilly Circus. At Eros the traffic whirled around the Loomparettes and the Adverts and the same girls still stared at the sky. If you stand at Piccadilly Circus for long enough you will always meet someone you know. His dad had told him this. His dad also said that London is a vast and spreading cancer of cardsharps and greedy so-and-sos on the take, stabbing you in the back and the front and slicing your legs from under you, leaving you to the wind. His dad would not have found himself here, intimidated by undernourished children and fretting about foreign skirt like V.

Grant made two more orbits and realized that she'd probably arrived while the heroes of philosophy were chasing him around a bollocks mall. She'd think he was messing her about. She would have stropped off to drink all day in some crap country-themed bar that he'd hate. Now he would never be able to say it, change her mind, get her to stay in Berlin because of how he felt about her. He decided not to linger any longer with the Loomparettes and the Adverts. This time he couldn't bring himself to phone V and listen to the message. He already knew that her phone was switched off. He would go back to the flat, meet Alex after work and talk it through over a pint. In the Underground station, in the tunnel and recorded by CCTV Grant dawdled hands in pockets towards his platform as a Scots piper in a black kilt and Tam O'Shanter played a stuttering drone.

When the tube came the carriage smelt of bleach and hospitals. Grant sat swaying gently among the other passengers. He felt again a rush of anger about the Reverses and being forced from Eros for no bloody reason at all and missing V and his last chance. Then he took a few deep breaths. She hadn't turned up because she hadn't wanted to. He shouldn't have followed her here. If she didn't even want to meet up and visit his old haunts then she certainly wouldn't want to live with him in Berlin or anywhere else. It wouldn't be like he imagined anyway, living with V, like where he was heading now was not like he imagined beforehand. The flat was in Island Gardens, a place that like the coffee shops hardly seemed to exist much before Grant left London. But it conjured images of actual islands. Islands connected by elegant bridges like the Ponte Vecchio or the Bridge of Sighs, a low and watery city of balconies and drooping foliage and calm little squares never far from the river. Venice and Amsterdam. Those islet-parks that float in the Danube at Budapest. The St. Petersburg that Peter the Great magicked from a swamp by the sheer force of his charisma. Grant had always wanted to live in a city like that and love in a city like St Petersburg. When he was seventeen he used to lie on his bed and listen to the sound of an ice cream van prowling the estate playing the theme music to *Doctor Zhivago* and he had dreamed of St Petersburg and its islands and girls. Varvara was from St Petersburg.

When he'd first arrived in St Petersburg it had only recently changed its name from Leningrad. Walking the Nevsky Prospekt or pacing the streets between the Hermitage and the Admiralty during those first few months he thought he had changed, too. He'd escaped from the world of Alex and chums like he'd previously escaped the world of home. But he had not been able to experience St Petersburg with V. He had not waited for her bundled up in fur hat and coat outside the Moscow Railway Station, or stood hand in hand as melting icicles fell from the facade of the Kazan Cathedral, or stood on Anichikov Bridge watching that particular light that glints on the Fontanka River. He didn't even know her then. He met her in Berlin, in class.

He had walked with her along an avenue of tall trees where ahead the streetlamps high in the branches shone like fireflies. They had walked together around the Victory Column and the Tiergarten, talking, laughing, analysing, comparing. They shared a bottle in his kitchenette and drank wine out of whisky tumblers and when she leaned across the table and kissed him he felt something that he'd not experienced before or had forgotten. Her climbing out of bed in the middle of the night woke him and he'd watched her pale body, her moonlit hips and the shadow that clung between her shoulder blades. At the window she breathed her cigarette smoke against the glass. It gave a bluish shine to the silhouette of her hair. He had been stupid, he knew, to place such emphasis on that one night.

As he got off the train at Canary Wharf he wanted to somehow meet V earlier, in St Petersburg. But when he was there he couldn't have known her. It would have been more than culturally difficult but horribly wrong to have known her. She wasn't even herself then. She was only three years old.

This made him feel pathetic and middle-aged as he crossed the plaza and headed for the overland station where he would make a connection for Island Gardens. The plaza was hectic with people, its bars and restaurants bustling and full. Later, several of the young men and women enjoying a Friday afternoon drink on the plaza – none of whom, as Grant noted, were Loomparettes or Adverts – would confirm that they remembered a man as distinct as Grant going in the direction of the station, locked up in his own thoughts, muttering to himself, unswerving and never once looking back.

On the platform he studied the departures display and the destinations of the oncoming trains: Mudchute, Mudchute, Island Gardens 5 Mins. He paced around the benches and the clustered office workers paused in the silvery light. He started to think backwards from V and about Eli from Helsinki who was ten years younger than him but still wanted to dedicate herself to filling condoms with plaster of Paris to make weird alien egg-like sculptures. Then Franka from Delft. They met in Spain. She was four years younger but wanted a baby right this minute and that couldn't be when he was still looking for somewhere he'd not yet found, somewhere luminous. And then Alice. They were the same age as each other and students and there were strange rituals like punting and college balls. She had talked often about what they were going to do for the rest of their lives together. That all collapsed in a pulse of acrimony that still shamed him seventeen years later.

When the second Mudchute train slipped out of the station he crept to the edge of the platform and stared at the rails. It occurred to him that maybe he was still trying to impress Alice. That feeling of *ahnen* recurred, but this time it made him shiver. He heard the train approaching. He felt himself swaying. The train curved into the station, disturbing the air. The grey streak of it flowed inches in front of his face. The people inside were blurs and smudges. He looked to his left as if bracing himself. He blinked as he noticed the stairway leading down to the platforms. At first he thought it couldn't be them but then the cue case gave them away. Halfway down the steps already, The Reverses picked up speed as the doors of the train swished open.

He was relieved that the carriage was so crowded that he had to stand and could keep a watch on the doors. He couldn't see The Reverses as the train shuddered onwards and everyone inside jostled this way and that. They might not have made the train in time, he reasoned. Nor was it beyond the realms of possibility that their reappearance was a coincidence and they lived on this line or further south of the river. He still thought of Island Gardens as a terminus but the railway had been extended while he was away. As the train coursed through three stations oblongs of glass and tessellated steel shunted past. He noticed how the new office buildings, stacks of black and white sugar cubes dwarfed what was left of the original dockers' housing. A sequence of sharp, triangular roofs morphed into a treeline of poplars that dipped and rose against the sky like waveforms on a heart monitor. At Mudchute, when the doors closed he felt a jolt that stiffened his shoulders and coiled in his stomach. The Reverses were standing at the other end of his carriage, a few metres away. They were holding hands. They let go of each other and their arms fell to their sides. The case was strapped to the Reverse English's back like an archer's quiver.

They didn't seem to notice him. They did not hunt around for him like they had in the mall. Nor did they acknowledge or even seem to notice that he was there. They sat down on a two-seater bench. The boy removed the case from his back and put it between his knees. Knuckles took off her hat and draped it over the dusty black square at the end of the case. Her hair fell free. It was long and golden-red; crimped tresses that reminded Grant slightly of the girls in Pre-Raphaelite paintings. Without the brim or the frown and the grimace she was actually quite pretty. He imagined her as a cut-out in a girls comic and removing the vest and the sweat pants and the mannish grey trainers and clipping to her outline a flowing maroon dress, soft pumps and a daisy chain for her hair. He could place her in a diorama: an orchard on a hillside with standing stones and the moon. A flicker of a smile passed over her face as she patted the cap on the case and then turned towards the Reverse English. They started at it again. The knuckles bristled at the nape of his neck. His hand snaked up her vest.

She could probably do better for herself than the Reverse English with his skullish head and mangled diction. And V could do better than the barman from Auckland or Galway who she was by now no doubt already falling for, or the scary Russian hitman she was still in bed with. It had always been so hard to negotiate for him, so slippery and faltering, so boom and bust, and then for others so easeful and expected that the public could become a private place.

He tried not to spy on them. He tried looking at his shoes or out of the window but his gaze was quickly drawn back. They were going somewhere. Dazzled, they would alight soon, somewhere at the end of the line. They were probably as happy as they could be at this moment in their lives and were wrapped up in something that if only for a moment was much bigger than they were. He tried to forgive what had happened at Eros and in the mall. He tried to accept that they were not yet fully formed or responsible. He realized then that he could not imagine what their lives were like, could not even speculate on how the Reverses saw the world or this carriage, this journey, the others here, the man beneath the statue and the sky that was becoming grey as the afternoon faded.

The train came to a halt at Island Gardens. People shuffled off. People climbed aboard and others shifted to accommodate them. The Reverses did not stop what they were doing, still engrossed in themselves and their bodies and warmth. Grant felt something lift from him as he stepped off the train.

Outside the station he hesitated on the concourse and took a long look at where he'd already decided he would live from now on. There were unpretentious curved apartment buildings, only two or three stories high, a convenience store, sycamore trees and a little park to his left. The flat in Island Gardens was between tenants. Alex would let it for a reasonable rent. He wasn't sure he liked the idea of turning Alex into his landlord but it wouldn't be forever, only until he found himself a decent job. He could retrain. He could teach languages in a proper state school and give something back. He wouldn't even have to socialize that much with Alex's friends if he didn't want to and there were millions of women here, millions of women staring up at the sky.

He became aware of the dryness of his throat as a dull pulsating sound that seemed to have always been there grew louder and louder behind him. He was about to cross the road to buy a carton of juice when the sound of footsteps vanished. He turned back to the station. They were standing in front of the ticket barrier, flushed and breathless, her hair concealed by the cap again and the Reverse's face gripped with some anger or intention. He reached for the case, swung it around to his thigh.

At first Grant headed for the park to get out of their way. There was no one sat on the benches to see that he kept to the path. The City rose up behind the railway, the gigantic silver stake of the Canary Wharf tower and a bar chart of subsidiary buildings. Red cranes clustered at ground level like the limbs of a giant crab. He was heading for a statue on a plinth; a broad and busty Earth Goddess thing crouched into an almost foetal ball. Behind her a line of laburnum trees shivered and the tops of long yellow grasses swayed. It must have been here that he felt again an upsurge inside him and the desire to halt and shout them down and then if necessary pummel the idiots and if he needed to, kick them to pieces as they sprawled on the pathway. And then he probably thought that he must stop running and talk this through with them, clear the air, appeal to the dazzle that he knew was inside them.

They must have met somewhere between the gate and the statue. When the boy took the blade from the case it must have looked much longer and sharper than it actually was. Grant Woods would have had no time to describe its impact to himself. For a moment he may have found himself able to see the way the sculptor had moulded the crown of the Earth Goddess's head, and then the intersections and the butterfly-roofs of the Isle of Dogs, the bow of the Thames and what must have looked like a mosaic of golden islands glittering out to the east and the sea. After the descent, in the dark at the end he would have felt only the vibrations of the footfalls fleeing away from him and the footfalls rushing towards.

Storming the Bastille

For hours, since they came back from the Sacre-Coeur, Greg has coaxed her. Nikki is still being coy. Their relationship has always been like this. Two years they've been boyfriend-girlfriend, though not, strictly speaking, lovers. He can't imagine being closer to anyone – they get on so well – yet, in private, she is all brinks and delays. She never undresses fully. He is always asking 'when?' She is always saying 'soon'. This 'soon' has recently become a promise. He squeezes the seat of her knickers, licks her breasts, again, strokes her nape, again. She breaks away. 'Fireworks,' she says. 'We're going to be late.' Nikki will always be a stickler for plans and timekeeping; Greg believes in carpe diem. He's read about it in books. He isn't interested in the fireworks display that celebrates the one hundred and ninety-ninth anniversary of the storming of the Bastille. He wants her to fulfil the pledge. It's why he's invested his savings – earned by eighteen months Saturday work in a menswear shop in Croydon and better reserved for university; he will leave for Oxford in ten weeks – in this double room in the Hotel Vivienne, at the head of the Passage d'Enghien, off the Boulevard Montmartre, twenty-two francs a night, breakfast and, more importantly, bed.

'Oh Nikki, you said, c'mon.' He snuggles against her.

She wrinkles her nose. 'I said the Hotel de Crillon.'

'Don't be so mean.'

'It's our last night. I want to see fireworks. I bet it's already started.'

'So, we'll miss it then.'

'If this was a nice hotel we could see it from the window.'

'Don't start that again.'

Nikki pushes him gently aside and gets out of bed. Later she will regret this decision, as she panics on the pavement, with Greg on the road, the car between them. But now she runs her fingers through her hair, arches her back and loosens her knickers with a tug. Greg watches her. Silvered by dusk light, her body toned and muscular. She is seventeen. She looks like a Man Ray model, except for her problem with nudity. Why couldn't she be more like a Man Ray model? Why couldn't she be like Kiki of Montparnasse, Man Ray's mistress, the naked pink girl in the painting by Kisling? Kiki slept with whomever she liked. Sleeping with Nikki means sleep.

But Nikki had promised, when he asked in his bedroom in New Addington, with David Sylvian's *Secrets of the Beehive* LP down low, she in just her underwear, and he said, 'You know, there are times when I really want to make love to you. I want you to be the first that I do it with.' She demurred: 'Only at the Hotel de Crillon. I'll only let you if you take me to the Hotel de Crillon.'

The Hotel Vivienne is not the Hotel de Crillon. The sweltering room looks inward, over an enclosed lead-coloured roof of skylights and chicken mesh. The pipes sputter. The carpet doesn't reach the skirting. The sheets are rough and threadbare. The whitewash is dirty and fissured. The breakfast croissants are stale and the staff curt and huffish. Greg thinks it has a bohemian down-at-heel charm. Nikki thinks: where are the gorgeous salons and elegant marble restaurant, the master bedroom and the view of the Place de la Concorde? The Vivienne's lobby, with its mauve and cerise paisley wallpaper and dirty bronze mirrors reminds her of a brothel in Turkey. It was the last holiday they had as a family. Her father was looking for a bar. He needed a drink. When they came out, he said, 'If I ever catch you in a place like that, babes, I don't know what I'd do.' This was before the day he smashed up the house he had bought with the money he'd made from his roofing firm, the day he destroyed the rocking horse, the dining table, the cabinets, the rabbit hutches with the rabbits in it, before he staggered off down the street, leaving a twelve year old Nikki with her unfaithful and flighty mother. Nikki's not seen him since. She's not even had a birthday card.

Nikki is not sure it would feel any different in the Hotel de Crillon. But she doesn't want to be like her friends, too easy, too keen. They have lost it in the back of cars or on sofas at parties with other people in the room, with boys they don't know, that they don't see again. So she says she's set her heart on the Hotel de Crillon. But what does she expect from Greg, who has just left school, has limited funds?

'We've seen fireworks before,' Greg says.

'Yes, in Carshalton Park. I want to see the Eiffel Tower. When will we get the chance again?'

'We can come back next year. For the bicentennial.'

16

Nikki frowns, staring at Greg's coiled, lithe body, the kiss curl concealing an eye. She watches him roll on his side and spread his legs. She breathes in. But you won't be with me next year, you're going away.

'I'm getting ready,' she says. She disappears into the tiny bathroom.

The water takes ages to run hot. She soaps her thighs, neck, stomach and breasts. She powders her face, applies make-up, moisturiser, roll-on and perfume. She puts on mascara and earrings. She brushes her hair and sprays lacquer on it. She lies on the floor, peers up at the cobwebbed striplight, masturbates, holding her breath so Greg won't hear, then changes her underwear. On the other side of the wall, Greg shuffles to the edge of the bed. The teardrop lamp casts a shadow across his torso, a deep wedge beneath his chin, dimples in his shoulders. He likes his black chest hair and hard waist. He lights a Lucky Strike. He loves these soft packs and American brands. You can't get them in Croydon. They are a Kerouac accessory to his image. He sits and smokes in front of the mirror, just like he will do so later, with other women he hardly knows in Oxford and London, when an urge to explain will overcome him, awaiting assurances of his worth. In six years time he will visit Paris hotel rooms again, always alone, aimless business trips. He will sit like this, cigarette in hand, listening to the sounds of traffic, murmurs behind partitions, a sink filling up with water.

Greg gets up and, with less sense of hygiene than Nikki, wipes himself down with a towel still damp from the morning's bath. He puts on a black T-shirt, cream chinos and a black second hand jacket. He likes his image, the dark colours, an artist, an intellectual. For him it is a glimpse of what he will become, when he leaves. Oxford. Languages. Then a career in The Arts, translations, books, maybe even the Foreign Office or Reuters. No driving taxis like his dad; not a clerical job in a Croydon insurance office like his brother, his cousin, his aunt. This is the Eighties. We are different now. He looks back at the bathroom door. It was you who wanted to hurry up.

At this age, eighteen, Greg feels old. Not old as in weary, but old as in accomplished. He has left school. He has a bank account. He can drive. He smokes. He gets served in pubs without ID. He buys records that are not in the charts. He's had a girlfriend for two years whom he loves. He understands her primness, her reserve; he sympathises, they talk. He's fluent in French. He's read Camus and Sartre. He's read *The Interpretation of Dreams*, *The Communist Manifesto* and *The Economic Consequences of the Peace*. He appreciates Moise Kisling and Man Ray. It was he, not Nikki, who knew that the Bastille wasn't there – the bet over breakfast meant she paid for lunch – that it had been razed to the ground in 1789. Greg knows everything. But at twenty-five he will despair. His aspirations will have been cauterised systematically, replaced by routine and malingering. Then, at twenty-nine, he will be younger and fresher and more vivacious than ever before. At eighteen he feels old. The only thing lacking is sex.

Nikki emerges in bra and pants. 'You look scrumptious,' she says, and squirts him with perfume from her make-up bag. He doesn't smile and looks about himself as if she is talking to someone else. 'Fireworks,' she says, as she dresses. 'What time is it? I bet we've missed them.' After he lobs the room key onto the reception desk she tries to take his hand, but he pretends not to notice. Night has long fallen in Paris. Without speaking, they make their way across the boulevard to Bonne Nouvelle.

Greg is morose on the metro. He conspicuously eyes up Parisian women until Nikki pulls his hand into her lap and kisses him. He dips away when he feels the tip of her tongue. She won't allow such public displays of affection in The Oval or Ponderosa's. Why should it be different here? He engrosses himself in the impromptu show of a puppeteer who gets on at Miromesnil. Nikki lets go of his hand.

At Iena they disembark, flap Carte Oranges at the ticket barrier, emerge from the station into a crowd of boisterous youths who jostle and shove them. Traffic careers across the Place d'Iena. Everything is crackles and flashes, gunpowder, exhaust. Klaxons and horns blare from the multi-lane Avenue de President Wilson. Something explodes close to Nikki's heel and, startled, she turns full circle, almost losing Greg. Someone has thrown a banger at her. Little bangers are going off around their feet, the bangers that are illegal in England, the ones schoolboys buy on daytrips to Calais, along with flick combs and nudey playing cards. Greg's sense of direction skews. *Cordon Sanitaire* is the only French he can remember. He knows he should be making for the bridge, the Pont d'Iena, but he's not sure if they're going the right way across the Jardins Trocadero. The Eiffel Tower, illuminated and ruby-golden. He pulls Nikki towards it. Use it as a guide. It's where we're going. Someone pinches Nikki's bum, but when she looks back there are dozens of figures receding into the dark. Greg glances up. There are no fireworks in the sky. They are moving against the crowd. The crowd is leaving the Eiffel Tower.

'Oh no,' Nikki says. 'We *have* missed it.'

Slowly walking back to the metro, Greg says, 'What shall we do now?' Nikki doesn't answer. He goes onto the next thing, she thinks. He doesn't care what I want. He only wants what he can see, and what he wants when he wants it. She wanted to feel his arms around her waist as they look up into the sky and see crimson and turquoise, violet and emerald, fireworks above the Eiffel Tower, the night sky over Paris, their last night here. As she often does, Nikki fears what Greg will be like after he leaves Croydon.

They quit the park, re-enter the Place d'Iena. Cars are smears, zigzagging into the six exits. Bangers still go off around them, making them wince and shuffle. Now he tries to take her hand but she refuses. At the metro, a posse of denim-jacketed, longhaired kids are pelting the stairs with fireworks. A pink flare dazzles Greg. He covers his face with his sleeves, rubbing spangles from his eyes. It is Nikki who notices first. An iron gate blocks the entrance. The metro has shut down.

'Oh, how are we going to get back now?' Nikki says.

'We can walk,' says Greg. 'It's not too far. We can go to a cafe on the way.'

'I've had enough of cafes ... I want, I want to go home.'

'It's not the end of the world, Nicola.'

She hates it when he calls her Nicola. It sounds parental.

'This is your fault,' she says. 'All your fault. If you hadn't made us stay in bed all evening we wouldn't have been late.'

Greg cranes over, as if distracted by something far more intriguing on the other side of the road crossing. The lights are changing colour, the traffic slowing. Then he says, 'Nobody forced you.'

'Yes they did,' she says. 'You did.'

Greg snaps, 'If you weren't so frigid we'd have been on time.'

Nikki, twisting, kicks Greg in the shin.

'Ow ... Nikki.'

But she's already making across the road, the Avenue de President Wilson, where rows and rows of Renaults and Citrons are revving and rattling and blasting their horns, as if the English girl and the English boy chasing her prevent them from raring headlong into the night.

Three kilometres away, in the Place Vendôme, where Greg and Nikki kissed two days ago beneath the column, other teenage revellers also hurl bangers, scaring one hundred and eight pigeons into a whirling, aerial flock. Buzzing the Tuileries, the birds corkscrew over the Seine then soar eastward, over the Petit and the Grande Palais, over balconies and roof terraces, gables and spires, before following the shimmering, traffic-snaggled route of the Cours Albert. All its lanes are static, held up by the lights ahead, apart from the inside channel, where one battered white Fiat hurtles along the asphalt. The Cours Albert becomes Avenue de President Wilson. The Fiat increases speed. The pigeons swoop Place d'Iena and spy Greg tracking Nikki on the crossing. The drivers thump their windscreens; jerk their vehicles back and forth. Before dispersing across the 7th Arrondissment, the flock sees Greg stop Nikki in the middle of the road. But she only wants to reach the other side. The other side, a news kiosk and a doorway there. The noise disorientates her. She fears that the headlights make her loose, long white cotton skirt see-through. That's what the noise *is*. Greg calls her name. He needs to apologise. She breaks away. A car behind them lets off a long wail of the horn. Just as they reach the last lane, with Greg now yanking Nikki along, the Fiat reaches the lights. It doesn't stop at the line. It skids to a halt on the crossing. The driver's window is open. Greg and Nikki freeze. The Arab in the car, arm outstretched, eyes hidden, points a Luger pistol at Greg's chest.

Fingers. The barrel. The fin above it. A red and white chequered scarf around his neck. A ring on his other hand, draped casually over the steering wheel, glints in the interior of the car. When Greg sees the eyes, the eyes gape. Greg cannot move. He wants to but he cannot. Place d'Iena seems to rotate. Buildings gloss into the night. But it is the lights that have changed. The traffic hares forward, apart from the Fiat. Screaming horns try to oust Greg from the road. Cars veer rightwards, almost colliding with one another. The Fiat stays put. A salvo of bangers fizzles from the pavements, along with whooping and chanting, scampering feet. Nikki runs. Greg sees the gun tremble. Standing-on-a-beach-with-a-gun-in-my-hand, reversed . . . *But I'm not French, I'm not French.* Greg is to be the Frenchman shot symbolically on Bastille Night, by Hezbollah, Polisario, the PLO. Greg is waiting for the stench, the last thing he will ever know, as the bullet detonates in his chest, before the blood loss reaches his brain, at the final heartbeat: cordite.

The Arab laughs. He tosses Greg the pistol and drives off. A car swerves and Greg feels its wing whoosh his hip. He stumbles to the kerb, trips, gashes his trouser knee, dropping the sort of toy Luger with which he used to play war in the alleys around his parent's house.

'Oh my God,' Nikki cries. She is weeping. 'Oh my God.' She crouches down. They hold each other on the pavement, oblivious to the throng and the couples parting to avoid their huddle. 'Oh my God, oh my God, I thought ...I thought ...'

Hand in hand, they walk up Avenue d'Iena to the Arc de Triomphe, where the feckless circling traffic causes Greg to shiver. They follow the Boulevard Haussman. They pass cafes and bars, but do not stop, even though parched and footsore. Greg's knee is bleeding; he smokes one Lucky Strike after another. There is a full moon that seems bigger than the one over Croydon. Nikki can clearly make out the craters on the surface. She pauses in Place Diaghilev, at the rear of the opera house, says, 'I thought you were gone. I thought you were ... he was going to ... I thought I was never going to see you again.'

Greg is still numb but is trying to show Nikki that he wasn't scared.

'It was only a toy,' he says.

'But I didn't know, you didn't know, you went white, I saw you, I've never seen you like that before, just then, when you were still in the road, I thought, I'm never going to see you again, I'm never ever going to ...'

He puts his finger to her lips, kisses her beneath the statues and buttresses. Without speaking, they return to the Hotel Vivienne.

'Does that hurt?' Nikki is before Greg. He has his trousers off. They've opened the window but pulled the net curtains. The other guests can see in, see the bed, if the curtains aren't drawn. Greg knows. He's seen them, sprawled out and lolling when he's smoked out the window. He looks back at Nikki. He looks down at her now. The curtains flap into the room. She kisses his knee.

'Does that hurt?'

'No.'

'Liar.'

She stands up, lifts his T-shirt over his head. He puts his arm around her waist, kisses her, and kisses her. Still kissing her, he unbuttons her blouse and tosses it onto the bed. He strokes her cheek and ear, still kissing. She wiggles as he passes her skirt over her hips. She feels it trace her calves and her heels. He runs his palms up her sides. She's ticklish; she giggles, with his tongue in her mouth. She feels his hands between her shoulder blades, her bra straps ping, her breasts widen and swell. She raises her arms above his shoulders. He pushes her onto the bed and she bounces and laughs, rolls on her side and her body now is pale and pink and imminent. He takes both her ankles and slides off her shoes. She flexes her feet. He tickles her soles and she writhes. He kisses her ankles, her shins and her knees; he kisses her navel, her nipples, her neck. And she says, 'Let's do it.'

Greg will never make love to Nikki. He will go to Oxford, become disillusioned and jealous. He will lose his virginity to a second year student from Exeter College, in a basement flat off the Iffley Road with a red light bulb and a *Fish of the North Sea* mobile. He will be drunk and will never remember her name. And Nikki will wait until a Sunday stock-taking a year after tonight ends with her and the deputy manager of Next, Sutton, on the storeroom floor together, a kink in the lino rubbing a strip of skin from her lower back. She doesn't have to explain herself. It seems easier, more honest. He doesn't even buy her a drink afterwards. She wouldn't want him to stay around anyway. Six years later, in a hotel room in the Marais, Greg will pace and fret – the room reminds him of her, this night, the two years – and Greg will sit on the bed and write her a letter, an update, what he's been doing, that he'd love to see her again. She will not reply; the letter's pompous, self-pitying tone. She will be preoccupied with her job as a junior conference organiser in Vauxhall, her mortgage, her flat and juggling her boss and the other man who says that he wants to move in with her. Greg will shuffle around many Paris hotel rooms, naked, smoking, his memory running over, blowing his hands as if freezing. He will wonder what exactly were his intentions, when he was eighteen, at this moment in his life.

Greg flips Nikki onto her side and pulls her hands up so they rest on his neck. She blinks as if startled. He kisses her. He says, 'Let's wait a while.'

A Short Story About a Short Film

Exterior[1]. Night. We TRACK across rows of windows and the white façade of a vast Soviet-style apartment block[2]. We glimpse living rooms and stupefied-looking people. We ZOOM in on a window to the left, then WHIP to a central

---

[1] So, first things first, Lucile. Ease yourself into your seat. Get comfortable. Slip off your heels. We're the only ones here, so you can slurp your Diet Fanta and scoff a packet of M&Ms as big as a boxer's punch bag without disturbing any snoggers or cineastes. You don't even have to turn off your mobile and can text your mates throughout the whole film if you like. I hope you don't, though. Because look, up there, moving and flickering, with its soundtrack and dialogue and beautiful black and white print. We did it. We made it. We finally finished it. Or, to be more precise, I did. I made it. It may have taken two and a half years, but I did make our film, Lucile, the film that on our first date I promised you we'd make. You remember our film, Lucile? No? Really? You do, surely. It must all be flooding back to you now. Our first collaboration. Our shot at fame. This screening is just for you. Welcome to our private cinema. Enjoy your personalized director's commentary.

[2] OK, as you know, we never did raise the money to go East, let alone get permission to film there. Amberley Terrace, your old halls of residence, does have a brutalist, megalithic quality. Your suggestion that we use it as the principal location was your outstanding contribution to the production.

window[3]. We look down into an apartment from a stilted angle. Snow[4] flutters around the window casement.

Inside is a BEAUTIFUL WOMAN. She is young (20s), dark-haired and beautiful even from a distance. She folds her arms and taps her feet on a rug, as if anxious that someone has not yet arrived[5].

Interior. Pokey Room. Night. CLOSE-UP of a GRIZZLED MAN[6] (late 20s) using binoculars. His elbows rest on a bulky desk pushed against a window. A camera with a long lens lies on the tabletop. An angle-poise lamp in the foreground causes both his outline and a pile of notebooks on the desk to cast

---

[3] 414 Amberley Terrace. Your old room before you met me. To my knowledge, and my knowledge comes mainly from our pillow talk, though I can't say that I've not dug a little deeper since, the list of people known to have slept here includes: Ben Sprake, Carlos Paine, Olaf Godalminger, Dirty Cheryl, Benedict 'Eggs' Rache, Hoggsy Hogg, Stu, Latvian Chemist Man with Overcoat Worn on Shoulders for Most Efficient Circulation of Air, Dr. Torquil Mizer, Armistead 'Lamby' Shanks, Joz Bovrille, Martin Bock and Specialneedsbi (I suppose you've also forgotten that Specialneedsbi played a significant part in getting us together in the first place). Otherwise, despite staring at it through a lens on and off for two and half years, I can't imagine the inside of 414 Amberley Terrace, or what went on there.

[4] And, of course, it wouldn't snow when we wanted it to snow, and Andre Font-Lackstone's uncle who works at Pinewood never actually delivered that snow machine, so our weather effects were achieved by cunning use of grated polystyrene scattered in front of the camera. The Font's acquisition of the snow machine was supposed to be his contribution to Fernfont Films, mine being the purchase of the camera used throughout. One thing I have learned is that a film as ambitious as ours quickly eats into an inheritance.

[5] This is you how I want to remember you. On the night that we met you were working behind the bar of the Flensborough Theatre. We, the old Film Studies posse, came out for a crafty one during the intermission (budget performance of *Look Back in Anger*) and there you were, demure and flustered in your serving wench mode. Specialneedsbi was slumped at the bar in his stovepipe hat and the black and yellow-hooped jumper that made him look like a Colorado beetle. He was muttering and flashing his arms around, saying things about your mother that I'd probably agree with now. He was so drunk it was simplicity itself to take him out onto the terrace and dump him there. You were so relieved when I returned, so appreciative. That's when you asked me what I do. And I, rarely this suave, said I'd tell you when I met you for a drink. I got the line from a film. Stole it.

[6] Sergei Brodin, who is not actually Russian. His parents were *Socialist Worker* types from Colindale. I often lie awake at night and wonder what would have happened if I'd not cast Sergei and followed my instinct and played the part myself.

mountainous shadows on the bare wall behind him. He grimaces and adjusts the binoculars.

The Beautiful Woman paces[7], her back to us, and holds up the hem of her dress.

We PULL BACK to see her through the window, dancing on her own as if to music that we cannot hear. We see her through two overlapping circles, as if using binoculars. We hear a doorbell ring. There is a BLUR for a second.

The Grizzled Man puts down his binoculars. He is shivering and lights a cigarette. He stands up, but still stares at the window as if hardly able to contain some impossible longing. FADE TO BLACK

Run titles.

---

[7] And there you go, Lucile, pacing that room (not actually 414 Amberley Terrace for the close ups; that's The Font's ground floor flat in Peat Cutter Street) in the same way that you paced up and down outside the Stray Cat Café as you waited for me. I was late when I am never late. In fact, I wasn't late. I was in the Jar and Pocket opposite, keeping a sneaky look-out, checking to see if you actually turned up. I skipped out the back way and sauntered around the corner towards you, swinging my brolly and whistling a happy tune. Inside, we sat at one of those heavy wooden tables enclosed by a wrought-iron frame. We drank coffee, then red wine. You thanked me for saving you. Specialneedsbi was hassling you, you said, been at it for weeks. You didn't say why, of course. You told me then that you were an actress, just passing time behind that bar, waiting for your breakthrough. Since drama school, this recession, paucity of roles, yadda bla bla. You felt like an enclave behind that bar. 'Enclave or exclave?' I said. 'Are you an enclave, smothered by the masses, or are you an exclave, away from the flock?' You didn't answer, just smiled. Nor did I get very far with my next question: what are your favourite exclaves? Mine: Cabinda, Oecussi-Ambeno and Kaliningrad Oblast. The latter is my favourite, a little nub of Russia squeezed out onto the Baltic between Poland and Lithuania, once the capital of Old Prussia, then East Prussia, formerly Königsburg, city of Kant and annexed by the Soviet Union at the end of World War Two. I had always wanted to live there. In photos it looks pretty similar to my hometown, the place I liked to call Slutsk, a sprawl of concrete blocks separated from Mother Russia by geographic and temporal accident. I then told you how I worship East European cinema and films from the former USSR, love a bit of snow and bleakness. *A Short Film about This. A Short Film about That.* Lots of following and longing. Tarkovsky. Kieslowski. It was then that you asked me what I do.

Selina Hackett   Merlin Prebble[8]

Kaliningrad[9]

Screenplay by Lloyd Fernery and[10] Lucile Delph
Directed by Lloyd Fernery

Exterior. Day. Overhead shot of the communal entrance of an apartment block. Three concrete pathways meet at the foot of the steps, segmenting a patchy lawn[11]. The Beautiful Woman exits the building wearing a trench coat.

---

[8] i.e., not you. You'll get yours at the end, in more ways than one. And not Sergei either, for reasons that I will reveal in good time if, that is, you still can't work this one out for yourself.

[9] 'I write and direct films,' I said. That's what I told you in the Stray Cat Café. I was sure that an electric current passed between us then. Later, sauntering through the town that I like to call Nurmansk on a night that winced with an enigmatic *Last Year in Marienbad*-ish atmosphere, your hand dangled perilously close to mine and you first articulated the idea that had already transfigured me but I was too cautious to share. We should write a film together! A film that I could direct and you could star in! It would make us. It would give we two poor bedraggled graduates something to do on our own. Otherwise we would soon be found playing cardboard violins on street corners for copper coins, pleading 'what will become of us?' in mouse-like voices. I came up with a plot in a flash. During a sojourn in the Bar Zurich I scribbled out a treatment on the backs of four tourist information leaflets for a shire horse centre near the hamlet I refer to as Lersk. *Kaliningrad*. A love story. Surveillance and guilt. Escape and passion. We could go there and make it. We could go there and fall in love. You were up for all of that, you said, especially the starring in a film part. Soon afterwards, in between your shifts at the Flensborough we would meet at my flat on Red Stallion Street. You would sit on the bed and chip-in while I typed. Best moments of my life. You with your mahogany-coloured hair styled like a forties film star, your tea dance dresses in muted colours, your Mary Jane shoes, your schoolgirl slang, a string of pearls, a subtle hint of cleavage. That night the songs of Vadim Kozin overcame us and we found ourselves rolling around the floorboards and pulling off our clothes. We were like Marilyn and Miller but from colder places and more pressurized times. That was the joke we shared, how it was between us, until we began to assemble the cast and the crew.

[10] Notice the use of 'and' here, not the ampersand. In screenplay etiquette, this means not a true collaboration but that the second writer played only a MINOR PART.

[11] Back of skanky flats near the recycling centre in Nurmask, filmed from roof. The Font was bitten by a dog called Kanye and we were chased away by marauding anarcho-chavs, hence the slight camera wobble.

Seven or eight of the apartment blocks[12] stand behind her as she walks towards us along a concrete path. It is clearly freezing.

She stops, as if unsettled. This close up she's incredibly pretty, with rosebud lips and smoky eyes, the sort of girl you might only encounter once in your life. She walks right through us. FADE TO BLACK.

At the top of the path stands the Grizzled Man, tall and pale.

Exterior. Market[13]. From behind we see the Beautiful Woman saunter through a concrete precinct laid out with market stalls. The stalls are manned by burly types but there is hardly any produce. Low mist hangs and creeps[14].

The Grizzled Man furtively trails the Beautiful Woman on the other side of the stalls, smoking.

Exterior. Cafeteria called Automatik[15].Day.

Interior. Automatik. It is a spare place with round plastic tables[16]. The Beautiful Woman sits at a window table. She is in mid-conversation with A MIDDLE-AGED MAN IN A SHABBY

SUIT[17]. She laughs. The Middle-Aged Man lights her cigarette.

---

[12] Actually what remains of the Pump House estate in Kroykov, near Slutsk.

[13] That precinct near the bus station, the part of Nurmansk that's like downtown Tirana and has its own weather system so it's permanently overcast and spitting with mineral brown rain.

[14] Courtesy of smoke machine borrowed from Nurmansk's third best goth metal band, Funeral in Carpathia.

[15] Inventive use of the laundrette on Builder's Row.

[16] All Bar One in Slutsk with the lights down low. A mate from school works there and let us in. The Font was seriously underwhelmed by the wine list.

[17] I didn't tell you this at the time but I always had Dr Torquil Mizer in mind when I wrote this part. I found out later that you still only achieved a lower second class degree.

He leans over and whispers something in her ear.
We PULL AWAY to reveal the Grizzled Man leaning against a
concrete pillar, smoking. From over the shoulder of his
overcoat we see the Beautiful Woman almost skip from the
Automatik. The Grizzled Man lights another cigarette. Mist
coils behind him.

Exterior. Vast Concrete Expanse[18]. From above, we see the
Beautiful Woman striding diagonally. We linger until the tip
of her shadow vanishes. The Grizzled Man follows it.

Exterior of giant office building like something out of
Metropolis[19]. The Beautiful Woman saunters up a flight of
steps. She disappears into the building.

Interior. Hanger-sized office[20]. Rows of girls are typing,
making a clattery racket. The Beautiful Woman finds her
desk. Her face is now devoid of expression.

We PULL BACK and LINGER, as if someone else is staring and
staring at the Beautiful Woman. The rhythm of her typing.
The shudder of her shoulders. The tapping of her heel on the
grey, grey floor.

---

[18] Carpark near the medical centre at the University of Nurmansk. Filmed by me while
waiting for The Font to have treatment for dog bite and sprained ankle sustained while
escaping the Death's Head Legion of the Erridge Park West Anarcho-Chavs.

[19] The façade of the now disused Platinum House in Kroykov filmed from an oblique
angle so it doesn't quite look so much like a pile of fifty pence pieces made out of concrete
slabs.

[20] The inside of the Platinum. That's why it looks a bit damp and disordered. We couldn't
lift the old coffee machine and had to cover it with a sheet. That's why it looks as if a fat
ghost is frozen in the corner of the shot (something that will surely crop up in cable
TV *Yuri Gellar's Real Life Ghost Mysteries Caught on Proper Film* documentaries in the
future!). I know the girls all look about thirteen. That's because they are. The guy from
the Kroykov School of Speech and Drama let us down on the extras front and we had to
approach the drama soc of Saint Perpetua's High School for Girls. They all looked up to
you, for some reason. You and I later had an argument in Café Rouge, that night Sergei
sulked at the bar on his own and The Font walked off to let us get on with it. I later
found The Font with three of the Saint Perp girls in MacDonald's, telling a lie about how
his uncle designed that big explosion in *Superman II*. After I prised him away from his
fillet-o-fishes and we returned to Red Café, as I prefer to call it, both you and Sergei had
vanished. We didn't see you again until we reconvened in Nurmansk three days later.

Outside, The Grizzled Man sits on the plinth of the monumental statue of some general or strongman. He looks up, sorrowfully[21]. The giant office building LOOMS.

---

[21] And so he should look sorrowful, considering that this is Sergei's last scene. Yes, as you remember, he quit after this. Well, not quit, actually. When I finally caught up with you after the Kroykov shoot – and I know this is immature of me and doesn't fit with your idea of the Hollywood life or whatever you have read in whatever biography of whichever silver screen diva and what she was allowed to get away with on set – I had suspicions about you and Sergei. I couldn't get them out of my head. You and him. Those three days. In some caravan or something. Taking your clothes off nice and slowly. That look on your face. I didn't quite believe that you had been at your Auntie Diana's in Hastings, or that your mobile's battery had run out without you noticing. I should have believed you, I know. I could have believed you. I wanted to. But you had been staring at him and he had been staring at you since we began. Sergei did insist that it was his motivation to stare at you obsessively. I sacked him anyway. See how much I loved you, Lucile? I got rid of our leading man for you. Then, of course, we had to find another one, which proved harder than I imagined. I thought everyone would be dying to star in *Kaliningrad*. Then, given what had happened with the dog, the Death's Head Legion of the Anarcho-Chavs and still being sore about me ruining his chances with the St Perps girls, The Font refused to reshoot the film again with a new actor. He assured me that no one would notice if we just carried on with a different lead in the second half. It's, like, he said, a comment on the shifting sands of identity and life in a police state where people disappear and reappear all the time.

31

Exterior. Dingy Bar called Eighteenth Brumaire[22]. Day.

---

[22] If you remember it was about this time that things started to get tricky. While we looked for a second Grizzled Man, we obviously couldn't continue with the film beyond shooting hours of footage of the ugliest buildings in Nurmansk. I even had to go fishing in your old drama school pond for a new Grizzled. Ben Sprake and Carlos Paine both turned me down but it was a close thing with Eggs Benedict. For about a week I thought he'd commit and told myself I could handle him joining us. Eventually, though, I had no option but to cast Specialneedsbi. A sober Merlin Prebble (he'll always be Special to me; slips of the tongue, both by myself and The Font would cause a little on-set tension later) was fresh from his life-affirming stint as an extra in a soft drink advert in which he'd pranced about in a maroon hoodie alongside a youth with cockatoo-like hair spouting vaguely sexist lifestyle statements. The experience had helped him get over you, he said. And at least, unlike Sergei, he was definitely your ex. I was raring to go but a hitch occurred when Special went all Christian Bale on me. He needed to inhabit the part, he said, and decamped for three months to stare at a concrete office block in the town I like to think of as Mordski. It was during this interlude that you started to get restless, didn't you, Lucile? You started to moan about the screenplay. Saying it was static. Saying it was boring and nothing happened. Saying that it was taking too long to get anywhere. This surprised me, because while we were writing the screenplay (note the *we*; you can hardly accuse me of foisting it on you) you raised none of these objections and seemed more concerned that the writing made you seem not just stunning but also smart *and* imaginative *and* good in bed *and* funny. Maybe this was it. Maybe I failed on the last score. I did make her the prettiest girl in Kaliningrad; I made her look intelligent *and* dreamy. But witty lines and comic banter are not my forte and perhaps – I have a point I think – not quite in keeping with the whole *Kaliningrad* mood. But you wanted another writer brought in during the hiatus. OK, anything for you, my love. Enter Shoutybollocks, the performance poet with the aviator mirrored sunglasses and the flak jacket and the wrong beard (think Grover from *Sesame Street,* think Grover looming over you in the dark, Lucile, pushing your head into your pillow with his blue, furry, lipless mouth). I wish I could say that he did something more than just confirm my prejudices against performance poetry or slam or . . . wank, sometimes just **wank** will do . . . a form of light entertainment I consider the bastardized hybrid of second-rate poetry and second-rate stand-up comedy from which emerges a chimera of arse that beguiles only the impressionable and those with short attention spans (two and a half years to make *Kaliningrad,* Shouty-B; two secs to scrawl an abruptly promoted, rhyming pub joke on a beer mat and bellow it at students who would laugh at a Spetsnaz firing squad if it was billed as *Shoutybollocks's Grover Face Rhymes Tit with Shit Show*). It's not Shouty-B's fault, I suppose. It's the world that he comes from. But as that's the same world as one Lloyd Fernery, it's not an excuse, is it? Like me he was raised in the Home Counties (or The First Circle of the Mercedes Archipelago as I like to call it), educated privately (not in the Magnitogorsk School of Mining and Metallurgy) and his father is not an exiled Russian Futurist or defected SMERSH operative but the chief executive of a Dorking-based firm selling kiddies' paddling pools and plastic slides. We both have an income to fund our dreams but unlike me the man has no romantic imagination or eastern sensibility. That impresses you, Lucile? That's enough for you? You started to spend a lot of time with Shoutybollocks, editing the screenplay while I waited for the return of Specialneedsbi. Meanwhile, strangely, there was no obvious ramping up of the script's comedy value.

Interior. Eighteenth Brumaire. A face, round and overfed,[23]
stares out at us. PULL BACK and he is sitting at a bar,
sipping from a tumbler. He is joined by the Grizzled Man[24].
The Grizzled Man flicks a note held in his fingers, as if
summoning a barman. The Over-Fed Man pulls the arm down.

>   THE OVER-FED MAN
>   As the promised cognac is just as
>   terrible as the last shipment, this
>   lot is on me.

A drink is placed on the bar.

>   THE GRIZZLED MAN
>   Come the Revolution, come the worst
>   of the cognac.

>   THE OVER-FED MAN
>   When you come up with results, you
>   can have what the capitalists drink.
>   What have you got for me Vostok[25]?

>   VOSTOK
>   Impatience, Limski, is the sign of a
>   narrow man.

He hands over a large envelope. Limski eagerly takes out the

---

[23] I'd always thought of Martin Bock when I was writing this part. He was operating the de-heading machine in a turkey factory when I asked him to audition. I like to think that I gave him his break.

[24] And there we have it. That's not Sergei. It's the far less grizzled Merlin 'Specialneedsbi' Prebble. Don't fret, Lucile. No one will notice the change. It happens in other soap operas all the time. And before you get all snarky and accuse me of using cruel and inappropriate language, you first called him Specialneedsbi, because this would-be actor and ex-fling fodder of yours "thinks he's special and is in great need" (your words in the Stray Cat). I won't here also remind you of what you said about Davros-Street Hawk, the bloke in the invalid carriage who kept spinning into shot like a bumper car struck by lightning when we were filming at the market.

[25] Ah, so his name is revealed. Named by me after another of my favourite places, another place I'll never visit. Lake Vostok in Antarctica, a vast body of pure water sealed under the ice for millions of years. Understand the symbolism? See why I'd be drawn to such a place? Why I would identify with it?

contents.
INSERT of big glossy black and white pictures of the Beautiful
Woman doing routine things.

Limski takes the sheaf of photographs and SLAPS them across
Vostok's chest.

                    LIMSKI
          I must know. Everything. Everything
          about this Natasha[26]. Get it all, or
          the March of History marches over
          you.

FADE TO BLACK[27].

---

[26] And that's her name. Natasha. You chose it. Compared to Vostok, though, it's a spanking great cliché. Couldn't you have done any better? Don't you know any other Russian names?

[27] The last straw snapped for me after we shot this scene. Let's go back over the end, just so we're clear, so there are no disputes about the facts. I'll cut all the times that you appeared not to be talking to me on set. I'll cut all the times that you failed to show up at Red Stallion Street or appeared really, really late and drunk and just fell into bed and started to snore. I won't mention your giggling at texts sent by someone who I suspect was *him*. Let's whip to that Fernfont Films production meeting at your house. I let myself in. I had bought free trade coffee and pastries for one and all. You were still upstairs, the bedroom door shut. Considerately, I let you sleep. The others arrived. The Font set up his laptop on the kitchen table. Special and Martin rolled in. We were supposed to be going over the revised script. We sat there for an hour watching Special practise his spy face. The bumps and creaks started upstairs. Then down you came, your hair a mess, wearing only leggings and a T-shirt, and poured yourself a mug of the coffee that I had considerately brewed. You were shortly followed by a barefoot Bollocks, all tousled and satiated. The two of you snuggled up together at the table and drank out of the same mug. When you peered over at me through slitty eyes and then turned away, I knew it was the end of us and the end of *Kaliningrad*. It was considerate of me not to put the cafetiere through Bollocks' head. It was considerate of me not to shove a Maison Brun croissant up his khyber. It was considerate of me only to shout at you in the street.

Exterior[28]. The Window of Natasha's Apartment. Night. A small
table with chairs has been pulled into the middle of the
room. There is a chessboard on the table. Natasha[29] and a

---

[28] Maybe a disruption of some sort is obvious in the final cut, given that the old Natasha disappears and is replaced by another actress (though I hope this has an effect similar to that in *Chungking Express* where the audience is not sure if a new narrative has started half way through because the direction is so intentionally enigmatic and cerebral). I can't say I knew what to do after you left. I wandered around parks and smoked like a zoo animal. I couldn't sleep. I couldn't get you out of my head. I was like a writer. I was like a writer in the fifties or sixties. I was like a writer lost in Europe somewhere. I was like a writer sodden with gin, wandering up and down the Karl Marx Allee trying to get *that* girl out of his head. I was like Holly Martins in *The Third Man*, just a hack writer who drinks too much and falls in love with girls. Lucile had left me. *Kaliningrad* was not to be. *Kaliningrad* had been recaptured by the Nazis. This went on for three months that felt like years. Beautiful things –movies, snowflakes, breasts – seemed acid to me. My friends tried to console me. I sat up one night with Special and Martin and we all agreed what a beguilingly fickle thing you are and wished a plague on the house of Shoutybollocks and his couplets of toss. The film was still dead though, the film was over. I tried to write another screenplay about a writer wandering up and down the Karl Marx Allee in the fifties or sixties trying to get *that* girl out his head but it petered out. I ate a lot of pizza. I cried. I went to the doctor and asked for a cure for heartbreak. Meanwhile, The Font, bless him, was out every day, filming hours and hours of background footage of shops, concrete and manky patches of lawn (thirty hours, in fact; turned out to be bastard to edit). Special was still in so deep that he was practically inseparable from Vostok (recently, Martin said that it's hard to see him ever having a normal life now). Somehow, somehow, I regathered myself. It struck me that I'd not only lost you I'd let down my collaborators. I was depriving The Font of his first film and Special of his first leading role. I knew I could make Martin a star as well. The Phoenix Kaliningrad was born. This was where we stormed the Winter Palace. Enter Selina.

[29] And there she is: Selina. Recasting Natasha proved as difficult and forced a similar delay to the replacement of Sergei's Vostok. Two bloody months. Two months of looking at disinterested, talentless waitress-cum-actresses (though from my perspective that sentence could as well sum up our relationship, Lucile). Then, suddenly, like thunder that signals the end of an arid spell, she smashed into our lives. Selina Hackett. Sister of Miles Hackett who The Font knew from his foundation course in Bournemouth, the self-same Miles Hackett who received a two-year suspended for stealing three suitcases and a set of skis from a baggage carousel at Lutonov Airport. We didn't hold that against the sister (and they were my skis!). We thought of her as a lifesaver, a lady of the lamp come to rescue our dreams. You will notice however, that she's quite a petite thing, and given your height and presence, this scene makes it look like Natasha has shrunk in the wash. Moreover, unlike you and Natasha, Selina is blonde. We had to dye her hair. It kind of works in black and white but her hair is much straighter than yours and lacks that tendrilly, wispy thing that you've got going on. Her hair was quite a bit shorter as well, more of a bob really. Anyway, here she is, her first scene (I know she still looks nervous, as if playing chess with Weed is a Room 101 job but we couldn't keep reshooting; at take fourteen we had to settle).

THIN MAN[30] are playing chess, studiously, not talking or laughing. There is a BLUR. The concentric circles of the binocular lenses return.

Interior. Vostok's Apartment. He puts down the binoculars and reaches for one of his notebooks.

Through the window, we see the Thin Man take Natasha's White Queen. She throws a huff and swipes the pieces from the board[31].

In profile, Vostok's pencil is looping and angling all over the page of the notebook.

Natasha, smiling now, saunters towards the window. She seems to pause and peer out into the darkness. She pulls the curtains with an abrupt swish[32].

Vostok stands and rips the page from his notebook with the same abrupt, precise gesture that she used on her curtains. He reaches out and sticks the page to the window.

---

[30] A dead-ringer, I think, for the Latvian Chemist with Overcoat Worn on Shoulders for Most Efficient Circulation of Air. I did try to track him down and cast him for this cameo, but according to Martin he'd gone back to Latvia to do paid and rewarding work.

[31] Not in the script. I think Selina had some sort of minor panic attack.

[32] This is where I think she first got it right and radiates the Natasha Effect. When we were filming this through The Font's bedroom window I felt like Vostok. Looking at Natasha but not being able to get to her. Looking at you, I mean Natasha, and finding a gulf between us. I began to realize that just like old Alfred had his Hitchcock blondes, in the future there will certainly come into critical parlance a distinct type of lady called the Fernery Brunette. I had a little tête-à-tête with Selina after this scene. I flattered her in the direction of the Stray Cat (not trying to relive anything, Lucile, you understand). I'd like to be able to say that it was as simple as two bottles of very good Shiraz and one thing leading to another. It was actually a case of two very good bottles of Shiraz drunk by me and a lunge into withdrawing arms. Outside, in that little square, where a classic half-moon hung above the ice cream kiosk, Selina explained to me that she was too professional and focussed on the role to get involved with anyone on set. Natasha is a mystery, her activities inscrutable. She must be like that. She must become Natasha. Full of respect, I walked home and must admit I had a cry, not sure over whom. It became clear soon afterwards that Martin was already giving Natasha II the benefit.

Interior. Supermarket[33]. Day. Natasha browses an aisle. It is lit by overhead lamps. The shelves are mostly empty. She carries a string bag with onions in it. She pauses to examine turnips. Behind her, at the end of the aisle, Vostok, camera raised, nips out and takes a photograph.

Natasha stands in the queue for the till with blank, unfathomable expression and a glass bottle of rank-looking soft drink under her arm. Vostok is behind her.

Exterior. City Square. Day. Natasha[34], string bag at her side, walks across a concrete square. Drunken lads[35] sprawl around a rubbish fountain, swigging from bottles. She stops when the lads start to jeer. They stand up and menace her. She drops her bags and her onions roll all over the paving.

Vostok jogs over. His presence scatters the drunks.

Natasha is a little flustered. Vostok collects the onions and returns the string bag to her.

                    NATASHA
        Thank you. And what is it that you
                      do?

                    VOSTOK
        I work in one of these shops. Are
        you OK? Would you like to come and
                  sit down?'

Natasha looks disappointed.

                    NATASHA
        No, I am fine. I go home now.

----

[33] Filmed 5am Happy Shopper, Bolingbroke Road. Turnips and onions courtesy of farm shop in Lersk.

[34] Whoops, that's actually you, Lucile, not Selina, as this bit was filmed in Tirana market after the earlier scene. That flicker in the lower right of the frame is of the invalid carriage Street Hawk flashing into shot.

[35] Navi's mates (paid in lager and the onions).

                        VOSTOK
        Maybe you would like a game of chess
        sometime?

Natasha laughs politely and walks away.

Exterior. The Window of Natasha's Apartment. Night. Natasha
sits on her chair again. An EFFETE MAN[36] appears to be reading
something to her from a book as he circles her chair.

Interior. Vostok's Apartment. He has the binoculars in one
hand and is writing something in a notebook with the other.

Natasha creases over laughing, forcing the Effete Man to
pause his reading.

Vostok, leaning back in his chair, scribbles furiously in
his book.

Natasha jumps up gleefully and rips a page from the Effete
Man's book. She holds it high in the air. He reaches up,
trying to retrieve it. She laughs and spins around like a
schoolgirl playing a game. She sticks the page on the window.

Vostok, now kneeling forwards on his desk, pushes the
binoculars to the window, clearly trying to read what's on
the paper Natasha has stuck to the pane.

Exterior. Window of Natasha's Apartment. Behind the paper
stuck to the window, Natasha and Effete-Looking jostle.
It's impossible to tell if they are play-fighting, actually
fighting, remonstrating or in the throes of love.

Vostok has set aside the binoculars and has pressed his face
and hands to the window. He looks like he wants to glide
through the glass and float across to her.

Exterior. Window of Natasha's Apartment. She approaches
the window, her expression neutral. She briskly pulls the
curtains.

---

[36] This is Stanislaw Pantz, half-Australian, half Transylvanian and the part-time librarian
at the Nurmansk Film Archive. I couldn't get anyone else. He's not a great actor but he's
certainly effete. If you study Selina's face you can see that she's clearly terrified of him.

Vostok sits at his desk, staring into space, smoking.[37]

Exterior. Street. Night. From behind, we see Natasha strolling between low-slung, oblong apartment blocks[38].

Exterior. Deserted Tram Stop[39]. Night. Natasha waits in a cone of white light thrown by a street lamp. We PULL BACK, watching her from a distance now. A tram arrives, rattling and groaning, then obscures her.

Natasha moves towards us up the aisle of the tram[40]. When she swerves out of shot to sit down, we see Vostok in a Breton cap and upturned collar following through the tram.

Exterior. Another Deserted Tram Stop[41]. Night. The tram pulls away from what appears to be a more suburban and less concrete-infested place.

[37] What happened during and after the filming of this scene is still open to interpretation. Selina was so shaken up by Stanislaw (the rumours did turn out to be false, as you know) that Martin insisted on taking her 'somewhere safe' as soon as I wrapped. He draped a trench coat over her head and hurried her away before I could even shout, 'the brewskis are on me!' Otherwise pleased with the night's work, The Font, Special, Stanislaw and I decamped to Tiger Tiger for promised brewskis. Until this point, I'd been feeling great. Lloyd Fernery was back, wielding the megaphone, making art, forging a rapport with the actors. Then across the seating area I saw you, your bare shoulders, your black dress, that flick of your hair. Opposite you was Shoutybollocks, who had slipped off one of his flip flops. His bony foot was pressed on your shoe and his toe ring glistened down there in the dark. Too vividly it reminded me of the scene at the end of Bertolucci's *The Conformist* where the assumed-dead pederast is revealed to be alive and about to seduce an innocent and hungry young boy in a colonnade. I was sick, Lucile, physically sick. Hurled my guts in the washroom of Tiger Tiger in Nurmansk.

[38] Selina looking terrified as she walks through the Larkton Estate. I wanted 'imperious and frosty' and kept whispering 'Catherine the Great, Catherine the Great' to gee her up. This only made matters worse and caused S to dash for the nearest pub – The Boxer's Brace – where we found her cowering in the ladies, muttering 'not the horses' over and over again.

[39] I know. It is that bus stop where Hot Black Avenue meets Little Mullard Street. Be quiet. Don't break the spell for the others.

[40] Interior of semi-burnt-out coach found on heath. You can't really tell the difference in black and white.

[41] Bus stop where Hot Black Avenue meets Little Mullard Street filmed from other side.

Exterior. Leafy Lane[42]. Night. Natasha walks. Owls hoot. Gravel crunches. We PULL BACK to see Vostok tailing her at a discreet distance.

Exterior. Mysterious Lakeside Villa[43]. Night. Natasha approaches a MYSTERIOUS VILLA with pillars and statuary. Mist seemingly parts for her. She reaches the portico. The door opens, throwing a plank of light over the gravel. A MYSTERIOUS SMUDGE OF A MAN appears. He ushers her inside.

At the end of the driveway Vostok squints, smoking.

Interior. Nightclub[44]. Vostok sits alone at a table, many empty beers bottles and tumblers at his elbows. He is clearly disinterested in any of the other women here, oblivious to their Aeroflot uniform-style clothes and bouffants[45].

Interior. Eighteenth Brumaire. Day. Vostok and Limski in profile at a window table. Vostok knocks back a cognac.

---

[42] I'm sure you recognize this location, Lucile. That's the lane that leads to your parents' house in Sussex. You know when you have an image for a scene in your mind and nowhere else will do? Probably not. Filming here did cause a lot of discussion. The Font was against driving this far and hiring such expensive kit for such a short scene. I think he also thought it a bit unwise to revisit a place that although I'd only visited once provoked such potent memories. We were held up a little, I suppose, because I couldn't help creeping up to the house to check if you were back. Then your dad came out and there was an unpleasant and unnecessary exchange of words. The police were called because of the lights in the woods and Selina started to cry when she thought she saw a badger with skeletal paws writhing in a ditch. The footage we filmed here, I agree, is a bit unsteady and *Blair Witch Project*. I'm glad we made the effort, though.

[43] Actually Font-Lackstone's family home out near Piltdown (where they once faked the missing link). We went there after the Leafy Lane Debacle. We all slept in this huge lounge. We were like a proper film crew, all in it together, and Red Army-style camaraderie broke out as cast and crew mingled freely. Except for Martin and Selina, who slept upstairs, and The Font, who retired to his old bedroom. Special and I had a right old bonding conference. This went on for some time, until we found that all the bottles were empty and we were shouting at the tops of our voices (about who I cannot conceive) and Mrs Font-Lackstone appeared in the world's least fetching nightdress and told us that she was 'getting jolly annoyed'.

[44] *Fluids* in Slutsk.

[45] Your friends.

Limski knocks back a cognac. Vostok lights a cigarette. Limski lights a cigarette. Vostok takes out another big envelope. Limski removes, then fingers the prints.

INSERT of b&w photos of Natasha playing chess with the Thin Man and listening to the Effete Man read from a book[46].

Limski slams his palm on the table. When a waiter rushes over, he's waved away. Limski throws his cigarette on the floor, stands up as if about to erupt, then slowly sits down again. Vostok's expression is blank, as if he's going through the motions of pretending not to know whose side he is on.

> LIMSKI
> This is not good enough, Comrade
> Vostok. I want to know what she does.
> Understand. Does. If it is dirty, I want
> the dirty. If it is nasty, I want the
> nasty.

> VOSTOK
> I think she just plays chess. And
> sometimes she lets an imbecile read to
> her.

> LIMSKI
> Do you want me to have to find out from
> her myself? You know what happens
> when I commit myself to the cause of
> information.

---

[46] Even without audio this is clearly the sort of wank verse that only impresses a simple-knickers jellyhead.

He gets up and leaves. FADE TO BLACK[47].

Interior. Vostok's Apartment. Night. He uses the binoculars to stare out of the window.

Exterior: Natasha's Window: She sits on her chair wearing a night gown and is maybe naked underneath. She is relaxed and unguarded, perhaps deep in thought. It's impossible to know if she is alone. The doorbell SCREAMS.

Vostok's Apartment.

---

[47] I suppose you need to know that the little contretemps we had at the New Creatives Forum bunfight occurred at this point in the shoot. I am assuming that you remember it. If not, please cover your ears. I would also like to make it clear for the record that being a serious auteur I do not usually attend such events, a networking junket for local wannabees and has-beens with a bit of so-called light entertainment thrown in to make it all seem less vulgar. The Font fancied it for some reason. Special wanted to check out any 'spare muff' as he so delightfully confessed, and Martin and Selina, well, I suppose they felt rather obliged to attend if The Font was going, not that they were fishing for other opportunities or anything. Anyway, the Fernfont Films posse arrive and clique magisterially around the bar. Everyone wants to talk to me but I am studiously aloof. Soon I am in my cups. I am on great form, tossing off *bon mots* like some latter-day Orson Welles. And then something horrible happens. There, at a table in the middle of the room, I see you, you with your back to me, you with your hair and pink tube dress, you being bored to death by that parvenu Shoutybollocks. I break out in a sweat. My *oblige noblesse* kicks in. This has to stop. You need rescuing. This was my reasoning, Lucile. I honest to goodness, hand over heart thought you needed me. I drew my party into a huddle. I gave instructions. We would rush the table, encircle the Shouty-B pocket and do the Muppet dance until he fled from this ridicule. They all agreed. We rushed. We surrounded the table and put on our best mental hospital grins and dangled our arms and knees as if on strings and chanted 'Shoutybollocks, Shoutybollocks, king of piss'. I realized that maybe this was not to be my Battle of Kursk when you looked up at me and your eyes were buried in a dark deadness that I usually associate with politicians or celebrities presenting a piece to camera. Shouty-B had this whiplash sneer going on. I realized that I was alone, that the Fernfont Films gang had not followed me into the breach. They were all still at the bar, standing there, hands over their mouths, all clearly trying hard not to laugh. Then some bureaucrat-commissar woman got up on the little stage and announced her delight that Shouty-B was about to regale us with a short set of lame, rhyme-based shtick. When you clapped, you did so in my face. Shouty Bollocks was on stage, going through the motions, a monologue-dirge called *Lady in Red Crocs*. Then I found myself in an alley and had dropped my kebab and was crying because I would never now be able to eat those red cabbage strips.

He scribbles in the notepad, furiously[48].

Exterior. The giant office building like something out of Metropolis. Day. Vostok sits on the plinth of the monumental statue of some general or strongman. He looks up sorrowfully at the giant office building.[49]

Exterior. Market. Day. Vostok is leaning against a pillar, smoking. We PAN to reveal Natasha[50] walking through the market.

Vostok drops his cigarette and approaches her.

> VOSTOK
> Hello, miss. I trust our little market
> is safe for you today?

> NATASHA
> Thank you for your concern, but I am in
> a great hurry.

> VOSTOK
> Would you not like to stay for a
> cigarette and perhaps a cup of our
> world-famous coffee?

She laughs, like she's making herself laugh to conceal that she's scared[51].

[48] The upshot of the whole Muppet Dance Forum Reversal was that everyone gathered the next morning at Red Stallion Street and stood around my bed while I shivered under the covers. The Font had been nominated to tell me that cast and crew had decided that I needed a break. The burden of writing, producing and directing a project as grand as *Kaliningrad* was clearly getting to me. I had undertaken a task akin to digging the White Sea Canal single-handedly. We should have a break. We should recharge batteries, bank accounts and bravado. I agreed. I didn't see much in the way of daylight or people for a while.

[49] This scene was actually filmed earlier in Kroykov, so that's Sergei. Don't worry about it. It looks fine.

[50] And, yep, you're right, that's you. Close your eyes if you don't like it (actually, if I ever write a sequel to *Kaliningrad*, this would be its title).

[51] Selina would have been much better in this scene.

43

                    NATASHA
        I know what you're after.

She tries to walk off. He grabs her elbow.

                    VOSTOK
        Why don't you tell me what you're
        after?

                    NATASHA
        I'm not after anything.

                    VOSTOK
        Then tell me, why are you spreading
        yourself so thinly?

                    NATASHA
        I consider myself lucky to be so
        thin. Now, leave me be. I have
        friends. Seriously.

He lets go of her elbow and watches her saunter away. We
LINGER on his face.

Exterior[52]: The Mysterious Lakeside Villa. Early Morning.
A car stands on the drive. The front door opens. Limski
emerges, followed by two small girls who run after him and
try to pull him back. A mousy-looking woman follows and
gathers up the children. He kisses her briefly on the cheek,
slips into his car, revs the engine and drives off.

PULL BACK to reveal Vostok behind a tree, now looking stern
even for a Kaliningrader.

Exterior. The Vast Expanse of Concrete. Day. From above we see
Limski stride across, swinging a case until he disappears.
We LINGER until Vostok appears and follows him.

Interior. The Hanger-Sized Office. Day.

---

[52] And of course, this was filmed earlier, during the Piltdown-Jolly Annoyed Adventure.
Sharpishly, I have to admit, as Mother Font wanted to see the back of Specialneedsbi and
Lloyd Fernery.

Natasha[53] types amid the clatter and racket. Her fingers spider masterfully across the keyboard. She is either very bored or daydreaming deeply. We ZOOM in to her slowly, as if we are approaching her, cautiously, with intentions, with itchy fingers and an aching tongue. CLOSE-UP of her face, its radiance and allure as she smiles. It is as if someone has just turned on a light in her mind.

Interior. Poky Room. Night. Vostok is using the binoculars.

Exterior. Window of Natasha's Apartment. The flat seems empty. It's dark. A light comes on. Natasha sashays across the window[54].

Exterior. Communal Gardens. From overhead we see the three pathways meeting at the entrance steps of the Soviet-style apartment block. Limski arrives, walking briskly. The concentric circles of the binocular lenses surround him as

---

[53] You again, not Selina. I was able to edit this stuff together during the enforced break in the proceedings which turned out to be six-months. Six months, during which The Font told me he'd used my camera to make a series of corporate videos for a company making hand cream (actually, I later found out that The Font was being economical again and had actually been sub-contracted to work on a bizarre portmanteau film called *Twenty-Eight Wanks Later* directed by the dubious local zek I like to call Stephen Polyorkokov). Martin went back to the de-heading machine and punishing fourteen hour shifts in the turkey factory in Lersk. Selina went to Spain and posted many photos of herself wearing a bikini on Facebook and Special returned to Mordski and stared at that building. I suppose I must admit that at this point I did concede that our film, Lucile, would not be completed and would remain one of those great conundrums often speculated about by critics and academics (like Cronenberg's *White Hotel* or Kubrick's *Napoleon*). I had got so far. All I needed was the end, the final sequence, the climax.

[54] Ah, I hear you sigh with relief. I hear you gasp. That's Selina. She's back. They did start again. They all returned to Lloyd Fernery to complete the masterpiece *Kaliningrad*. This is true; I did manage to reassemble cast and crew, the circumstances of which I will relay to you in good time. The first thing to notice here is that Selina, after all that time sunning herself in Barcelona, has a tan. Natasha looks suddenly dusky, more fan dance than polka. We did try to lighten S by rubbing talcum powder on her face and arms but she started to look like Kinski's *Nosferatu*. I had hoped that I wouldn't have to use Selina at all. Again, more on this topic later.

he enters the building[55].

Interior. Poky Room. Vostok slowly puts down the
binoculars.

PULL BACK to reveal that all over the walls of the poky
room, all over the walls that surround him are drawings
of Natasha, of her face and her hair and her body, of her
lying and sitting and standing and walking, of her clothed
and in the nude, surrounded by flowers, surrounded by
mists[56].

Vostok, his face full of chivalrous energy, slides a pistol

---

[55] How did this come about? How did I recover? It was like this. A horrible, grey afternoon
and I have nothing to do so I drift into Nurmansk and in a horrible, grey bookstore I find
staring out at me from the 3-for-2 table a pile of a book called *Let the Snakes Crinkle Their
Heads in Death* by the writer and performance poet I like to think of as Shoutybollocks.
Let the Snakes chronicles his rise to the top, complete with self-effacing accounts of all his
early failures and unlikely seductions. "Brilliantly-observed, couplet-based mirth," it says
on the jacket. Numb, feeling like a ghost haunting my own life, I was forced to purchase a
copy of *Let the Snakes* because I noticed a chapter called *Making Movies*. I wedged myself
into a corner of the in-store Starbucks and read very slowly Shouty-B's hilarious account
of his time 'buffing up a non-budget weepy', the 'particular craziness' of which he can't
re-emphasize frequently enough. It's a project that he soon realizes is 'doomed' and he's
soon side-tracked by the attentions of the 'honcho's squeeze', a girl he lovingly refers to as
Luce Lid (it was 'easy to get her top off'). If you've not read this worthy tract, this veritable
manifesto for modern living (Shouty-B is after all, a shark evolved to swim comfortably
in the shit that's left when Living is Commerce and Art is Over) I suggest you do, Lucile,
and then remember that I wrote the beautiful story of *Kaliningrad* for you. I can't say
that sitting in that Starbucks, reading Shouty-B's side of things was a particularly morale-
boosting experience, especially his version of the Muppet Dance Forum Reversal where
'the honcho had clearly gone tonto/ but I knocked off their socks/ with *Lady in Red Crocs*'.
He went on to describe how he soon afterwards 'traded Lid for another model/funnily
enough a real model/love and fame for me a doddle'. Then it struck me. You and Shouty-B
were no more. You were free of his grasp. Moscow and its onion domes had been saved.
The Panzers ran out of fuel at the gates.

[56] On the way home that afternoon I tossed *Let the Snakes* into the river and found myself
possessed by a strange energy. The scales of the snake must now have fallen from your
eyes. You would come back. You were Natasha. I wrote the part for you. We could start
again. Start the whole film from scratch with a consistent Natasha and me as Vostok. I
even had a fantasy of kidnapping Shoutybollocks and forcing him to play Limski (the idea
supplied by Kim Jong Il's habit of kidnapping actresses and directors from South Korea
and having them make private films for him). I wandered the streets and thought about
you. Later, I determined that I would have to track you down. A Fernery Brunette needs
a constant supply of propositions after all.

from his coat pocket, holds it up to his face and cocks it[57].

Interior. Lobby. Limski strides towards elevator doors. He presses a button and waits.

Interior. Concrete Corridor. Vostok runs towards the elevators.

Interior. Elevator. Limski is going up, leering.

Interior. Elevator. Vostok descends. He is looking down, both his hands crossed over the pistol butt that is pressed to his groin area.

Interior. Corridor. Limski knocks on a door. Natasha opens it and lets him in.

Interior. Lobby. Vostok DASHES towards the elevator.

Interior. Living Room. Limski and Natasha embrace. His head rests on her shoulder. Her face is hard to read. She is maybe scared. She perhaps more lets him hold onto her than she holds onto him.

Interior. Elevator Door. A strip of light emerges with

---

[57] You know that I called you. You must have heard the messages I left on your voicemail. You didn't reply to my texts or my e-mails. I suspected that even though I'd spelt out my motive for contacting you (*Kaliningrad*, Lucile, *Kaliningrad!*) you suspected me of having less than pure intentions. I say that these things run on tramlines and that is how it should be. In any case, failing to make contact I knew that I had to see you in person. If you would just let me take you out for a skinny latte and perhaps some waffles or tapas I could explain. Adopting the role of Stasi Lloyd, I found myself drifting past your house on the off-chance that you were coming in or going out. I took to sitting in the park opposite your house. I saw nothing. I pulled up the collar of my coat and prowled around the Flensborough but you didn't seem to be working there any more. I rang your parents' number from a phone box and put down the receiver as soon as I heard your dad's voice. I listed the sort of places you liked to go (patisseries, perfumeries and boutiques) and stood around, kept watch and waited. I thought that you might even have left town, perhaps shamed by the Luce Lid thing in *Let the Snakes*, but then I did catch sight of you, drinking coffee in Red Café with Dirty Cheryl. I lost the two of you in the street and saw you whisk off in a taxi. You were around though. I saw you outside the chemist on Vantage Street but you blanked me and jogged away quickly. I knew that I was going to have to return to the front. I decided that I'd have to go to your house and knock.

Vostok slam in the middle of it. His face is pure hardman[58].
The door hisses open.

Exterior. Natasha's Window. Natasha pulls the curtains.

Interior. Corridor. Vostok, pistol lofted, KICKS-IN Natasha's
door[59].

Exterior. Natasha's Window. Behind the curtains, three
indeterminate figures sway, push and shove.

---

[58] It was hard to get Specialneedsbi to follow my directions and act like Jason Statham but more hard.

[59] And so there I was, Stasi Lloyd, standing on your garden path, the blood thumping at my temples, the glittery moon above me and a breeze stinging the nape of my neck. Your light was on. The curtains were drawn and behind them I could see your outline pacing up and down. I was scared, I have to admit. I was only doing this for *Kaliningrad* (this is what I kept telling myself but even I realized that I was drowning in visions of our reunion and what we would say to each other and then some caravan somewhere and you taking your clothes off nice and slowly, that look on your face). I was Vostok and in there you were Natasha. This seemed so right. I took a breath. I smoothed down my coat and was about to take the final step to the door bell when someone called out my name. I turned. In front of me was standing Joz Bovrille. Joz, tall and primped and Jude Law-a-like, a bottle of wine wrapped in crepe paper under his arm. He was smiling, as well he might, as even I knew he'd just scored a plum role in the sure-to-be-smash hit British comedy *The Great Leap Forward* (or *Lesbian Machine Gun Nest* as I like to think of it). 'Lloyd,' he said. 'How you doing, squire?' 'Just dandy,' I said, backing away. 'What are you doing out here?' 'Nothing,' I said. 'You here to see Luce?' 'No,' I said, 'does she live here?' 'Of course she does. Come on in. We'd love to see you. Have a drink.' 'Er . . . you and she, you back on?' 'Between us, I'm cashing in on my success.' He winked at me, like a co-conspirator. 'I couldn't impose,' I said. 'I couldn't.' 'Lloyd . . . Lloyd, come back.' But I was over the road and running through the park in the night, mud splattering the tails of my coat, my head in flames.

We PULL BACK. Things darken. GUNFLASH[60].

FADE TO BLACK. PAUSE. FADE IN[61].

Exterior. Communal Gardens. From overhead we see the three pathways meeting at the entrance steps of the Soviet-style apartment block. Limski departs, walking briskly.

Exterior. Window. There is no movement within. Then: SECOND GUNFLASH.

PULL BACK from the window to reveal the whole block and then the other blocks behind the block as we PAN across the communal gardens[62], then ZOOM in on Limski, walking off

---

[60] I must admit that when I arrived home my face was sore and I felt like blowing my brains out like that Czarist officer in Franklin J Schaffner's *Nicholas and Alexandra*. I tried to console myself by thinking that we are alike, both of us always on the hunt for a leg-up to help us realize our dreams, both of us, apart from me, who never seeks, let alone gets a leg-up. In fact, it was I who had been providing everyone else with the opportunity: Special, Selina, Martin, The Font, you. I knew now that you were never going to come back to *Kaliningrad*. I felt something in me wither and crumble. I stared out of the window at the terrace opposite and the passing cars. The world seemed suddenly provincial and English. Eventually, I found myself digging out the script we had written together, or, as I ought to say, the script that I wrote while you watched me write it and dreamed your little dreams of what it was going to do for you. I realized then that I ought to have better understood our differences when one evening you told me that your favourite films were not Eastern European, snow and bleakness, Tarkovsky, Kieslowski, but *When Harry Met Sally, Love Actually* and *Sliding Doors* (or, as I like to think of them: *When Lloyd Shouldn't Have Met Lucile, No Love, Actually* and *Doors Slammed Rudely in Face*). I should not abandon my film so close to the end because of you. I sat up all night then, revising and attending to the script's climactic sequence.

[61] I rang cast and crew each in turn. I put the last of my money on the metaphorical table. They came. Selina even came back from Spain.

[62] Not a ridiculously expensive crane shot but library footage of Reading City Centre Hexagon.

into what passes for a sunset in his head[63].

Roll Credits[64].

---

[63] You notice, Lucile, that the ending has been changed since our original script. In that version, the final scene is of Vostok and Natasha, all dolled up in opulent fur coats being lovey-dovey in some Orient Express style train carriage, en route to the West, where a better life awaits them. I couldn't help feeling that this was too optimistic and untruthful. In Paris or West Berlin or wherever, Natasha would probably become an underwear model and leave Vostok for a rich banker or a singer in a German Schlager band; and Vostok would become no more than a night watchman or a small-time villain's muscle. Or, Vostok would fit in perfectly in Lisbon or London but moody, never-satisfied Natasha, like Tereza in *The Unbearable Lightness of Being,* would dump him there and return to the Land of the Weak and Vostok would be forced to go back for her (perhaps this is the baseline plot of *Kaliningrad II: Close Your Eyes If You Don't Like It*). This is what I learned from you. You changed the end, so I changed the end. And I realized that my fixation with the East and all that cold and suffering and grainy films is decadent and wrong. Now I've got a new project, *Upper Volta*, based on my love of countries that keep changing their names. A man and a woman and their struggle to be free, lots of sand and clay huts, a falconer on a roof in a head scarf surveys white buildings, heat hazes, a sidewinder coils across a dune, a jeep appears on the horizon, a sickle moon sparkles and lifts.

[64] Selina Hackett has gone to better things and is now a Human Resources Officer at the same sprawling poultry business that employs Martin Boch to work a de-heading machine. Merlin 'Specialneedsbi' Prebble is still trying to emigrate to Kaliningrad. The Font is now working full time for Stephen Polyorkokov (with my camera). Sergei Brolin, I have no idea. Shoutybollocks appears on Radio Four too frequently for my liking. Joz Bovrille won a BAFTA for his role in the film I like to think of as *A Date with Yuri Andropov*. I was surprised that you were not in it, too (I hear that nothing came of you and he). I thought I did see you the other day, though, in a film called *The Stockholm Climb*, thought I saw your backside, tightly bound in a nurse's uniform, wiggling along a corridor while the lead actors walked towards the camera. There's my girl, I thought. There's Lucile. I wonder if she ever thinks of me. I wonder if she ever finds herself on some railway platform or cheap, melancholy restaurant, late at night, alone, moonglow and sleet seeping down the window, thinking of me, remembering and saying to herself, 'We'll always have Kaliningrad'.

Post-Leading Man

The glow on the horizon could have been sheet lightning, but as Blue focused on the skyline, as his eyes adjusted to the distance, there was no thundercrack, no tailing boom. The glow was still out there in the dark, brighter than all the neon and the receding pinpricks of the city. Directly ahead of him, as far as he could see, it shone between the uprights of two high-rise blocks. He'd been separate and wordless since the phone call and couldn't tell if the glow was there when he drifted to the window, or if it appeared while his eyes were glazed. Neither could he work out what it was. It might be a fireworks display, or an open-air gig, or an historical building illuminated for the tourists. But somehow he knew it was none of these, and it had been there for as long as he had.

Dipping his forehead to the pane, he squinted to bring the glow into better definition. He remembered other times, on trains and coach journeys, on taxi rides and night-flights and previous trips away for auditions, when if he saw a light outside in the dark he experienced an urge to strike out there to find it, to be there, there in the light elsewhere. He remembered flashes of sodium-lit industrial parks sighted for an instant. The stark empty kitchen of a farmhouse glimpsed in a break in the trees. The street-lamps he'd caught for a second as a plane took off and rose and soared and suddenly the suburban grid-plan below spread into a blur of yellow and crimson, then white. At that point he'd wanted to jump, to disappear into the lights.

He removed his head from the glass. The reflection of the hotel room swam across the image of the city. His face peered back at him: Blue Swanson – post-leading man. Beyond his face was the ghost of the wall that ran down one side of the room until it formed a sort of hallway between the en-suite and the door where his leather coat was hanging. The double bed was behind him. Nina lay on her side, one elbow resting on the pillow, her ankles crossed at the footboard. She'd taken off her tanktop. Earlier, she had slowly, slowly slipped off her knee-length, black suede, high-heeled boots. She would want one last Sly rehearsal before she held him to their bargain. Afterwards, they would have the conversation. He concentrated on her picture in the glass. The glow on the horizon blocked out her face.

It hovered there until Nina shuffled off the bed. He watched in the glass as she wiggled out of her loose black trousers. The calf muscles flexed as she stalked across the room to become the first woman in history to put her trousers in the Corby press. The machine started to hiss. Her image approached him. She put her hands about his waist and squeezed the newish six-pack that he'd developed when he was preparing for the part of Sylvester 'Sly' Ramos-Pintos in *Gentleman's Relish*, the part about which his agent had phoned an hour and a half ago. He'd said that he was just as disappointed as Blue. They didn't think he inhabited the part. He said he was sorry. He would be in touch should something come up.

Nina rubbed her fingers on the muscular ridges that lurked beneath the surface of his shirt. He knew what she was going to say. She was going to say that they should put Sly to bed for one last time. She would then take Blue's hands and hold them clutchingly to Sly's washboard stomach – the only aspect of Sly that met her approval – and she would tug him from the window and down onto the bed, and caress and console him with her kisses and thighs. And subsequently, with the sheets wrapped around them and clothes everywhere and the mini-bar's extortionately priced Cava bottle empty in the bed beside them, she would matter-of-factly state that Hannegore had mentioned it again. He could manage the bar if he wanted to. The job was his. Come on, she will say, you've not had a part for two years. If it walks like a duck and it quacks like a duck, it's a duck. Nina – who before she ditched her acting career to become an actuary was once a credible Alison to Blue's Jimmy when they first met on the set of a student production of *Look Back in Anger* – Nina would say that he'd promised to stop if he didn't get the part of Sylvester 'Sly' Ramos-Pintos in *Gentleman's Relish*, a cable channel drama about three stud-hunks working for a male escort agency called, funnily enough, 'Gentleman's Relish'. Sly Ramos-Pintos: a right dirty, ripe-and-ready, half-Portuguese, half-east London geezer shagmonster in it for the fun and the riot and the birds when one of his co-stars does it for the money (wife, kids, debts etc) and the other is a bit pretty, a bit confused and a bit of a bender, and deep-down has a thing about Sly.

Blue could have played it. He knew he could have played it. *Gentleman's Relish* wasn't *Glengarry Glen Ross*, but he could have downgraded to Sly, and it would have been the breakthrough. It was good money and would have led to other parts and TV work. And of course he'd inhabited Sly. He knew

Sly like he knew himself. He had Sly behind the eyes. But Sly was gone now, and Nina was going to ask him to stop and settle for managing Hannegore's bar, where he'd been working in the evenings to make some contribution to the mortgage.

Nina nuzzled his neck and some time soon, in room 1207 of the Alpha Star hotel, she was going to finish off Sly. As she fiddled with the lowest button on his shirt, Blue found himself asking: what would Sly do here? What would he do? Sly wouldn't hesitate. He'd get the job done, then head back to his pad for a joint and a scotch, to strip off and lie on his bed and stare at his body in the mirrored ceiling. In the glass, Blue practised Sly's most wolfish grin. Outside, the glow was still there, shining in the moonless night.

He turned, and now facing Nina kissed her on the lips. What would Sly do here? What would he say to his best girl, the one he always comes back to? Nina was about to speak. He traced his finger across her mouth and popped his eyes and smirked. In his head he repeated lines from the script: let's play lion, you kneel right there and I'll throw you my meat … His finger trickled down her chin and her neck to her breastbone, skimmed the front of her blouse. The trouser press hummed and clicked above the white noise of the air-conditioning. She draped her hand around the back of his neck and crushed her chest to his chest.

'Hang on,' said Blue. 'I'm just going to brush my teeth.'

In the en-suite, he heard her pacing around the room, no doubt considering the phrasing of her ultimatum. It had been easy for her, the choice to quit a straightforward one. He pulled the door ajar and ran the taps to muffle her.

He studied his face in the mirror, the swoosh of his jaw and the flinty cheekbones that had marketed 250,000 units of *Hombre!* shaving gel in Spain, France and Portugal. He undid his shirt and tightened the torso of the man who'd modelled bikini briefs and appeared, head in shadow, crotch lit-up, on advertising hoardings from Helsinki to Copenhagen. He was still the man. He could have been Sly. He should have been Sly. But he wasn't going to be, and he'd promised Nina that Sly was the last throw. He was older than Christ now, and older than Homer Simpson, and in a few short years he would be older than James Bond, and that really was a psychological marker; just like when he was seven at the Queen's Silver Jubilee and his aunt had whispered to him that at the next one he'd be thirty-two, and being that old was inconceivable then, but now thirty-two had passed without event, without fanfare, without notice to anyone but Nina. When she'd bought him a birthday meal in Hannegore's bar, she'd talked about a new direction, a different career, a reality check. 'You've got a scarf, Blue. You can wrap it around your neck, or you can use it as a slingshot.'

As he rebuttoned his shirt he listened for her call. She'd get bored of waiting soon. She knew when to let him brood for a while. Men, she once said, are either sulkers or shouters. He tried to imagine how she would appear to him when he went back into the room. Her ash-blonde hair undone now and free around her shoulders as propped up on the bed in just her underwear she'd have the look on her face. And he wanted to gain something here, some old flush of urgency, the surrender and melancholy that he used to have whenever he walked back from her halls of residence in those first few weeks when he rarely stayed over, and all he wanted to do was return to her and start it all over and never go home again afterwards. But he couldn't feel this, he couldn't. He couldn't visualize her either, and as he was trying to think of her in the room outside, all he could imagine was the glow at the edge of the night and the city.

All tension dropped from his arms and his muscles. In the mirror, his face was starting to tighten and tremble. If he didn't find the glow now, he knew he never would.

That's what Sly would say. That's what Sly would do. In the character bible: never regrets; never feels guilt; always takes what he wants; total control.

Blue flushed the toilet and used its rushing to tiptoe out of the en-suite unnoticed by her and pick his leather coat from the hook and silently open the door and pad along the corridor to the lift.

Going down in the lift, sadness needled him. She would be alarmed, worried, letdown. He found his mobile in the pocket of his coat and fingered a text message about needing some space, but Sly wouldn't do this. Sly turned off the phone and put it away and when the lift reached the ground floor, Sly glided across the foyer to the street.

Outside, the night air was damp. There were specks of rain, whispers of autumn. His coat flapped at the back of his legs as he paced up and down the taxi rank outside the Alpha Star. He was at ground level now and couldn't see the horizon, only the low-down glimmerings of restaurants and bars on the other side of the road. Sly was street and smart though, as he knew that Nina's room was at the front of the hotel, and so behind the restaurants and bars, somewhere out there, was the glow.

He crossed the road, swaying his shoulders as if the night owed him something. He imagined the camera behind him, the title sequence of *Gentleman's Relish*; the throbbing electronic soundtrack; 'Blue Swanson as Sly' supered on the screen; the hem of his coat coiling at his boot-heels; the flashes of sheen up his back as Sly and Family Escort and Closet Bender Escort strode into the night like Norse gods for hire.

Sly aimed for the mouth of a thoroughfare, one of the arteries of the city. When he arrived there, sweat began to tickle his hairline as he powered up the long, straight street. He swaggered, chin-up, hands thrust in the pockets of his leather coat, checking his reflection as it flowed across plate glass windows, a habit he'd picked up at drama school. He passed pavement cafes and the vacant, eerie showrooms of furniture stores and Greek restaurants.

He felt nothing but energy inside him, momentum, purpose as he forced clubbers and late night shoppers and idling couples to move out of his way. Sly here would be on his way to a rendezvous in a penthouse or wine bar or cocktail lounge, to a pretty, logical thirtysomething lawyer or sales executive who beneath the Chanel and the body powder and confident flirtatiousness would stink of a work/life balance out of kilter and body clock issues and frequent flyer ennui, problems he would make her forget for a couple of hours (until a beat in the script when she turns out to be his long lost sister, or a long lost man, or a Christian fundamentalist serial killer with a particular grudge against male prostitutes; her father was a male prostitute, her mother a needy, pretty, logical thirtysomething lawyer, etc, etc).

As he crossed a canal bridge, Sly clocked a line of hanging fairy lights that like will-o'-the-wisps disappeared into the blackness past the towpath pubs and the houseboats. A gang of hen night girls jostled him, brushed him with their long bare legs. Grinning his way through their catcalls and shrieking, he thought: wolfish, I am wolfish, wolfish. He made sure that they each saw the whites of his eyes and the white of his teeth. Sly Ramos-Pintos: remember this face, ladies. Their voices softened behind him as beyond the canal bridge the shops became low-key, more functional – unmarked entrances, solicitors, financial services – and the street began to climb. Far away ahead, above the camber of the road, he spotted the tips of the two towers. At the summit of the rise he had a vantagepoint and stopped and stared and felt a pitch of feeling inside him. The glow was there and closer, waiting for him.

As the road bottomed out and he picked up his stride, the feeling lulled. In room 1207, Nina would be fully dressed again and sitting on the side of the bed, a tumbler of extortionately priced malt whisky from the mini-bar clasped in both her small hands, her hair tied back, waiting for the turn of the key in the lock. She would be worried and disappointed. He was avoiding her. He wasn't letting her help him. But he'd done this before. She knew him. She would not be happy, but she would understand. He said this to himself as he passed through miles of nondescript offices, their anonymous doorways reminding him of the theatrical agencies on Charing Cross Road and Longacre and Shaftesbury Avenue that used to intrigue him and excite him so much when he was just starting out, when he'd left drama school and was doing provincial plays and lunchtime theatre in Soho and the Edinburgh Fringe, when he was an understudy and a walk-on, when he was reading, reading, reading with Nina, and auditioning every week, when the big break was always out there somewhere and he was waiting to be discovered.

To be discovered. How he had always loved that phrase. He would recite it to himself in the mirror every morning after he'd done his tai chi and his press-ups and stretches. To be discovered. To have always been there in the wings with his talent and presence and commitment, and suddenly the spotlight sweeps and double takes and veers back to rest upon Blue Swanson, leading man.

Ahead of him, the road smudged into a hotchpotch of squat, ground-hugging buildings and warehouses. Behind them, the two tower blocks were closer and taller. He could see the fluting and the architecture, the wink of glass, and could almost make out the corporate identities emblazoned at the summits. The glow was stronger, white and sharp; a giant half-shell shot through with spokes of grey. He could feel it inside him as he entered a strip of manky dance clubs and specialist dives emitting smothered bass-lines and dim beats. At the corner, a corner some way off, fifty metres or so, there was a figure crouched on the ground.

His boots slithered to a stop on the pavement. Some sort of small box rested at the feet of the figure on the corner. The hands dangled over the knees and the head was thrown back, lifted towards the sky. Behind, the glow beamed out from the two tower blocks. He let the glow spangle in his vision until the grey lines in the shimmer waxed into turquoise shafts.

The figure on the corner had moved its head. As Sly advanced he realized that the frame was slight and the ankles narrow, the shoes open-toed and kitten-heeled, the breasts full and impossible to miss. As he reached her, the eyes of the woman glinted up at him as she nudged her Tupperware box with the tip of her shoe and rattled the small change within it.

She didn't like doing this, he could tell. Her smile was false, but she tried to mask this by flashing her eyes. She was in her early twenties, he reckoned, and she had a round, moonish face and full lips and a smooth nose with a single silver stud. Her fingers were grubby and there was a smear of dirt across her shoulder half-hidden by the strap of her black vest top. As she looked up at him, the smile seemed to lose its plastic feel, seemed to warm to him, and he thought for a second that she would actually scrub up well. This is what Sly would think. He had radar. What would Sly do here? He would be moved, or at least some part of him would feel sorry for her, he himself having lived by his wits, hand-to-mouth, on floors and in hostels in his late-teens before he island-hopped along an archipelago of broken beds as he discovered his mission and his talent. Sly would take her home. Make it up to her. Take her home and fuck her in the shower and fuck her in the bedroom and for a while she'd be a kind of sidekick-confidante until she got too close and too jealous and he sent her on her way. This is what Sly would do. But Sly's pad was not an option and for a second he found himself scanning the manor, checking for some secluded spot, an alley or doorway where maybe he could do his thing for her in fast-forward: sink and grasp and release and they would be happy. He looked down at her and thought: wolfish.

Smiling still, she said, 'Nice coat.'

A feeling crept up on Sly. This was where he was going. Not the glow, but the street. Not Sly, but Blue. There was someone slumped on a street corner and that person was Blue.

'Are you all right?' he said. When she didn't answer he reached inside his coat pocket, found his wallet and counted out three twenty-pound notes. He pushed them into her hand and slipped Sly's leather greatcoat off, folded it over his arm and let it drop into her lap. 'Here, you look cold. You have it.'

He swung around and started to walk. There was a scrabbling behind him and a tug on his elbow. The woman was wearing the coat now, but she was a slight, petite thing and it dwarfed her like a sou'wester. The sleeves hung over her hands and the coat tails pooled around her feet.

'Hey you,' she said. 'Can you take this in for me?'

Blue slung his arms across his chest. He stood up to his full height and toughened his body, felt the six-pack ripple beneath his shirt, a tactic he'd learned from playing an extra-intimidating bouncer in some midweek crime series that bombed like an anvil from high altitude.

'I'm sorry,' he said. 'I've no more cash.'

'I don't want anymore.' She delivered a very mannered little pout. 'Why don't you come and help me spend it? You look like someone with something on his mind, and I've got a very sore bum from sitting down, and maybe we could both use a drink.'

'No, I'm sorry,' said Blue, checking over his shoulder for the glow.

'There's nothing down there,' said the girl. 'Unless you're looking for grief. C'mon, I just want to say thanks, that's all, and not be on my own all night. There's places open down by the river, and you've been very nice, and …'

'Sorry, I need to be on my own.'

'What's your name, then? C'mon, at least tell me your name, so I can say thanks to a person?'

He was about to say Sylvester Ramos-Pintos, but you can call me Sly, then Blue – Blue Swanson, I'm an actor, doing some research for a part here and you're spoiling my method – but he wasn't, not anymore. He thrust out his hand and shook hers.

'I'm Graham,' he said. 'Graham Longrigg.'

Graham Longrigg. He'd not used the name since he'd changed it to Blue Swanson by Deed Poll – Blue being the name of one of the cooler kids from school that he was always jealous of, being a Graham. Who'd ever heard of a leading man called Graham? Graham Valentino? Graham De Niro? Graham Di Caprio? And Longrigg? Long Rigg? The comico-genital connotations. The way they used to stomp around him and swing their arms between their legs in the changing rooms. The phlegmy Lon Grigg. The 'g's' that hung like haemorrhoids from the sphincter of his name. Blue Swanson, however, had a classic vibe, an intimation of Hollywood, a charge to the syllables. Blue Swanson was a leading man

'Well Graham,' said the girl. 'Cheers again. You sure you're all right?'

'Take care,' he said, 'look after yourself.' Without waiting for her reaction, feeling the chill on his arms, he walked away, soles scuffing, towards the glow.

The road funnelled out into a business district. There were loading bays and clusters of high metal bins. Tumbleweeds of shredded dot-matrix paper rolled around the tarmac. The glow was so near now that he could make out its crest as it drizzled into the night sky. It was near, only minutes away.

He lost himself in a network of alleyways and open-air car parks, ending up on a gravel pathway. A fenced-off wasteland and a low brick building with slit-windows of opaque, reinforced glass flanked it. In the distance, the pathway merged into pavement. There was a street-lamp with some sort of wall behind it. Thinking about the river the woman had mentioned, he looked up at the glow in the sky to the right of his position, and the towers and the logos on the towers: *Magnatech* (bold and violet letters looped by atoms) and *ellipsis* (a filament-like, adobe-red font). As he approached the lamppost he started to worry about the river. He realized that his footfalls on the gravel were echoing around the buildings. It sounded like there was two of him, then four of him, not two, and then eight of him, not four, and a prickly heat-like sensation on the nape of his neck made him look over his shoulder. A group of youths, boys in baseball caps and sweatpants and skanky sports tops, chains glinting around their necks, and rings on their fingers were prowling up behind him.

A voice called out.

'Yo, Hasselhoff.'

Graham turned and walked backwards so he could front them. Their thin, angular faces were grimed with wispy stubble and their skin was pallid and zitty. If John Carpenter's *The Fog* had featured an undead hip-hop crew, it would have looked like these boys.

'You sorted, Hasselhoff?' said the Head Undead. He'd left the rest of the Zombie Massive at a standstill behind him. He was pacing after Graham.

'You sorted?' he said. 'You sorted, mate?'

Graham whirled his forefingers like Yul Bryner in *Westworld*.

'I'm sorted,' he said. 'No hassle.' He swirled around and carried on, but the Head Undead was still behind him, closer now.

'What you got then? What you got, Knight Rider? What you got, muppet? You fucking mug? What you got? Give me what you got. Giiiiiiiiive it.'

Graham stopped, feeling nothing as he sized up the Head Undead. He was young, seventeen, eighteen, but bulky, his face more potato-shaped than the rest of the Zombie Massive. His face was stark in the half-light, the features pulled back against his cheekbones and the bulb-like knob of his chin.

'I'm gonna break your nose,' he said.

So Graham, Graham Longrigg, a long way from home and close to the light, weary and sore-footed from his trek, Graham Longrigg coiled his fist, and with a forearm worked for years by morning press-ups and ergs and weight-training and fencing, felt a surge of Charles Bronson and *Deathwish* as he smashed his fist into the Head Undead's ugly face, and the Head Undead crumpled and fell to his knees on the grit with his face in his hands. Way back down the path, the Zombie Massive stood up and jolted their necks like hyenas when there's blood on the breeze.

Graham ran, ran like there was nothing else in him but running. Gravel ricocheted off the brickwork and the chain-link fence whizzed into a silvery stain as he kept up his rhythm, unable to tell if they were behind him or not, and as he reached the cone of light thrown by the street-lamp, he almost crashed into an embankment and could smell cooler air tinged with a stagnant vegetable odour: the river. He was running on flat and straight paving now, pistoning his arms and lengthening his stride and he was running, running, running alongside the river, past offices and pubs and shops shutdown for the night, and as he ran he could see them, see the two buildings on the other side of the river, *Magnatech* and *ellipsis*, giant monoliths of steel and glass, and around them, haloing them was the stunning, sky-high, crown-shaped, mightily intense power of the glow.

He came to a halt; caught his breath. His throat and his ribs felt scraped out and red-raw and the muscles in his calves wanted to pop out and bubble up his legs. There was no one behind him, no Zombie Massive on his tail. He shambled now, lumbered up the embankment, a kind of awe inside him, awe and fear and regret and worry for Nina that subsided into a dullness as he reached a wooden jetty protruding ten or so metres out over the slosh and glint of the black river.

From the end of the jetty, he could see the glow clearly. Between *Magnatech* and *ellipsis* there was a plaza where flagstones gleamed like wet marble in the unnatural light. At the furthest point, resting on a plinth or stage was a bank of huge searchlights struck up to the sky, brilliant and blazing.

A kind of emptiness overtook him. There was no way of crossing. He scanned up and down the embankment for a bridge or underpass, but he could see nothing from here. He thought of walking further along the embankment as there must be a crossing somewhere, but he decided against it. He'd come this far. This was enough. This was it. He would go back now, retrace his steps, skirting the Zombie Massive, of course, and return to Nina at the Alpha Star and explain it all to her, how he felt, and he would tell her he would take up Hannegore's offer. It was either that or flab-up and weather until he could palm himself off as a character actor. Or take the downward mudslide into porn, and reinvent himself as Miles O'Member or Michael J Cox, but that would be the negation of the negation, that would void his pride and his self-esteem and his ideals, and in any case that particular career move would register seventeen-thousand on the Nina Scale. Standing at the end of the jetty, he looked into the heart of the glow and felt for a second that he must, to a casual observer, resemble Robert Redford in *The Great Gatsby*, Redford at his most miscast and stilted, and he didn't want to be this way anymore. The walk back would be long, but he would make it.

A slithering metallic sound came from behind him.

'Yo, Hasselhoff.'

He spun around, a sizzle of fear pulsating from the pit of his gut to thrum at his temples. Blocking the end of the jetty was the Zombie Massive. Twelve at least of the fuckers in their prison-white trainers and racing stripes, their *Stone Island* sweatshirts and cheap-shit bling. Head Undead was at the front, blood on his top and his neck and his face. Head Undead brandished a retractable metal cosh that was raised over his shoulder as he rampaged up the jetty with the Massive in tow.

Stepping backwards, Graham's heel failed to impress on the boards. His arms floated out from his sides in mid-air as he snatched a glimpse of the Massive at the end of the jetty above him. Their jeering faces became blobs of flesh that his boots wiped as they shot up above his head. He hit the surface of the water with a smack.

The jetty and the Massive warped into a haze, then into glimmers as he sank. Strangely calm, now that he'd dropped some way without smashing his skull on the riverbed or some jagged object dumped here in the dark. No sound, only a burble in his ears. Sludge in his eyes, so he shut them. Saw stars now. As his body drifted, as he cruised down to fronds of weed and felt maybe fish or eels flicker against him, unsure if this new sensation might be the cold or the impossible weight of the water; as he sluiced down further to the bottom and the current swept him further from the embankment and away from the jetty, he thought that this was right, right to vanish like this and see only stars at the end. What else, in the end, was there to see?

He opened his eyes. They were flushed with silt, but it cleared. The surface was miles above him. He imagined the real stars a trillion miles away; how he was always going to be one of them, and that he soon would be. He imagined Nina asleep on their bed, balled up like a shrimp. And the mobile phone that he should use to speak to her now in the pocket of Sly's leather coat that was draped around the corner-woman as she huddled in some alleyway. An oval widened above him. He saw giants, their fingers outstretched, holding banknotes, the smiles on their faces. They were the people he knew, friends and acquaintances. They were the people from Hannegore's bar, people who came in and spent their payslip money on bottled beer and wine and company. They were reaching down to him like they reach out to him at last orders and in his head last orders clanged.

Rolling on his front, he plunged further, then resisted the descent, forcing his way upwards, pumping his legs, holding his breath in his lungs and ballooning his cheeks to fight the black river. His arms scooped out great swathes of watery space, pulled him up towards the surface that was a patch of sheen above him, wide there, wider now, paler, then whiter and there was a rush at the end, a rush when he broke the surface. The buildings bobbed and jostled all around him as he gulped. He went down again, came up to tread water and float for as long as he could as he orientated himself. There was one last push, one last Burt Lancaster job to a landing-platform for speedboats and launches on the other side of the river. He heaved himself up and the dead-weight of the water fell away as he sludged onto the platform, coughing up river-water, his limbs finished and spent, his stomach flooded, his eyes clenched shut and gritty; filthy, freezing and sodden.

Crouching, he spluttered and threw up sediment. He rolled on his back and opened his eyes and looked up into the night sky for the stars. No stars. The night was bleached. Light pollution in the sky. Light pollution caused by the glow that was this side of the river, just up the steps from the platform.

   At the top of the steps, the breeze nipping along the embankment hit him. It thickened his bones and chattered his teeth. He wrapped his arms around his chest and ducked his head and started to jog. The glow would be warm. The glow would be hot. The glow would save him from shock and hypothermia. His feet seemed as soft as slices of cold meat that squidged against the paving. A deep, inconsolable gloom fell through him as he reached the first of the grand towers. The offices inside were hidden by mirrored glass that reflected his shivering form. The glow was at the end of the wall of mirrors, a shaft of light that fired out over the river from between the buildings. He found himself laughing as he made it to the mouth of the concourse. Standing now between the *Magnatech* and *ellipsis* buildings, he was suddenly laughing, and laughing made his stomach clench and hardened the taste of river and bile in his throat. The glow was a white core; a star that sent blade-like shadows radiating out to him from the stone benches that littered the concourse. He had to squint as he stumbled towards it. He shielded his eyes with his hand as he wandered between the benches and stone troughs full of wavering plants. The feeling inside him found neutral. He could not sense his feet or his face. Closing his eyes, he kept going and let his hands drop and felt them slap against his thighs, but not his thighs impact his hands. It was dark now, dark behind his eyes as he kept walking blindly. He couldn't hear his breathing anymore. He couldn't remember his name. He was nothing but a heartbeat as he stepped into the glow and the glow engulfed him.

Tomorrow Belongs to Me

Each time the phone rang they lay in the darkened bedroom, not speaking, and waited for the click of the ansamachine. They would listen to the tinny message as it whispered up the stairs and then to its flatlining hum until that too, fleetingly, gave up the ghost.

It was long past midnight when the quiet held long enough for Scarlet to fall asleep. The night was humid and David's back had stuck to the undersheet. A car pulled up outside. Shafts of light strobed the ceiling. The room seemed to tilt. He tensed. It was only the briefest of journeys to here. There were voices, though, and two slams, not one. Laughter faded. The car drove off. David thought he felt Scarlet wriggle in her sleep. She, too, would demand an answer in the morning.

Earlier, David had pulled down the upper sashes of the windows to circulate the air but no breeze disturbed the curtains or the pile of papers on his desk. The desk was still the wallpapering table liberated from a dead uncle's garage. It was spacious and broad and when covered with a cloth looked like any other table. In the evenings he could sit in here, vigorously researching the subjects of his classes – never, he felt, could you know enough about the past – and meanwhile keep an eye on the street. The notebook he'd bought to record neighbourhood events and flashpoints sat unopened by the desktop fan. During the only visit she'd made to his house his new colleague, Karen Harris, had giggled over the condition of the fan and the wallpapering table. Both looked rubbish, she said. He could definitely afford a proper desk. And why was it up here when there was nothing in his backroom downstairs? 'Boys and their bedrooms, eh?' she said as she spread out slowly across his bedclothes.

In silhouette, the fan looked like a miniature radio telescope. It too had been rescued from the same uncle's garage at a time when the white goods of the dead were often foisted upon him. It was a noisy contraption that emitted an irregular drone. Scarlet would wake up if he switched it on. He felt around for a hand. If he rolled over he might be tempted to trace with his fingertip the soft groove between the top of her arm and her shoulder blade. Should he rouse her, though, she would reel out her priorities. She would speak of Berlin.

The phone had remained quiet for some time. He didn't realize he'd got out of bed until he was halfway to the window. He found himself hiding behind the curtains, afraid that a spying-eye might see his nakedness.

The street was deserted.

No one was standing at the end of his path.

He had met Scarlet at the Dawkins' fancy dress party. He hadn't wanted to go. The idea of fancy dress embarrassed him. In the end he opted for a character from a film no one remembered. He'd arrived with Karen. He'd left with Scarlet.

What was supposed to be a costume still dangled on a coat hanger hooked to his wardrobe door. The party had been organized in the upper rooms of Broadhurst Hall by Terri, the wife of Godfrey Dawkins, Head of History at the school where David taught the same subject. Its theme was *Silver Screen*, a celebration of Godfrey's passion. He was the brains behind the Sixth Form Movie Club and the organizer of trips to the National Film Institute to see venerable classics that bored the boys and most of the girls and prompted disappearing acts and small-scale riots on the walkways around Waterloo. Godfrey had bragged that he would be coming as Hawkman from the eighties re-make of *Flash Gordon*. The costume David chose for himself was easier to assemble: M, the eponymous killer played by Peter Lorre in Fritz Lang's masterpiece. All he needed for M was his black suit, a white shirt and a fedora. The hat was the only item that cost money, apart from the chalk he used to scratch a big, accusative M for Murderer on the shoulder of his trench coat.

Selecting M made David remember the first time he'd seen the film, when he was sixteen, late at night on Channel 4, and how the forbidding, dark streets of Berlin seemed impossibly gorgeous and futuristic to him. He loved the scene where the machines in a toyshop window glitter in the night. He desired to experience the atmosphere of the film and feared the trial. He knew then that he would live in Berlin one day, where there was intrigue and romance and stark choices and human extremes. The girls, with their hats and their feathers would be more exciting than the girls he knew. He would love one of those chorus line girls.

He never actually went to Berlin, though, only read a lot about the twenties and thirties, Weimar Berlin, its novels and histories, art and cinema. There was something comforting about losing himself in a culture that flashed so brightly before it was crushed. Recently, he'd found himself drawn to those books again.

On the night of the party he'd arrived early at the Broadhurst, an ugly Tudorbethan mansion that loomed over a village green called The Knock. At the downstairs bar, waiting for Karen, he felt relatively pleased with his ensemble as he watched Magnus Lingard, Head of Physical Education, and his usually demure wife Miriam lumber past as Shrek and Donkey. They were followed by a pisspoor Tinman (newly qualified geography teacher wrapped in BacoFoil) and a cardboard Darth Vader. In all likelihood, the colleague inside Darth had a taste in films that had not matured since he was seven years old.

In the mirror under the optics the face of a more intriguing alter ego glinted back at David. He liked this face most when he pulled the brim of the hat down low. This wasn't Mr Foss, a history teacher with a crap desk and fan combination stumbling into something unwise with the wrong type of flapper, but a more glamorous doppelganger. A city dripping in scarlet neon thrived in the corner of his eye.

Someone flicked his earlobe, a frump in a shaggy wig and tweed jacket.

'Guess,' she whispered, 'and buy me a G&T if you get me wrong.'

'Don't know,' he said.

'It's a double then. And double-doubles until you guess me right.'

'What Norman Bates keeps in the fruit cellar?'

'Ooh doubling, doubling.' She threw both her arms around his neck and squashed her chest against his back. He made himself laugh and craned to see if any other strangely-dressed colleagues were traipsing through the bar to the party of the decade.

'Come on,' she said. 'Your favourite TV programme.'

'Oh God, not that woman from Cretin Pit.'

Karen started to laugh and needed to rest her hand on the bar to steady herself. She would laugh at anything. At a dinner party at the Dawkins' house a few weeks ago Karen had laughed until she hiccupped at his story of being shortchanged by the bloke with the squint in the Gusto di Rimini delicatessen. A similar story of thrills and cosmic irony – that a chemist had been shut by the time David arrived hoping to buy athlete's foot powder – had reduced her to a helpless state. By this point he had worked out that the whole evening was a set-up. A select gathering, Godfrey had said on the phone. Beyond the hosts, the select gathering included only David and a new Media Studies teacher fresh from two years in chaste Singapore and a stranger to this kicking little town.

Terri had provided a succulent rustic chicken with pasta, followed by a summer fruits pudding. Godfrey, with goblet raised, announced the forthcoming fancy dress extravaganza. While they all drank and cooed over Terri's sauce David tried to act the geek and listed for no sane reason the names of nations overrun and assimilated into grander entities that in turn had been long since renamed (Dacia, Navarre, The Far Eastern Republic et cetera). Godfrey wouldn't play, though, and only wanted to discuss his Hawkman costume with his wife, forcing David to provide for Karen a dreary fact sheet of local inconveniences and a black list of the most unfriendly pubs. She laughed a lot and then described, in anaesthetizing detail, her love for the Saturday night TV show that David knew only as *Cretin Pit*. He didn't know how to respond without encouraging her, so explained that, really, taking all into account and with a view on the long term and communal utility, everyone – and he stressed *everyone* – who auditioned on *Cretin Pit*, and the judges, the studio and production crews, its entire audience and all the people who went out afterwards and bought the resulting and dismal compact discs should be deported to somewhere remote and freezing. Karen laughed so heartily that she spilled a whole glass of rioja over the table. Godfrey or Terri or some awesomely devious PR firm in their pay must have spun out of control when they pitched him to Karen. In the conservatory, as the evening turned to night, the Dawkins left him alone with Karen. After several high-pressure silences, she still suggested a drink the following weekend. He didn't have a reason to decline. Meeting up couldn't do any harm, could it? It couldn't lead anywhere. They had nothing in common.

Ten days later he'd been patrolling the football pitches at lunchtime when Georgi Shakos from Year Nine shouted, 'Oi, Fosspot, you giving that Miss Aris the benefit?'

In the bar of Broadhurst Hall David bought Karen her double gin and tonic. As she sipped she stared up at him and rocked from side to side.

'Is I a good likeness?' she said.

'Not as good as that,' he said and indicated that she should glance over her shoulder. Swaying through the bar was the Religious Studies teacher, Kristoff Crawford, a gangly garden cane of a man slouching towards retirement age and here dressed in scholar's gown and stripy scarf, as Harry Potter.

'Yikes, Charles Hawtrey,' said Karen. 'Love your Blues Brothers outfit by the way. I can always tell a soul man.'

David sighed and twisted, pointing with his thumb at the chalk M.

Upstairs he hung back as Karen launched herself into the room like a bouzouki dancer. Applause followed each shimmy of her hips and flourish of her hands. David didn't know if this routine had anything to do with the woman from *Cretin Pit*. He'd only watched it once for ten minutes, at Karen's flat, and it had induced a terrible spasm that made him rant and swear. Before then he'd only caught glimpses of the woman from *Cretin Pit* on the front pages of newspapers that he didn't read. During David's spasm, the woman from *Cretin Pit* was singing *Up, Up and Away in My Beautiful Balloon*, a performance that Karen was impersonating now as she swept past the Pisspoor Tinman and Shrek and Donkey and Darth Immature and always-too thin-looking Judy Mystere dressed as an Oscar statuette and Big Baz Gummer in an England rugby kit – a spurious choice, thought David, unless 'screen' meant anything on the telly, in which case he could have saved the others from confusion by coming as a yoghurt drink full of friendly bacteria – and then Karen swished by a random centurion and a character smeared with bright blue food dye that David did not recognize and around and around until she clicked her heels and slapped her thigh and stiffened abruptly in front of Godfrey Dawkins.

David had come to teaching late. He'd told Karen on the night in her flat when he'd sworn at *Cretin Pit* that initially he hadn't wanted to grow up in front of much younger people. He had tried his hand at many unsuitable jobs – telesales (fired), advertising copywriting (fired), bicycle courier (two months in hospital) – before he finally settled on teaching history. Three years ago the career pedagogue Godfrey Dawkins had taken David under his wing. This, though, was ridiculous. Godfrey's wings were a papier-mâché cast smeared with black feathers and attached to a leather harness. More than a suggestion of paunch poured over the waistband of a tight pair of leather hot pants. The bushy beard was clearly held in place by elastic strands clipped to the twin-spiked helmet. Hawkman's club was a long, thin pepper grinder that belonged in an Italian restaurant. At his side, Terri's Dale Arden wore a black gown and Aztec-style headdress. Karen curtsied before them, sedate and regal, as if drinking in her one moment.

'Up, up and away,' boomed Godfrey and proceeded to knight each of her shoulders with the pepper grinder. 'By my giddy aunt, you're astounding, woman.'

David watched all this from the doorway. He felt shivery and again pulled down the brim of the hat. Karen revolved on the heels of her court shoes and raised both her arms, powering out another chorus of *Up, Up and Away* until she faced David. The walls of his throat tightened and his shoulders contracted. He found himself suddenly buttoning up his trench coat and fastening the belt. It was only the poignant enthusiasm in Karen's face, and the stares of the Dawkins and their guests that prevented him from retreating into the better darkness of the evening outside.

'It's Men in Black,' shouted Godfrey. He pointed the grinder at David. 'Don't just stand there, lad. We're waiting for you and Miss Harris's duet.'

Karen held out her hand to David, laughing again. He winced and shuffled forwards to where she and the Dawkins were standing in their pomp.

'Are you the Singing Detective?' said Terri.

'God knows who he is,' Karen said. 'He doesn't even know who I am.'

'Where've you been hiding, lad?' said Godfrey, slapping at David's backside with his club. 'Everyone knows who she is.'

'Everyone,' said Terri.

'You know what he calls her?' said Karen. 'The Brush, as in "daft as a . . ." .'

'Oh that's mean,' said Terri.

Mortified, David could just about flick his eyes from side to side to scan the party and the Dawkins and Karen dressed as The Brush. He didn't, he knew, have anything against The Brush. The woman looked on the point of collapse. It was the jeering, bread-and-circuses element to *Cretin Pit* that he hated. At that moment, surrounded by costumes and with Karen, he could tell, about to grab his arm and coerce him into singing *Especially for You* or *Islands in the Stream*, he reached what he would later describe to Scarlet as the pinnacle of loneliness.

He made an excuse. At first he thought he was going to the bar but he skirted along it and around the back of the guests and headed for a pair of French doors that opened out onto a balcony overlooking The Knock. The town's distant lights shimmered in his eyesight. He must have been deep within himself here, he would reason later, because he did not realize at first that someone else was on the balcony. She seemed to have run from a distance, right through the reception room, and leapt at the last moment to hang from the rail beside him.

'M,' she said. 'How sweet of you to come! I was feeling most terribly lonely.'

He had seen them both before, the costume and the girl, though he couldn't remember her name. She was petite, her hair dark and sharply bobbed and she wore a black silk dress with white collar and cuffs. A pageboy hat was angled on her head and her fingernails were painted emerald green. He hoped against hope that she was not someone he taught but she was in her mid-twenties, thank God. He thought about university and those jobs, remembered a pretty girl he'd never spoken to who sat in a room at the end of a corridor in a building that gave him the creeps. She wasn't that girl and she wasn't Maya Braun who one Wednesday night during a half-term had him reading *Jazz Age Goddesses of Decadence* in Nando's for two hours before he eventually gave up and sloped off home. If Maya Braun hadn't stood him up he would have suffered her in Nandos all night wishing she was a Jazz Age Goddess like this girl here.

'Sally Bowles,' he said. 'And not Liza Minelli, the English one, from the book.'

In his bedroom a slight breeze puffed out the curtain, lifting it over the frame of the desktop fan, snagging it there. Sat on the side of the bed now, he went over and over the time he met Scarlet on the balcony and asked himself how it could come so quickly to this, to an ultimatum, a horrible choice? He would like to sleep as she was sleeping but feared that if he closed his eyes the phone would ring. The phone would ring in his dreams. He lay back. The night they met: a conversation on a balcony overlooking The Knock. A warm evening and distant lights. A girl called Scarlet dressed as Sally Bowles who recognized the M straightaway. A discussion about whether M and Sally ever rubbed shoulders in Berlin and where they might have met: The Lady Windermere bar; on the Kurfurstendamn; a cinema in the Bülowstrasse showing *Metropolis* or *The Blue Angel*. A joke about prairie oysters and seductions over the telephone. A promise to show him her bowler hat. Party noise in the background and someone singing karaoke, Karen probably, her voice no doubt inferior to that of Scarlet, a real cabaret singer. Slipping through the party, unseen, their footfalls accelerating over the laminated floor of the downstairs bar and out across The Knock and into the trees.

Two hours on, after the pair of them emptied the best bottle of red in the rack, in the room where he waited now, she took off her black dress. Her thigh above her stocking top was a white stripe that glowed in the moonlight. In the morning, dishevelled and smudged around the eyes she lingered and kissed him by the telephone stand. When she finally left there was a sense of shock. She was someone he had anticipated all his life. A girl from a vintage photograph or a black and white film. A girl a young man meets on a train, between the wars, in Mitteleuropa, what they unleash in each other in a room in a hotel on Lake Maggiore. This girl is called Scarlet. She even answered her phone when he called her later at dusk. They met in the Cantina Reggio and over a bowl of mussels and a bottle of pinot noir she told him the story of her short, incandescent life.

Home-schooled in the wilds by an opera-singer father and a mother with experience on the West End stage, she knew at the age of eight that she must sing and act. Music college: she plays banjo, piano and the ukulele if she has to. Starring roles. Her voice. Plaudits and garlands. Older men drawn to her old-world charm. Much time in front of the mirror and with make-up artists; a tour of Germany and Austria playing Sally in *Cabaret*. Small parts in long films. She was here now to promote a feature called *Lost Causes* about a man beset by ghosts in Berlin after a war. She laughs, but not like Karen. Scarlet did not laugh but leant in and cupped his knuckles with her palm when he told her about the pinnacle of loneliness and what he saw in his face under the optics. He would afterwards realize that Berlin first occurred to her here. The charge of it almost ruffled her hair.

Later that week she led him down a flight of steps in a side street he must have previously ignored and into a cellar bar with brick arches and long oak tables. A packed-in crowd of men in suits and girls in tea dresses clapped when she got up and sang *Tomorrow Belongs to Me*. Silvery and lilting, her voice overcame the song's connotations, made it seem that the future owed the pair of them. She isn't as annoying and testing as Sally Bowles;

this is what he realizes. She isn't flighty, or promiscuous or unreliable or unrealistic. She doesn't smoke, she isn't camp and she can definitely sing.

One Sunday afternoon in his lounge, tipsy, in pink feather boa and sitting with her thighs pressing a chair's backrest she had moved so it faced him, she said that she loves his inner flamboyance. She wants everyone to see it so she can marvel at their faces as they gasp. In his bed, later, she first whispered what she wanted, her playful little dream.

On a weekend break in Oslo, marooned in the hotel because of the rain, naked and side-by-side on the floor, she told him that he grounds her, makes her feel that all is possible. She needs him. She wants her M, her darkly handsome, inscrutable, misunderstood and criminal counterpart. At the top of a ridge, in the park, the Broadhurst and The Knock visible in the distance, the taste of her tongue was still fresh in his mouth when she first said it as if she meant it. We must leave, David. We cannot stay here. It will sap us, whittle us down. It will break *you* anyway, because I am not staying. I am going back to Berlin. We are going to Berlin, where we belong.

Berlin, she said, is best approached from the east, from Moscow, on a cramped train full of refuseniks and dreamers, after thirty hours of travelling through flatlands and forests. You arrive in Alexanderplatz – just roll that name around your mouth – and come out from the tunnels and into the sunlight that shimmers on the concrete. We now find our eyes open for the first time. We run through the streets, the graffiti blurring into blue and yellow streaks either side, through crowds and spectres. In Prenzlauer Berg we rent a flat with high ceilings and gaping rooms for nothing at all. We can live from the proceeds of my voice so that all day you can do whatever it is that you really want to do with your life. We can sleep late in the long brown winters, then bundle ourselves in coats and scarves, slip-slide up the Unter den Linden, past the statue of Frederick the Great to the Brandenburg and the Tiergarten to browse the monuments and look for ice-lakes and shell-holes. In coffee houses we'll meet avant-garde tract publishers from Arkhangelsk and jewel-thieves from Prague and surrealist painters from Bucharest and revolutionary separatists from Vladivostok and the self-proclaimed heirs to the throne of Navarre. In Berlin you can sweep up these people and draw them down into a nightclub you can only enter through a manhole. In Berlin you dance all night in crimson smoke and feel yourself rise and drift and become. In Berlin you clamber past the graveyard in the Hasenheide Park at four in the morning, a haze in your head, stopping at an all-night bakery on the way to another dive-bar where you can still drink champagne with Otto Dix or George Grosz. In Berlin, the night and we never end.

Cooler air started to infiltrate the bedroom. His clammy skin felt like it was hardening. He realized that he had taken the empty notebook from the wallpapering table and was flicking through the blank pages, an action that seemed to widen the space between himself and where Scarlet slept. He remembered what she had said earlier, when he had failed to give her an answer: *When did the child in you die, David? And when did the adult fail? When were you left only with the adolescent?*

He'd never had an answer to this question. There were no notes in the notebook. He couldn't remember the dates and the battles and wondered if this failure had anything to do with his curious decision to attend the Dawkins' party as a child murderer.

Another car pulled up outside. Lights again cascaded over his walls. The engine stayed running. Then it stopped. A door clunked. David flipped the notebook onto the bed and from the window saw Godfrey Dawkins tottering around in the road besides his Volvo estate. For the first time that night it occurred to him that he would have worried them, the Dawkins and Karen, when he'd disappeared from the party earlier. They would have been concerned and may well have not enjoyed their night because of him. Terri was still in the driver's seat. Someone else was in the back. Godfrey waved the pepper grinder over his helmet, staggering in a circle, and then he must have noticed David's outline at the window.

'Dispatch War Rockets,' he bellowed. 'Gordon's alive!!!'

He fell on the bonnet with a thump. His wings quivered and the helmet fell off. It rolled to the curb. Karen emerged from the rear of the car, wigless now but still dressed as The Brush. David couldn't make out her expression as she took her mobile phone from her bag and strode up his path. He didn't know if he was going to apologize or explain or move on or slide back. Scarlet was still asleep. She could sleep through this. He was going to have to close those windows. He was freezing now and it hit him: Scarlet would *not* sleep through this. He wanted to look away from the street and over to the bed. Outside, Karen paused to prod her keypad. The phone would ring, soon. There was only a moment left, a moment to climb through a manhole into a room of red smoke, a moment to join the tail-end of the Love Parade, a moment to hold hands, raindrops in their hair, rain thrumming on their shoulders as they scamper across a hemmed-in, cobbled square towards the lights of an all-night drinking den. He switched on the fan. The drone started and sounded like it had always been in the room but with its volume turned down ever so low. The phone rang in the hallway, once. Someone knocked on the door. Karen called out his name

Ultima Thule

Ansbro crossed a deserted market square, wary of slush and ice, the weight of his overnight bag and The Product drawing down on his shoulders. In what he assumed was the city's main drag he passed pubs and bars, all empty. Behind the windows of pizzerias and restaurants untouched wineglasses were arranged in shining squares on circular tables. It was Thursday evening. It was still snowing. The cold latched itself to his face as he paused on a traffic island to check his street plan. According to the chatty buff on the train the whole city had once been an island, an inland island that resisted The Conqueror. After it fell, no later campaigns followed, no skirmishes, uprisings or even an air raid. Ansbro didn't find this surprising, given its remoteness. It was only surprising, and more so inconvenient that his esteemed client was headquartered up here. Ansbro, representative of Bastion – the publishers of usually low-quality military history books – had left London early for an appointment that had taken over two years to arrange, the breakthrough being the acquisition of The Product. It would have to snow today. The train would have to stop about fifteen times and then, after an incident on the line, huddle for hours at the white outskirts of the city.

Moving off in the direction of his hotel Ansbro thought that if Big Dump, his manager, were here, he'd be too cocksure with The Product beside him. He'd eat a lot now and then guffaw through the appointment. On Monday he would crow that he'd rolled up the flank in a faceless divorcee's bedroom. He'd boast to Leonard Lovestone, Bastion's owner, about his acumen in placing The Product. The Product was Big Dump's name for it. Ansbro wanted to stop thinking about it like this. He wanted to stop thinking about

Big Dump as well and Big Dump's massive bowels. Big Dump and his bowels were envious that Lovestone had given Ansbro this job. This dealer had been out of circulation for years. Lovestone thought he was dead and had taken his lists and contacts with him. Communication with Ansbro had been by letter only, a genteel way of doing business. The dealer had agreed to view The Product tonight, at his premises, a place called Ultima Thule.

The street forked ahead, as if parting for the Hotel Aachen. From this angle it was a triangular wedge that tore the road in two. Snow swarmed in the orange glare of its carriage lamps. It would be a short walk from here to Ultima Thule. There was still enough time to make the appointment, if Ansbro was quick, snappish, sharp, a proper seller.

It seemed hardly warmer inside as he found himself shivering on a thin electric blue carpet identical to those he'd seen before in a hundred or so budget hotels. The carpet and the over-bright spot-lamps seemed at odds with a Victorian staircase with banisters as wide and sleek as funpark waterslides. It was as if the hotel had been only half refurbished. Maybe they had run out of money. Even the canniest of businessmen were running out of money these days, even Lovestone. That's why Ansbro was here.

He rested his other luggage in front of the reception desk but kept hold of The Product, afraid that it might walk if he put it down. He rang the bell and waited. He experienced a twinge as he imagined that he'd left The Product at home or in the office, or if after the stupor of the journey he'd abandoned it to some lucky opportunist on the train. Footsteps approached from an outer office. He put the case down and sank to one knee to check on it. For a second he felt that he could no longer remember the combination and only noticed that his teeth were chattering when the number came back to him.

'What are you doing down there, Mister Ansbro?'

When he bobbed up the woman wore a smile she asserted with mind and industry. She was a petite reddish-blonde and probably no older than he was. She wore faded jeans and a black, off-the-shoulder top that overlaid a lacy, turquoise vest. Something – like a crack in the surface of a sheet of ice – glinted in her right, blue eye.

'I'm Kay,' she said. 'Your concierge. I've put you in The Salon.'

'The Salon?' said Ansbro. 'I didn't book The Salon.'

'I upgraded you,' said Kay. 'Same tariff.' She placed a swipe-card on the desktop. Her fingers spidered over it. He had difficulty with the eye and focused instead on her unevenly varnished cherry-red nails. 'Oh yes, and before I forget, you had a phone call this morning. A Mister . . . a Mister Tool called for you.'

Resting his knuckles on the counter, Ansbro said, 'No, it's Thule, like hula.'

She laughed. 'I'm sorry, Elliot.'

'It's not important,' he said, even though it was, and then it struck him.

'What did he say?'

'He apologizes, says can't make tonight, but he'll be there for you same time tomorrow night.' The crack in her eye shifted. 'I am your concierge, though, if you need The Salon for another night, or if you need anything else, Elliot.'

Concierge. She wasn't a concierge. This was not the sort of hotel that employed a concierge. She'd used his first name as well; she was flirting and dressed like she worked in a smoothie bar. And the room that he stood in now was not a salon, just a room at the top of the hotel with slanting ceilings and a round window like a porthole. When he thought of a salon he pictured a vast, plush-carpeted affair with ornate mirrors and chandeliers and high windows that overlooked a deer park. Evidently, the word meant something else for Kay.

He left The Product on the bed and was now standing by the porthole. Snow thumped against the pane and half-obscured his view of the spires and gables and the lit-up buttresses of the city's cathedral. He would have to stay here longer than he wanted. The appointment would impinge on his weekend. There was a woman he was supposed to meet tomorrow night. He wondered what was wrong with Kay's eye. The snow reminded him of a piano tune he could no longer name, music that felt like falling down the stairs in slow motion, painlessly, without impact. He suspected he'd been sent here to fail. This mission was a pretext to get rid of him. That call could have been from Big Dump. This was cross-double-cross. Big Dump was setting him up.

Perched on the bed, he took out his mobile phone and left a message on Lovestone's ansamachine. Then he took The Product from the case. He'd bound it in a black silk wrap. He suspected that he might unravel it now to find half a paving slab in its place. That's the sort of thing Big Dump would do, or at least it was the sort of thing he said he'd done in the past. But from under the silk emerged the white custom cloth slipcase. He used the drawstring to coax out the book and then, scared he'd drop it if he opened it on his lap, knelt with it resting on the bed. He'd memorized its vital statistics, its contents, its accumulated sales. Seventeen and half inches by thirteen and a half inches of jacket. Four point two inches thick. One thousand and eighty-eight pages and one thousand and forty six illustrated plates, all by the same celebrated hand and only published within these covers. A uniformologist's delight, the Holy Grail of Napoleonic Buffdom, it had been much coveted since it first appeared in 1931. It had been reprinted only once, in the late 1980s. A mere two thousand were left. The American publisher had gone bust recently and Lovestone acquired the stock in the fire sale. It would never be reissued. *La Roche's Imperial Codex* retailed at £799. This would seem a reasonable price to Mr Thule, Ansbro was sure of this.

Everything he knew about Mr Thule came from Big Dump and Lovestone. Whenever Ansbro discussed sales with the old boss he would mutter ruefully about Ultima Thule. In the sixties and seventies both the shop and the mail order catalogue had sold thousands and thousands of Bastion Books. Lovestone would often pine as if some El Dorado or retail Atlantis still existed up here in the once-island city. He'd collapsed into a sweaty rapture when Ansbro confirmed that a meeting had been arranged. Ansbro was to sell the whole consignment of the *Codex*, play nice with Thule and suss out whether the shop or the list, or both were for sale. Ultima Thule was to be annexed to the Bastion Imperium. Elliot Ansbro was the outrider.

During an informal man-to-man strategy session in Big Dump's hutch of an office BD's *Shredded Wheat* hair looked especially wheaty and his Barbour jacket was still the colour of duck shit.

'Don't get up yourself here,' he said. 'The *Codex* is just another product. Pricey, like, but just product. Product for Buffs.'

For Big Dump the readership was divided in two. There were the Grunts, who would buy anything, literally anything, even *SS Underpants and Sock Suspenders of World War II*, or *Hell's Coming to Breakfast: Field Catering from White Mountain to Afghanistan*. Grunts were, in Lovestone's words, people who got 'hot about nuts and bolts'. Buffs, on the other hand, were more likely to get hot about Sexy Wars. They were of higher rank, rarefied and wealthy readers, attachés and ex-brass, the elite corps, the sort of people on the Ultima Thule mailing list. Big Dump could bollock on all day about Buffs and their buying buttons. He pronounced 'Buff' with a hard, punchy emphasis, as if the B was a projectile that wiped out not only the rest of the word but also the whole of the sentence.

For Ansbro, the word Buff conjured only nakedness. He frequently pictured naked Buffs reading Bastion Books in their shabby armchairs, curtains drawn at midday as they slotted and sliced their way across the ghost battlefields in their heads.

'Thule is the King of the Buffs,' Big Dump had said. 'Only met him once. Frankfurt. Weirdo. Must be about eighty now. Told Leonard he'd rather have been one of Napoleon's generals. Thinks he missed his time. Should have been born two hundred years ago. Don't go AWOL up there, you. This is the big tickle.'

Ansbro opened the *Codex*. The binding creaked. The pages smelled like fresh paint. He felt like a little boy again, kneeling by the bed, nose pressed to an annual or comic. The image on the plate was of General Massena, upright with his palm resting on a globe in a proper salon of hardwood panelling and august bookshelves. His face was stern and inquisitive and his hair short and Caesar-like. Scrupulous brushwork gave a tactile quality to the sash, the sabre and the gauntlets. The intensity of the colours amazed Ansbro, the nobility of the navy blue tunic, the shimmer of the braid and the fluid brown of the general's pupils.

Originally, La Roche's designs had been cigarette cards. During the First World War, all French army issue fag packets included one of these inspirational reminders of the nation's military past. At first La Roche concentrated on the ordinary soldiers: The Old Guard, Chasseurs, Marines, Lancers, the Elite Gendarmes. Later he painted the more exotic elements of the *Grand Armeé*: the Squadron of the Mamelukes, the Empress Dragoons and the Vistula Uhlans, and later still, during the twenties, he painted the personalities, the Marshals, Riskepanse and Kleber, MacDonald and Massena. This is what Ansbro had learned about the origins of The Product. You learned a lot when you worked for Bastion Books.

Massena's eyes seemed to blink the longer Ansbro stared at them, as if the General conferred some approval or understanding. Was it one of these pictures, or even this picture in the *Codex* that had once told Mr Thule that he'd 'missed his time', that he should have been one of Napoleon's generals spreading *Liberté, Égalité* and *Fraternité* by cannon flash and cavalry charge? Was it Massena who made him hear the whisper, or was it St Cyr, The Owl, who smashed two Russian armies one after the other? Or Rapp: so wounded in campaigns that his men called him 'the piece of old lace'? Ansbro would ask Mr Thule. This wasn't part of the pitch he'd prepared. It was another discussion he was now planning. Most of the dealers Ansbro sold to were arch-Grunts, bayonet-obsessives, bowel-irregulars and paramilitary fantasists like Wolfgang Carver of the Onslaught Bookshop in The Wirral. Big Dump was right about one thing only. Thule was not a Grunt. But he was not the King of the Buffs either. He was the Emperor.

Ansbro felt a sudden heat at his temples and dryness coat his tongue. Outside, the snow was still falling, thicker now, creeping up the windowpane. He was going to have to stay inside the Hotel Aachen tonight.

Later he found the bar at the rear of the hotel, an array of dark green padded alcoves and stained glass partitions that wheeled around a circular serving area. No one was drinking here, no other reps or lorry drivers. Kay was standing behind the counter in front of a wall of shining, yellow-tinged glasses and glimmering bottles and spirits. Around the walls were hung framed images of fairy-winged nymphs promoting aperitifs and infusions. As he approached, he felt that he was somewhere else, some other city and century. Prague maybe, 1921, or Vienna, Montmartre, Bourbon Spain. It was wrong, he knew, to think of the past as a more charged and exciting atmosphere. But what else was there to do with history? He didn't want to think of it as Sexy Wars. Nor did he want it to be an accumulation of overlooked lives, the biographies of unsung boys and lonely girls in service to this or to that now defunct institution.

He pulled up a stool and ordered a single malt with ice. He was glad to be alone. He wanted to brood.

'You've had a terrible time getting up today,' Kay said. 'And all for a cancellation, poor you.'

'Not a cancellation. A rearrangement.'

In the mirror beneath the optics he noticed her hand shake as she poured his drink. The ice cubes clattered against the sides of the tumbler. He had long since ceased to think of these trips as holidays or adventures. He was not Big Dump. All that kissing and telling. The not kissing and still telling. He was not, he hoped, going to park and ride. What were those lines in her eye? Would it be rude, intrusive to ask her? She put the tumbler in front of him and smiled again, this time as if she anticipated that he was going to suggest something.

'Kay,' he said, poking his finger at the ceiling. 'Can I ask you something a bit private?'

'Fire away,' she said. She clapped her palms softly together, then wiped them on her hips and ended up dipping them into the back pockets of her jeans, a motion that pushed out her chest.

'You're the owner, aren't you?' he said. This had occurred to him earlier, considering that she was so far his small-talking concierge and now barmaid.

'Sort of,' she said. 'Family business. We've been here for a hundred and fifty years. Just about.'

'That's nice,' he said, and sipped as she began to tell him about the history of the Hotel Aachen, its beginnings as a coach house; the haunt of Red Hector, a famous highwayman; an Edwardian heyday; an inter-war reputation for integrity and cleanliness. He wasn't really listening. He kept thinking back to Massena and the piece of old lace and Thule and manoeuvring Thule around to discussing a change of management.

'These pictures here,' said Kay, 'are insured for ...'

'Kay,' said Ansbro. 'Do you know where Ultima Thule is?' She looked baffled and tapped her cheek with her thumb. 'It's a shop.'

'I could ask Dad?'

'He might know my client.'

'Mr Tool.' She rested her elbows on the bar and leaned in close to him. The lines in her eyes were tiny lightning strikes radiating from a central core.

'Thule like hula,' he said. 'Vidkun Thule. Like the unpleasant Norwegian.'

'So what does the unpleasant Norwegian do?'

'He's not unpleasant. Or Norwegian. He's going to offer me a job.' Staring into her eyes, he tried to catch his reflection there. He shouldn't be doing this, and wanted to lean back but he couldn't.

'Confident,' said Kay. 'Like it. So we might be seeing more of you?' She lifted her shoulders and spread her arms along the bar and her knuckles paled either side of him.

'Maybe,' he said.

'More?' said Kay as she reached for his now empty glass. 'Dutch courage for the interviewee?'

The light behind turned her hair to golden coils, and then he was certain of himself, of what was going to happen, and he didn't care about anything else.

Upstairs, back in The Salon, he lay face down in the bed with his arm draped over the shape beside him. It was the middle of the night now. He couldn't sleep. Things that had been said came back to him and he found himself sniggering in the band of grey moonlight that cut across the duvet. He kept mulling over a day in the office a few months ago. Two nights before Big Dump had swallowed a king prawn vindaloo and fifteen bottles of Oranjiboom with someone possibly called Norbert Pogrom from Beer Hall Putsch Books and Figurines in Frisby on the Wreake, Leicestershire. The king prawn then fought a dogged rearguard action in the Wookey Hole-like cave-system that was Big Dump's bowels, morphing and mutating into a gigantic basalt millipede that slithered out segment by segment all morning and all afternoon, on and on while Ansbro was forced to take BD's appointments. One of these was the pitching of a new list to Maggie Dunderness of the Broadside Naval History Bookclub in Leigh-on-Sea. When Big Dump returned from sentry duty he looked pinched and peaky. He said, 'what you think of Maggie then?'

'Buff,' said Ansbro.

'No. As a woman. What did you think of her … as a woman?' He made a mauling, claw gesture.

'I was thinking about naval books,' said Ansbro, even though he hadn't been.

'Wuss,' said Big Dump. 'Me? I would have taken her to a lay-by and done her.'

Big Dump and his lay-bys and his stonk-on for Broadside Mags of all people. Even Mrs Dump was a more attractive proposition, and she was a gas mask fetishist – she'd have to be, wouldn't she? Each time he replayed the Lay-By Declaration Ansbro cracked up. If all went to plan he would never have to stomach this sort of idiocy again. The *Codex* was beside him, under the covers, safe and concealed. The *Codex* would now play a subtler role. He found himself laughing again, then heard something and stopped. Tentative footfalls approached in the corridor outside. He sat up and held his breath. He waited, sensing that the softened dark corners of the room had shrunk in closer to him. He mustn't laugh. She would go. If it was her. Could be another resident, but he'd seen no one else. And she'd made him stay in the bar for so long and seemed crushed when he went off to bed. The steps trailed away. He started to laugh again. Tomorrow he would capture Ultima Thule.

Then the time was finally upon him. He was about to ring Ultima Thule's bell, a big stubby black button that had in all likelihood once been the first ever, newfangled doorbell contraption in the once island city. Shoulders back, chest in, he focused on his breathing so he wouldn't appear nervous or intimidated by Mr Thule. He held the *Codex* in his left hand to keep his right one free for the introductory shake. The iron grill across the shop front was still in place, though there was a mess of slushy footsteps and zigzag bootprints around the doorstep. People had come in and out today. Buffs, probably.

It was dark now. Ansbro could make out even less of the interior than he had this morning. The window was so dusty that he could only imagine the shelves of bulky, cloth-bound spines and showcases for lead soldiers and dress-uniformed dummies that he was sure lived inside. He would get these windows cleaned. It would be the first thing he would do as manager. This had occurred to him during his earlier reconnaissance mission to find the shop. That had been at midday, after his lie-in and after he'd paused on the mezzanine and then tiptoed out swiftly while Kay was in her office, but before Big Dump called with some gruff threat about what would happen if Ansbro was having a day off at Bastion's expense. To get off this topic Ansbro explained that he'd done the concierge in a lay-by last night. 'Good drills,' said Big Dump and recommended a Mongolian All-You-Can-Eat in Crouch End. There was only an afternoon to waste before the launch of Operation Thule.

He'd walked the *Codex* around a snow-struck, half-hidden city deserted of people. He mooched cathedral cloisters and a covered market where the stalls were all shut for the day. Then in a fresh snow flurry on a hump-backed bridge he watched a wizened woman with her mouth smeared with thick red slap push a tricycle up the slope towards him. He thought then of the girl he was supposed to meet tonight – her name was Selina; she was an ex-actress and she'd once lived in Spain – and he suspected that she would like him more if he could fix a lawn mower engine. He sent her a text and cancelled. He ate lunch in a pub called The King's Shilling and pondered the Sexy Wars and how Lovestone thought that some wars were sex: Napoleonic, Zulu, World War Two in the West. And some were like a bad date where you got nothing because you couldn't fix a lawnmower: Bosnia, Latin American death squads, Nazis off the leash in Belarus and the Ukraine. There were readers who got hot about nuts and bolts: caterpillar tracks and weird bits of kit and special spoons. He would ask Thule all about this. Thule would have an opinion. Thule, he imagined, was tall and lean with a tight slot-like mouth and unruly eyebrows and long, silvery hair. In a local paper Ansbro compared the rents of one-bedroom flats and flicked through stories about the snow and the closure of the schools. Someone had won twenty-five quid for a photo of a red setter going mental on a sledge. The incident on the line yesterday had been a fatality. There were still no trains south. He walked the streets in the late afternoon. The *Codex* no longer felt heavy. He'd become used to its weight. As the light began to fade and the sky became a blue screen he stood transfixed by an evening star, delta-shaped, an arrowhead, glinting and distorted. He sat in another pub and drank coffee and waited for seven o'clock and made plans. Now it was seven o'clock and he was outside Ultima Thule, pressing the doorbell, waiting for Mr Thule to emerge.

On the yomp back it started to snow again. Unable to see, he nearly lost his footing twice and the handle of the case started to chafe the calluses that had long ago formed around the joints in his fingers. An upwardly swiping ache in his right shoulder blade became a spearhead of pain that had dug in around the top of his spine by the time he stumbled into the Aachen. The lights were off. The reception was unmanned. He dropped the case. The calluses stung and crinkled. His last girlfriend had complained that his hands felt scratchy when he touched her. An occupational hazard, he'd explained, when you heft a load of old cack around all day. When the case banged on the carpet the light in the outer office flashed on. He picked up the case and, head down, strode towards the stairs, his shoes greasy with snow and seemingly pressing on nothing. Halfway across, the spotlights above him sprayed the darkness beneath him electric blue. He kept on walking and didn't look at her.

'Elliot,' Kay called out. 'Oh Elliot … wait.'

Upstairs in The Salon he sat down on the bed, still in his coat and with The Product lodged between his ankles. He still couldn't feel his feet and his hand stung. He should run it under the hot tap but didn't have the energy. Snow pounded the porthole window again. He thought of the piano music, but this time saw himself smashing his elbows and chin on the stairs as he fell. He had rung the bell for an hour. He had thrown snowballs at the dim, upper storey windows. This was all a set-up. Big Dump knew Thule wasn't here; or that Thule was a crank or dead or bound to muck about any minion of Leonard Lovestone. And all the time he'd thought there was something else over the escarpment, another promontory, something beyond or improved. Better.

He realized that he was going to have to go home. He would have to slouch into the office on Monday and explain this. Even if he didn't end the day putting his stuff in a cardboard box he would have to keep this up, wander the streets and the shops and talk about books for Buffs and books for Grunts and Sexy Wars and nuts and bolts, and Big Dump would still lie about his conquests and his mobile phone would still have an *1812 Overture* ringtone and his bowels would still be massive and Lovestone's head would always be the shape of a sweet potato.

He'd left the door open. Kay said something courteous. He didn't answer. Her footfalls approached and she sat down on the bed beside him. Her feet appeared next to his. She wore cute flat-soled, leopard print pumps.

'I'm sorry, Elliot,' she said.

'What on earth for?'

'What happened.'

'Happened?'

'You don't know yet?' She took his hand, the left, uncallused one that didn't throb. 'I asked my dad about Mr Thule this afternoon, and he did know him.'

'Did?'

'I'm sorry to have to tell you this, but Mr Thule was the man who died on the track yesterday.'

His ankles clamped against the case. The snow outside the window seemed further away. Kay gripped his hand a little tighter.

'Apparently, he stopped trading ages ago and put all his money into stocks and that. Recently, you know, debts, nothing. Must have got on top of him. I am sorry.'

He bowed his head. Pressing his knees together compressed the case and hurt his shins. He tried not to, but couldn't help it and pictured Thule on the track. The barren white expanse on either side. The snow. The oncoming rectangle. The blue smudge. The rails hum. Gravel jitters. Thule in Massena's uniform as depicted by La Roche. He wondered whether in his last instants Thule considered himself fooled, perverted by spiel and oratory. He must have ended as tatters, wisps.

'I didn't want this for you,' said Kay.

'You couldn't have known.'

'No, but I didn't want this for our last.'

'Last what?'

'Guest. We're going, you know. Going under. All this time we've been here, and now ...'

'I'm sorry to hear that. It's a grand hotel.'

'I saw your name in the reservations, Elliot Ansbro. Bookseller. And I just thought, pull out all the stops, Kay. Make sure he has a great time.'

He sensed that she'd turned her head towards his, but he was staring at the case, the black oblong of it. He could sell the thing inside. Pawn it. Flog it to some second-hand merchant in the city. Cut some cash. Stay a few more days. Keep the Aachen open. He turned to her. There was still something in her eye.

She let go of his hand. They both sat there, hip to hip, and outside the snowflakes swirled, drifting down in the top panel of the porthole and then caught in an updraft in the lower half sped away out of view.

The Prettiest Girl in Berlin

It was starting again. The Usher couldn't keep his hands from shaking, this time until he meshed them together behind his back. As the truck juddered round the corner the skull and crossbones on its side turned a sharp white cheek. The vibrating chassis shivered the black uniforms and the brimless, almost Turkish helmets of the soldiers up top. The Usher locked his heels together. He wondered if they thought he was standing to attention in their honour. They looked away from him, their rifles pointed at the low grey sky. He raised his trembling hands to his face. His face felt even smoother and colder than before. She used to call it his handsome face, admired its dreaming aspect.

As the soldiers receded into Leipziger Strasse, they appeared to him a legless mass welded onto a steel block fitted perfectly onto the back of the truck. They would descend on a ramp and slide into battle on rollers. If Measure were here he'd say something about a Hydra of commingled metals and flesh, a Modern Centaur, rampant, virile, eternal yet indefatigably new. That was Measure for you.

It was late afternoon now. Smoke still rose from the direction of the Linden and to the south from the Newspaper District. The stammer of machine-gun fire and the distant blasts that unsettled the pavements drew closer to The Usher. Glassburg had lied. Or at least, Glassburg was mistaken. This was not Paradise Built. Measure was correct again. Measure was often infuriatingly right about things. The war wasn't over. They were all still at war, all of them, including the members of The Plenary that with himself included Glassburg, Measure, brazen Tempio and Hephzibah. He should have listened to Measure.

91

At least this time he had the luxury of standing still. In the Tiergarten, when that machine gun nested on the Brandenburg Gate had fired over the crowds he'd been unable to stop and fled in a cowardly, undignified fashion. He had found himself sometime later stumbling through fields of crab grasses in the Garment District, silver flashes in his head and not sure how either he or the grasses had materialized there.

Following the truck, a cohort of the black uniforms marched in quick-quick time across Potsdamer Platz followed by a horse towing an artillery piece. The contraption squeaked as it crossed the tramlines and split the puddles. His coat was wet. He couldn't decide if it was January or December. It must be January. Aunt Eva had recently grumbled about there being no money for Christmas illuminations. Blotches the size of coins disturbed the surface tension of the puddles. It had started to rain again. It had rained throughout the week, since the noises began and the newspapers vanished. Droplets spattered on the windowpane of his room, the room where The Plenary met. Measure and Glassburg were his regulars. Sometimes the alley cat Tempio emerged exhausted from someplace somewhere. Hephzibah? Once she had whispered on the edge of their conversation. And then last night Glassburg had finally betrayed her confidence. Not only did he know who she was, he knew where she was and what she wanted The Usher to do.

Behind him now the little flight of steps still led up to the terrace of the Café Josty. There was no one inside. Some of the tables had been overturned. He noted the determined absence of good cheer and cordiality today. There was a waiters' strike. He had been told this when he was halfway here and the shaking had first overtaken him, on Invaliden Strasse, in that café where an exception had been made, coffee served and then the waiter seemed unsurprised when The Usher only warmed his hands on the cup. He was shaking again now but if he walked into the Josty they would let him compose himself. They would serve The Usher. Of course they would. An artillery piece was being towed through the centre of the city.

Blue light and smoke shimmered over Berlin. The Usher was about to fragment, shatter, just like Measure predicted. He turned and was about to run up the Josty's steps and onto the terrace when he saw it again.

The poster. It was pasted to a wall. If Glassburg were here he would say it was another sign. The picture and the writing. *Who is the Prettiest Girl in Berlin?* And The Usher stared at the rough, reddish, vaguely Frenchified style of the drawing, the line of identical and anonymous high-kicking girls. *Who is the Prettiest Girl in Berlin? Visit the Caviare Flapper Dance at Stardust Cabaret at 8.30pm.*

The Usher already knew the prettiest girl. And he would not find her in some squalid den where once-nice girls danced like pistons and speculators guzzled champagne looted from the cellars of Odessa and Kiev. Glassburg would counsel that this was old Measure's miserly language. And would no doubt continue: you must nowadays find a new way of articulating. After all, like it or not, we are witnessing the birth contractions of a Golden Age. On the other hand, Tempio would positively revel in the possibilities of the Stardust Cabaret whether Hephzibah resided there or not and however she was feathered. Pandemic dance contagion? *Fantastique!*

Reflected in the window of the Josty his coat was a grey impression and its buttons sparkled like the eyes of a spider. He could just about make out the Dreaming Aspect of his Handsome Face that she had once commented upon here, on the day they walked across the square talking of books and other things and he had bought her coffee and a pastry before they hurried to his room for the first time. He remembered this and turned to follow the artillery piece out of Potsdamer Platz and into the Liepziger.

He lost sight of the artillery piece as the daylight began to fail. Shiny pinpricks glittered in the rain ahead but when he reached them he found only splinters of glass. Blood splashes trickled into the gutter outside the Reich Post Ministry. *The Prettiest Girl* was pasted again alongside a restaurant with smashed windows, the rain blowing inside and its chairs thrown out into the street. Distant shouting came from behind the shops and offices. And always that throb of machine-gun fire and the reverberation of mortars. A hissing. A whoosh. Not so far off. What were they doing in the side streets? When one particularly loud and nearby explosion forced him against the facade of the Wertheim Department Store – the interior of the shop vacated, rows and rows of shelves and stands and things he couldn't quite make out in the half-light, no customers any more, no assistants, not the pleasant and warm-hearted shop girl from whom he bought a brooch on the day that he also bought her a pastry and talked of books – he seemed to be somewhere else, before a red horizon, the crest of that ridge, back when The Plenary boys used to march into villages and tunnel down into the earth.

To the south, a great muster of smoke rose into the sky. Something was on fire near or actually in Kreuzburg. He would have to cross that district to reach her.

Further on now and something began to approach. At first he thought it might be a giant man in a hussar's helmet or the artillery piece coming back this way. Where Friedrichstrasse crossed Leipziger Strasse, where he would have to turn, he realized that ahead it was a horse pulling a carriage. And then he saw that from Friedrichstrasse, marching towards him out of step and out of line came a mob of men, red tabs lodged in their hatbands, their coats unbuttoned and flapping, their rifles raised and a red flag flourished at their rear. This must be the rabble that Measure had described.

According to Measure these plebeian degenerates were in thrall to some horror from the East. We have not seen their like since Islam burst forth and bloodied the lands from dusty Mecca to the promontories of Vienna.

This demonic breaker, like the Mohammadans before them is nothing but a torrent of zeal and brute force in the sway of some vague and pious utopian claptrap. They even bear the banner of their prophet and the prophet's catspaw here in Berlin is the traitor who, abetted by his Polish whore, stabbed us in the back not so long ago! It's fine for Glassburg to prattle as he does. He forgets that although the Romans had no stirrups they did discover the cement. The Kaiser did not desert us. He was usurped!

Glassburg, of course, explained this week's disruptions as a spasm of exuberance that would purge us all and then we will see what is left to mould and refashion. The new situation is a great opportunity. What a waste it would be if we did not grab hold of it with both hands, not to throttle the serpent in the cradle, as Measure would urge us do, but to embrace and nurture it. For justice, Usher. For peace and fairness and freedom for men and women of all standing and nations.

The Usher felt in no position to judge and as ever in The Plenary Hephzibah was silent and Tempio absent carousing and so neither offered an adjudicating perspective. In the café on Invaliden Strasse, however, the Striking Waiter with the lion-like head and pork-chop whiskers, after he fetched the coffee had sat down on the only other chair that wasn't upended. 'It is the young ones who strike. They think the new republic will fall just as surely as it did in Russia and then they'll have their say. I'm going along with them out of … I don't know what anymore … but like you, I'm sure I don't approve of such behaviour in the streets. They may have replaced the Kaiser with a saddle-maker but these Spartakists are worse than Ebert, I tell you.' And then he tried to convince The Usher that it was no day for anyone to be out in Berlin. The Spartakists may well have declared the General Strike on Monday and seized the Printing Office and the railway stations and the newspapers and ranted about revolution and the Soviet Union of Germany, but it was Thursday now. The Saddle-Maker had appointed a bloodhound and The Bloodhound had raised an army from the borders and his boys were hunting city square to city square, boulevard and alleyway and house-to-house and were dealing with these Spartakists. And if that wasn't enough, the poor were dropping like flies from this influenza. A thousand wretched souls last week and probably a thousand more by tomorrow. Soon there would be too few Berliners left to take pot shots at one another.

When it must have become obvious that The Usher was never going to drink the coffee, the waiter offered, formally and kindly to walk him back home in case there was any unpleasantness with Spartakists or the Bloodhound's boys. No one could tell who was who on Thursdays anymore. 'You don't want to go further than this, my friend. I beg you not to.'

The Usher put the money for the coffee on the table, including what he assumed was a generous tip, picked up his hat and left to head for the Tiergarten.

'The time for action has come. The time for action has come.'

The Spartakists thrust their fists at the rain as they chanted and staggered into each other, brandishing their flags and their guns. The Usher stepped back under a tattered awning to get out of their way but no one seemed to notice him. No one noticed the Dreaming Aspect, or they all chose not to as the vanguard rushed screaming towards the carriage as it turned at the junction. The horse whinnied as it found itself suddenly blocked. Over the ranks of fedoras and caps and although it was half hidden by a flag The Usher could see the horse wavering side to side like a punch-drunk prize-fighter. The men started to rock the carriage.

'The time for action has come. The time for action has come. All power to the Councils. All power to the Workers.'

The Usher reached out his hand to catch the attention of a sailor in a uniform streaked with oil and grime. He wanted to ask, find out who was in the carriage, but he merely flapped at the sailor's shoulder as onehandedly the sailor lifted his rifle and let loose a round that seemed to split the sky above the junction and scare off the rain. The Usher thought he could taste something coppery in the air though knew this was illusory, and that these fervid souls here had lost their minds as well and had no idea who was actually cowering in that carriage. Men had seized the roof of the carriage and began to thump it with the butts of their rifles. The horse clashed its hooves on the road and the carriage door swung free. Gunshots cackled above them and seemed to find sympathy with other gunshots that circled the city like birds calling to other birds. The men hauled a black bundle from the carriage that disappeared under the level of their shoulders.

The squall had blown over Berlin. The Usher turned his back to the carriage and started to walk. The men seemed sketched in charcoal as they passed, grey and fuzzy, and those who noticed the Dreaming Aspect changed tack and veered out of his way. As he progressed into Friedrichstrasse it was as if he carried with him a moveable glass dome that kept his distances, a *cordon sanitaire* that seemed to melt into the cold as he reached the very rear of the mob and the street stretched away in converging lines like rows and rows of books in a library stack. And this reminded him and in his mind's eye he saw the library stack at the Institute. Early evening, that rich odour of bindings and dust, tiny moths glittering in the pyramid of light that seemed to prop up the hanging lamp at the end of the aisle and Gertrude opened a book and stroked a page like she would a beloved cat. Something flashed in her eyes when she realized that he was watching her. But he knew already that this hadn't really happened and what had passed between them occurred not in the library stacks but in that bookshop on Jerusalemerstrasse, when he had bought her the poetry of Catullus on the day that he bought her the brooch and then coffee and a pastry in the Café Josty. Her face was close to his and she had whispered, 'You can stop buying me presents. Your duty is your duty. I'll come back to your home now.'

Behind him more yelling and stamping and shooting erupted and that horse heaved an almost metallic, grating sound from its throat. In the road ahead of him a soldier sprawled swigging from a red wine bottle and laughing at the wet surface while an older man in an officer's cap and dark glasses, a stick-grenade wiggling at his hip ducked down and tried to drag his drunken associate to his feet.

The drunk threw off his fellow's hand and lobbed the bottle. It stopped The Usher in his tracks when it smashed at his feet but made no more than a gentle click in the shouting all around them. The man in the dark glasses reached into his coat and took out a revolver that he raised at The Usher's chest. Then he lowered it, his shoulders relaxing. The man on the floor looked up and pointed.

'Look, comrade, we must have stormed the opera and kicked all the phantoms out on their arses!' He fell on his back. The man with the dark glasses put his gun away.

'Ignore him,' he said. 'My apologies. We must not forget our manners.' He nudged the drunk's head with his boot. The drunk's cap rolled away and hopped the kerb. It bowled up to the front of a looted cigar shop, and where the cap stilled, up above it, pasted onto the glass was the poster of *The Prettiest Girl*.

'And who is looking after you, friend?' said Dark Glasses, putting his hand back inside his jacket. The Usher could do no more than shrug.

'The Socialist Revolution,' shouted the man on the ground, 'will spread throughout the world.'

'Where do you want to go?' said Dark Glasses. 'Maybe we can help you?'

'Make the dream of a Socialist Republic reality!' The man on the ground was still shouting.

In the lenses of the dark glasses The Usher could see the Dreaming Aspect of his Handsome Face and the smile it radiated and how she would fall for it again.

'I suggest that you don't go any further,' said Dark Glasses. 'They do not tell friend from foe.'

But The Usher strode on, following a more frequent occurrence of *The Prettiest Girl* along Friedrichstrasse. The great muster of smoke he'd sighted earlier seemed to be coming nearer and nearer and every so often groups of Spartakists ran past him, men in overalls and galoshes, factory girls with rifles and blood-streaked faces and sometimes they didn't run but staggered in twos or threes, holding up a fellow whose head hung like a rabbit nailed to a door. One group collapsed close by and there was a smell, like the Sunday joint inside the oven mixed with something chemical and singed that crawled across the Dreaming Aspect. It seemed to make his mouth dry and taste dirty and he thought he could feel his tongue stuck to the roof of his mouth. He had to ignore this sensation and keep walking towards the smoke. There, again, between a looted dealer of postage stamps and a deserted milliner's shop was *The Prettiest Girl*.

'Your duty is your duty. I'll come back to your home now,' she'd said. They had walked across the Tiergarten and when they arrived he felt fortunate that they had the house to themselves, Aunt Eva being away in the south and this being the second year he had been without a mother and fifteen since his father had been killed fighting the Herero of Namibia. Upstairs, in his room with its walls the colour of bluebells and the bookshelves and the desk in the window under the eaves that made the most of the morning sun, she took off her coat, then her shoes and he felt somehow afraid when she unbuttoned her dress and unfastened her corset and sat down on the rust-red velvet chair to smooth off her stockings. She closed her eyes as he in turn undressed. He did not want to embarrass her by remaining clothed. She sat perched on the edge of the velvet seat, one hand behind her back, one gripping the frame of the chair, and tucked her chin to her shoulder. A black wisp of hair coursed over her collarbone. Her eyelids were tinged with a new turquoise shadow. She looked like she might be asleep. He couldn't imagine how she interpreted this moment, or how she'd foreseen or conceived it in her girlhood. He was naked now. Outside, the men of the continent thronged towards parade grounds and muster points, railway stations and sidings. He thought of the suitcase he had already packed and the small things he would take with him. Her waist was slender and her legs pressed together at the thighs but crossed at the shins. Gertrude opened her eyes. She said, 'I'd like you to come back in one piece, please. I like the handsome face as it is.'

After Kochstrasse, dead men lay in the road. A scorch mark covered the upper portion of the poster of the *Prettiest Girl* and all he could see were the legs, two disembodied right angles tipped by red dance shoes reproduced over and over to a vanishing point. Her letters had stopped three years ago. Aunt Eva said she couldn't be found. No one knew what had happened to her. Her family were no longer at home. Everyone had been blown this way and that by this war. But Gertrude was back, that's what Glassburg said. She was calling herself Hephzibah. She had asked him to come for her today.

Friedrichstrasse ended. The great blaze was somewhere to his left. The Usher stared out at the Bloodhound's boys now organized in Belle-Allianz Platz. It was so named, he knew, after the famous Prussian victory that to Measure's profound annoyance the English still call Waterloo. Dozens of the black-uniformed troops surrounded the truck with the skull and crossbones on its side. A machine gun mounted on its back faced a broad, four-storey building, some sort of office or premises with rows of slit-windows. Smoke soared from its rear-quarters. Tiny embers whirled around the soldiers. The Usher couldn't feel them on his face but heard them sizzle on the wet sleeves of his coat. He looked for an officer or commanding presence but couldn't see one. A group of soldiers started to haul the artillery piece in front of the building. The Usher's hands began to tremble again. When he linked them together behind his back, the chin of the Dreaming Aspect quivered and shook droplets of rain from the brim of his hat. She lived on the other side of Belle-Allianz Platz, in the south of Berlin beyond the canal. He would have to cross it or go round it. He'd have to negotiate the Bloodhound's boys or keep out of their way. They were everywhere, though, house to house, the city squares, in the boulevards and the alleyways, here in the Newspaper District.

The artillerymen adjusted and lined up the canon. The Usher knew again that he should have listened to Measure. A girl is merely a girl, a bauble for a popinjay like Tempio when for the love of God we are still at war, Usher. And the enemy is different now. It lays traps within. It estranges us from one another. It corrodes us from below like satanic rust. But Glassburg would say, remember the pictures, the posters, the signs, the Prettiest Girl for the most Handsome Face. We write our own destinies now, Usher. Love Heals. Love Reconstructs. Love is Godless. Love is Art and Art will save us and show us the way. Go forwards to it, Friend Usher. Advance.

The Usher wanted to advance but instead rooted himself to the spot. The artillerymen recoiled. The troops behind them covered their ears with their hands even though they wore the Turkish helmets. As they did so something gigantic and ancient passed over The Usher on its way into Belle-Allianz Platz. For a moment the buildings seemed to separate and hang as if kicked up into the sky. When they landed the Colossus stamped its gigantic heel. All at once the windows shattered.

Over at the besieged building dense smoke coiled in the breach where the doors had stood. In a pincer movement, four-strong detachments of soldiers scampered towards the building. One by one they tossed stick grenades through the ground-floor windows. Splinters of glass on the pavement waxed red and orange as the building shuddered. Then it shuddered again, and once more and then expelled a cloud of black smoke from inside as if girding itself against one last push. From the upper balcony someone waved a white shirt attached to a rifle. Another appeared at a window lower down. The Usher found himself on his knees now. The men on the square crouched en masse, as if joining him in a game of follow the leader. Everyone seemed to be waiting. Waiting for The Spartakists to capitulate, for a ragged and soot-stained remainder to teeter onto the steps and throw down their guns. The lower of the white flags still signalled but slowly, as if it was an effort to keep going. Something clanged from deep inside the building.

The men on the square kept perfectly still. They all seemed serene and the burning building rosy and sunset. The Usher felt for a moment that he was at one with them. He remembered when he had been made to wait like this for something that he assumed would happen but nonetheless threw him into confusion when it occurred. Something about the sky above the ridge that day. Something that he said about it, or explained to his compatriots, how some poet or notable had rendered such a sky, unaware that this would prove to be the last time.

The Bloodhound's boys must have heard a command. They lowered their heads and put their hands over their ears and braced themselves as on the back of the truck the machine gun jerked the chassis up and down until it became a blur and The Usher realized it couldn't stop and he was lost in a vortex of metal noise.

The gunner let go of the gun. The truck stilled. The architecture seemed to simplify. For a second The Usher imagined himself floating in a stone circle of megaliths and keystones with nothing beyond or beneath t but ash. The fire at the rear of the building stretched taller as the dusk gave in and the night sky crystallised above Belle-Allianz Platz. A network of stars winked into life. The crescent moon was like the grin of a dead man lying with an ear to the ground. Bullet-holes criss-crossed the façade of the building. The Usher couldn't see how it could stay standing for much longer.

He stopped shaking and climbed to his feet. As soon as he did so, the Bloodhound's boys stood up as well. On the back of the truck men adjusted the machine gun, feeding it more bullets. They looked up as the white flag struck out from the front entranceway of the building. Then out they came, The Spartakists, waving white flags not the red, showing their hands, maybe a dozen of them, maybe twenty, a mismatch of uniforms and factory garb. The Usher tried to imagine how unreal and distorted this moment must seem to them as they emerge under sufferance into the enforced silence after all that clamour, after for keeping faithful for so long to whatever it was they believed in, for so long maintaining their stranglehold on what was tactically important about that building and for however long they had been barricaded in there. How peculiar and warped the city must seem now, as they shamble out and show the white flag and give up their weapons. The soldiers look down their barrels at their defencelessness and their complete and intact faces.

The Usher let Glassburg carry the motion in The Plenary about whether to cross the Belle-Allianz Platz. He put his hands in his coat pocket to keep them still as he walked forwards. All around him muzzles flashed. Bodies twitched. Yelps. Screams. Tyre-tracks on the grass. Ditch-mud. That smell, again. And it was like before, when he would think of her as a sort of touchstone or good luck charm, so not to – in a phrase that could make him laugh now, if he could ever really laugh about it or laugh at anything again – not to lose his head. He would think of her commenting upon his dreaming aspect and handsome face and that he should come back in one piece. He was back. He had not heard from her. Three years. Measure said she was a coward, Glassburg that it had been a trauma for her, too. It is time to listen even if that means listening to silence. Tempio only gloated over that memory of her thighs around his thighs and the taste of her tongue against his tongue, the taste of tongues in any case, and the deep-down, ageless thrill of her that day she stripped in his room when the suitcase was already packed and standing sentry in the hall with all of Belgium and France waiting for it.

The Plenary had marched midway across Belle-Allianz Platz now, on their way to unite with their absent fifth member. In The Plenary Hephzibah and The Usher could talk. Talk to each other. Talk it over. The lovers could not do this in his room or a café. They all knew this. They all wanted this however hot-headedly or coarsely they expressed themselves sometimes. They approached the truck and the machine gun and the artillery piece. Up ahead were soldiers, the Bloodhound's irregulars, and five men lay dead at their feet. Fire in the upper rooms of the building turned the chambers into a beguiling reversed world, glaring, vivid, so white it looked cool and calm. The soldiers seemed to be staring up at those rooms as if they longed to bask and frolic there. Then they noticed. They noticed The Plenary and the fat one at the front of the group, the freckly, over-sweaty one gasped and ripped his revolver from his holster. The Usher did not flinch or feel as the bullet clipped the shoulder of his coat and he kept on walking through them as other soldiers wrestled the pistol from the fat soldier's hand.

When they finally reached the courtyard that dead man's grin of a moon was still above them. The stars seemed like smudges of milk against a sheet of black glass. Rainwater gurgled in the drainpipes and slicked the rungs and the struts of a ladder that lay abandoned on the flagstones. The trek here occurred in an instant, as if they had clicked along at breakneck speed once they were clear of the Bloodhound's boys. It had seemed like seconds, but it may have been hours when they paused and waited for the shaking to stop. They became transfixed by what seemed at first like a mass of dead seals drifting in the canal that turned out to be hundreds of bundles of newspapers dumped in the dark water. The streets then were mounds of soot. Her district seemed to have been abandoned. The Plenary had by now filed through dozens of these courtyards. No children played in the spaces. There was a smell of damp stone, vegetation and piss. The world was darkness; nothing seemed to cast this shadow. Measure had reminded them that they had become shadows even to themselves. Glassburg disagreed and said, 'Secrets, we are merely *secrets* to ourselves'. Tempio crowed that Hephzibah would show them her lamp, but they had seen not so much as a candle flickering in any of the apartment windows until now. The Usher had to crane right back as far as he could to focus on that singular light in the window of a flat on the sixth floor. This must be the address.

At the door they caught their breath after the climb up six flights and their march along the walkway. The Usher raised his arm to knock, but it started to shake and he didn't want to be shaking in case she thought he was scared of her or angry. Glassburg might suggest that she'd understand, and

Tempio that she likes to be shaken anyway, but Measure was correct that he should pull himself together. You are The Usher. You are our dreaming and our poetry. You just need to choose your side. There are no compromises any more. The Usher put his arms behind his back again and remembered how he hadn't imagined that she would desert him. He didn't believe Aunt Eva that Gertrude could not be found. He remembered that when he woke up the doctors and the nurses wouldn't explain to him how long it had been. They wouldn't give him a mirror, only a notepad so he could write down his needs. The others were dead; they were upfront about that. The look in their faces suggested he would have been better off dying on the ridge as well. He was shipped home and she didn't come. She stayed away. Now he had found her.

He raised his arm. This time he did knock. The double rap seemed to skitter from him and down through all the stairwells and courtyards. There was no sound behind the door but he still knew she would open it because he had come back for her. She would see him and realize that there had been no good reason to steer clear. She would see the Dreaming Aspect of his Handsome Face she had remarked upon before. It had rescued him, he'd been told, though he wasn't sure who had explained this to him, Aunt Eva or Glassburg. He was still waiting for Gertrude to emerge when he put his hands to his face and felt the smooth and hard surface of the Dreaming Aspect. 'Leave now,' said Measure, 'while you still have a chance.' 'Do not waver,' said Glassburg. 'All the fragments can be reformed, refashioned, reinvigorated.' 'Now, you are talking,' said Tempio. And just then The Usher asked himself what exactly was he ushering in here?

They stopped their babble. Glassburg and Measure, Tempio and The Usher. He couldn't hear them anymore. He realized he had closed his eyes and when he opened them he felt a tingling in his legs and arms akin to the sensations he experienced when he first identified the ceiling in the field hospital. His right shoulder stung and he remembered the glancing shot of the fat solider in Belle-Allianz Platz and the *thwip* sound it had made as it tore through the fabric of his coat. The door ahead seemed to slightly change colour, its bottle green becoming lighter, as if before him verdigris crisped over the panels. He wasn't sure where he was now. The hallways carried on either side of him. The breeze licked at the hem of his coat. Crackles and bangs drifted over from the city. He was suddenly footsore. His face felt nothing more than hot and he remembered where he was. Why was he here? She wasn't here. Of course she wasn't here. She didn't live here. She didn't live anywhere like here. And he didn't want to see her. Not true. He didn't want to see her like this. There was only dreaming about her these days and that was the best he could do. Dreaming was best. The best of it was now the dreaming. She wasn't here. She couldn't be here. But he didn't actually know that, did he? What if she was here? Did he want to see her? Could he go to his grave without ever seeing her? Could he endure her seeing him like this? He didn't want to see her. He couldn't. He mustn't. His aunt must be worried sick. He couldn't remember the last time he had been out of the house. He had not worn the Dreaming Aspect outside before, only when he had visitors. He turned to leave, pausing and staring at the hallway for some reason he didn't understand, somehow expecting that other ghosts would appear under the arches on either side, just as behind him he heard the door open.

'Is that you?' said a woman's voice.

The muscles in his shoulders contracted and his hands started to tremble again. He buried them in his coat pockets. She would be seeing him hunched and showing his back to her, quaking like a maniac, a lunatic, a screamer, but he couldn't put his hands behind his back to control his arms. She would see him doing this. The thought made the tremors intensify.

'If they've sent you, you're too late,' she said. 'You're too late.'

He did turn around now and there she was, smaller and looking much older and thinner than he remembered, her eyes sunken and ringed and her face a rough, parsnip-white and streaked with a siltish dark around her cheekbones and her hair unwashed and untied. She wore a once-white blouse that was now grey and where it was undone at the neck he could see the struts of her ribcage sinking into her skin. He realized that she must be shocked that he was staring at her so flagrantly because she gasped and hooked her thumb to her mouth as she took a step back into the apartment. He wanted to say that he was sorry but he couldn't. He expected her to slam the door.

'You are the doctor?' she said.

He wanted to say yes but knew this was not quite the truth. If it hadn't been for the war he would of course have finished his doctoral thesis, but he assumed that she did not urgently require the services of a Doctor of Romantic Literature. This seemed humorous to him but he couldn't laugh in front of her. The Dreaming Aspect of the Handsome Face was quivering again. She may have thought that he'd nodded.

'You're the only doctor? ... You're the doctor? You are the doctor!'

She fell to her knees and started to sob in her doorway with her palms pressed to the wooden floor, sobbing up something so terrible and stark that he felt a fellow feeling pass between them. This was good to him, it was right. She did not flinch or resist when he reached under her arms. She leant into him and let him take her weight as he half-carried her along into the sitting room. She was making a noise that reminded him of the horse in Friedrichstrasse. There was something animal about it. He pitied this, but envied it and then felt disgusted with himself for thinking this at such a time.

A single lamp on a table lit the room. He let go of her. She staggered backwards, for a second putting herself between him and the flame. He couldn't see anything beyond the glimmer around her outline. Then she moved and the room widened out for him. There was a green vase without flowers on the table and on the wall a painting: stern huntsmen with horns chased petrified stags across a hedge that divided a field from a forest. The brown curtain between the rooms was dusty and dirty, as was the floor, and arranged on the floor were four little clumps of blankets each headed by a pillow. A bowl full of water glinted in the lamplight. He watched her as she sat down in a chair draped in a blue cloth. He wanted to ask her now about how she ended up here and why she had not written, why she abandoned him. He was prepared to hear what he had always suspected, that Aunt Eva had warned her to leave him be in the circumstances. He would understand, though. It was understandable. It would be an honourable starting point. He wanted to say something now, ask her, but he couldn't.

'You're too late, Doctor,' she said and swept her hand across the bedclothes on the floor. 'And what were you going to do anyway? Give them a sugar lump each and keep our little fingers crossed?'

He wanted to ask her if he could sit down, but he couldn't. Her face was unrecognisable as he pulled up her second chair and sat down opposite her.

'Were you going to write out a prescription to bring back my man?' she said. 'And why don't you say something? The cat got your tongue?'

He shook his head, then put his hand to the Dreaming Aspect and between finger and thumb squeezed its ungiving sides. With the heel of his hand he pressurized its chin and felt it swing into the gap where his own chin used to be.

She stood up and at first he thought she was coming to embrace him, to let him know that it changed nothing. But she shuffled to the table and stood staring into the lamp with her hands pressed to her jaw. He could only hear her breathing. He wanted to go to her but it started again. The tremors began in his feet this time. The soles of his shoes clattered on the boards and his knees clunked together and then the hands, the arms, the Dreaming Aspect shook and he searched inside and asked The Plenary for help, for discussion, advice, but heard no voices, and he looked way from her for fear of adding to her woe. He noticed the arrangement of the blankets on the floor. You could still see how a child had lain, the curve of the hip and muddle of the feet and an impression of the head on the pillow. The Dreaming Aspect shuddered from side to side now and he couldn't control his arms enough to link his hands together. But he had found her now and would not leave. He wondered how long she had left and how long before she caught him too and then how it would be for someone like him. It would be best if it were simultaneous, as it should have been on the ridge. He doubted that it would be. She put out the lamp. It was starting again.

The First Suggestion of Night

'And now you can prepare my funeral oration.'
Giacomo Matteotti – speech to the Italian Parliament, 30th of May, 1924.

Three men loll against the black wing of the car. Every now and again they scrape their boot-heels on the running board. A fourth, Dario, the youngest, does not watch the street as they do. The Lawyer has slipped his mind again. He stares across the river and dreams of bridges. When the city expands it will need more bridges. A bridge here would speed the circulation of automated traffic and simplify a journey from the outskirts to the centre. And Dario is right. In five years time he will witness the grand state opening of the Ponte Littorio. A New Rome will surge with bridges, avenues and motorways. He will feel a part of this. He will remember today but keep concentrated on the bridge. Now, in his head Dario erases the less glorious of the buildings on the other side of the Tiber. He invents the space that each great edifice needs to impose itself. He still wishes he'd trained as an architect. An architect would have more scope than a painter of murals. There is suddenly movement behind him. The others have stepped away from the car. Rome is around them. Rome bristles. The man, upright, cream-suited, approaches their corner.

All afternoon they have waited. At first they kept watch from inside the car. Dario sat in the front, alongside Amerigo, the boss. On the backseat Malacria and Volpi told stories about the march across the border, the town

107

that they took there and the women from the villages. When it grew too hot inside, the whole squad decamped. They slouched against the Lancia, scanning the passers-by for that tell-tell popinjay's strut. The neck of the man. The pigheadedness. The Lawyer must realize by now. They know that every afternoon he walks this way to Parliament, and yet he continues to take this route.

Ahead, The Lawyer pauses. Dario notices the case at his side, that same hat. Over the last few weeks he has followed The Lawyer many times. During the election the patterns his wanderings created, the alignments of union halls and newspaper offices, the co-ordinates of muster points and society houses, the juxtaposition of his haunts and his residence became Dario's map of Rome. It is a city that until recently he knew only from pictures in history books. It is a city about to enter its third golden age, whatever The Lawyer's objections.

'If he will liken us to Mexicans,' says Amerigo, 'we'll take him to Mexico.'

Malacria and Volpi pull the brims of their hats over their eyes and let their arms hang at their waists. Dario turns away. It is unnecessary to see it again. The Lawyer will go through this tomorrow, and then next week and throughout the next month until he desists. Dario squints at the Tiber. The currents remind him of the swirls on a soda water bottle. He wonders how the river would have seemed to Augustus and Julius, to the War Pope and Michelangelo, to the great Italians before the miracle of mass-produced assembly-line glass.

Up ahead, The Lawyer swaps his case from right hand to left. He shivers, dips his head before striding headlong towards the car and their corner.

Last night, when Dario returned to their hotel, after he had tailed The Lawyer all day and reported that a bundle of papers had been passed from one hand to another in Piazza Navona, Amerigo had stood on a beer crate and given the most emphatic of his speeches. This time he did not merely proclaim the beauty of The Idea and the genius of The Leader. Nor did he spit fire about the parliament that keeps our peninsula in a state of decadence and weakness akin to that of Byzantium before it was swept from the atlases. He did not rail against the indignity of the Mutilated Peace, or against parasites, pacifists and moneylenders and those who do not believe. He did not denounce the squalid nature of this election, the outcome of which would mean not a cracked fingernail to the leadership. This time he spoke only of The Lawyer.

Not only had The Lawyer publicly insulted The Idea. Not only had he stood up in that Byzantine whorehouse Parliament and hissed scornfully at The Leader and whined about 'popular sovereignty' when it is we who are the very limbs and blood vessels of the national will. Not only has he compared us to Mexican bandits and betrayed our representatives in dung-heap France, but now he's handed over a dossier of lies to an agent of our enemies abroad. The Leader swears twelve bullets in the back for those of bad faith.

Amerigo's words always cause Malacria and Volpi to swig vigorously from their bottles before they salute and salute until ordered to stop. But Dario always forgets the words once he is outside, thrilled by something else as he follows The Lawyer. He'd forgotten the speeches today as they waited on the embankment. Yesterday he did not remember anything as he waited outside The Lawyer's house from dawn until the chauffeur drove the little boys to school. There was something beyond Amerigo's passion that he sensed as he tailed The Lawyer all the way up Via Cavour to a pokey little bookshop near Termini Station where he bought a copy of *L'Avanti*. Outside the Palazzo delle Esposizioni he conferred with Mutton Guts, the man whose house Malacria and Volpi had last week searched with the determination of bloodhounds. The Lawyer never seems to suspect Dario, always standing nearby, scribbling in a pocket book. He must look like just another architecture student sketching spires and colonnades, awed by Rome. He knows he was chosen for this task because he will not be recognized. He's too young to have fought in the war or marched across any borders. Back home in Florence last year, after the glassworks stayed open, his father owed Amerigo a favour. When Amerigo realized that this man's son was studying to be an artist he asked for a mural. In a villa in the hills, in a long grand hall, Dario completed the first of his masterpieces, *Vortex,* a pattern of overlapping, multi-coloured, angular shapes all cut from equilateral triangles. The effect was like staring into a well of shards. Kaleidoscopic. Prismatic. Pure. Amerigo had professed some liking for it, but said it lacked people and history and made Dario paint over it. Dario returned with *The Force of Destiny*. An image of The Leader stood on a platform at the centre of a framework of girders and gantries. The people massed behind him, uniformed, alert, roused, and around the edges floating motorcars, fighter planes, ocean liners and steam engines. When *The Force of Destiny* was unveiled, Amerigo fell to his knees, clasped his hands together and wept. Dario could not have anticipated that this commission would lead to another, a Roman assignment that in turn would lead to introductions and opportunities.

Outside the Palazzo delle Esposizioni, The Lawyer and Mutton Guts embraced and went their separate ways. The Lawyer took a circuitous route to the Piazza Quirinale. Dario almost lost him when the Egyptian obelisk there proved such a distraction, how it stands between the statues of Castor and Pollux. He caught sight of The Lawyer's pale suit rounding a corner and followed. The Lawyer entered the house that Amerigo suspected was used by the Bolshevik pamphleteer who spread The Lawyer's morally-typhoid book about The Leader. The Lawyer stayed for nearly an hour. When he emerged he was accompanied by a short, bald man who did not wear a jacket. Dario pursued them to the steps of the Casanatese Library. Here they spoke and even laughed with a young woman Dario had never seen before. She passed papers in a bundle to The Lawyer. The three of them then double-backed to La Terrazza on Via Vittorio Venuto. Dario loitered outside the café but could not get close to them. They met other people. These people were perhaps foreign. They ate a lunch. The Lawyer left alone. He handed over papers on Piazza Navona to a man who might be from somewhere other than Rome. The Lawyer returned to his house, to kiss his wife on the cheek before he made his daily, afternoon trek to Parliament. Dario has proved correct in his assumption: again, this afternoon, The Lawyer comes this way.

The city is drifting from spring into summer. When Dario tracks The Lawyer through the streets of Rome he thinks not of blossom and lovers. He thinks of Rome breaking over the hills and along the banks of the eternal Tiber, so huge and populous that it reaches the Tyrrhenian Sea. The world's greatest city with eight wide arterial avenues that connect the centre to the suburbs and the other cities and the new provinces of Italy: Vienna, Dalmatia, Nice. Rome as the pulsing hub of the world, beacon of the coming century, city of machines. New streets with new names and the slums and festering neighbourhoods cleared and sanitized. Grand spaces around Rome's great monuments and reminders: the Imperial Forum, Augustus's Tomb, the Theatre of Marcellus, The Capitoline and The Pantheon. Railways for speed and ease of transit. Massive green spaces for parades and leisure. More hospitals and airports than New York, London and Paris combined. And room set aside for devices and infrastructure as yet unimaginable.

This is what Dario dreams as he follows The Lawyer through a Rome that must be superseded as one mural must be painted over another. He sometimes wishes he could talk to The Lawyer, sit him down and over a glass of something explain the vision, the city that lives beyond the oratory of The Leader and people like Amerigo. If he explained, The Lawyer would understand. The Lawyer would revise himself voluntarily. He would get out of the way. He would be safe.

There will be a bridge here. In twenty-one years time, a hungry, footsore and almost ragged Dario, middle-aged now and suddenly without a salary at the end of the war will pass by this spot, quite by chance, and notice that the bridge has been renamed already. It is no longer the Ponte Littorio. It is now named after The Lawyer. He had not remembered The Lawyer while there were bombs and occupations, armies lost to the sand, the clownish execution of a circus war, as if during the years he had lost the ability to connect one point to another. But then he will picture The Lawyer striding up the embankment, grainy at first, then hard and resolute and suddenly so sharp that he could have slipped backwards in time, returned to his youth, to this moment when The Lawyer reaches the corner.

110

He does not see the precise moment The Lawyer and Amerigo come face to face. He is still staring at the river, thinking of glass and emperors. It will perplex him afterwards – when he lies in his room for nights on end unable to focus on anything else – why The Lawyer did not turn back. Maybe he only expected to be jostled again. This tedious ritual. Maybe something registered only when the tallest and oldest of the men ordered him into the car. This is the moment it strikes Dario that something is different today, when Amerigo shouts at him to open the car door. Malacria and Volpi seize hold of The Lawyer. Amerigo belts him in the stomach. When they finally force him into the car there is such a struggle that Dario ends up behind the wheel with all four of the others in the back. He doesn't know where to drive. He keeps a straight line south into a Rome that is hazy and baffling to him. The streets are a mess of yellow smudges. The car is listless, like it doesn't want to explore the shabby, packed-in, unknown quarters of Rome. In the rear-view mirror he glimpses an animal made from four men. The Lawyer part kicks out. A spider web of cracks appears on the side-window. Dario almost swerves the car into a queue outside a pork-butcher's shop. Something flashes in Amerigo's hand.

A strange, harsh sound is coming from Dario, so he turns the car into an alleyway between two tenements and stops it in a courtyard. The light down here is rusty and flecked. Ahead, barefoot children chase a hoop around a water pump. At first they do not notice the car. In the rear-view mirror Dario notices that The Lawyer is sat up and ready for chat but his suit is changing colour. Outside the car now, Dario is ill on the cobblestones and the children surround the car and press their hands to the hot chassis. Somehow he opens his eyes and Amerigo is driving, the track ahead is stony and squeezed by cornfields, the horizon studded by hamlets and windmills, The Lawyer unmoving in the back and ready to listen now. The Lancia's tyres throw up ribbons of dust. It passes through a village that when later questioned Dario will say he's never heard of. The police will release him, unconvinced that one so shy and bookish could have anything to do with the fearsome Tuscan squad that goes by the name of the *Ceka*. In the fields, beyond the last of the outbuildings, the car heads for three trees that stand out against the sky. They turn out to be stunted and small when the car stops. The day is ending. The sky is beginning to purple when Dario slides out of the car. Malacria and Volpi are digging a trench, their work made more arduous not so much by the dryness of the soil but by the hammer and carjack they have to use instead of shovels. The Lawyer lies beside the trench. Someone has removed his jacket and thrown it over his face. Amerigo then takes the hat and uses it to cover the bloated stain on his chest.

'Not so clever now, are we, eh? Not such a smart arse, not such a stubborn prick?' He kicks The Lawyer, then circles around and kicks again with more force. The hat hops up into the air, then flops out of sight. At the trial, Amerigo will receive eight years, for improper disposal of this body. He will say, not even with a straight face, that he had offered The Lawyer a lift in Rome. The Lawyer then unfortunately suffered a consumptive fit and sadly passed away on the backseat. Not knowing what to do, Amerigo and his boys took him here because they thought it was his home town and he would have liked to be buried close to the site of happy childhood memories. Unlike Malacria and Volpi, at this moment scratching in the dust with blunt implements, Amerigo will only serve eleven months. He'll then live in Tripolitania and Somalia and every now and again will remind The Leader of what he did for The Idea in the early days. During the war, the British will shoot him seventeen times. He'll still survive and escape. When the Germans return The Leader to the north of Italy Amerigo will be with him. He will make a fortune out of procurement and distribution. To Dario, here under purple skies, with the dust sweeping up from the ground and The Lawyer draining into the dirt, Amerigo seems not only like he will live forever, but that he has already lived forever. In fifty years time, though, Dario, decrepit, terrified still of being found out, will stand by the bridge as the city erects a monument to The Lawyer, this after his name has spread over streets and squares not only in Rome but in all of Italy. It is a small monument. Discreet. Amerigo will be ten years dead by then. He dies in Florence, at home. He has a wobble in his kitchen and bangs his head. But for a moment here, kicking, shouting, he's a Caesar, a Julius. 'You're forgotten now, pig brains. Forgotten. Forgotten. Forgotten.' He swings and glories and is still doing so when Dario stumbles away, over toward the farm shacks, to the outbuildings that rise like the shimmer of an oasis towards the first suggestion of night.

Marmara

'At sixteen years old she stood in court and heard her own suicide note read aloud: 'Dear Mother, please don't be angry but I can't stand it any longer. The world is against me. I am going to end it all. I am going to Hell where I belong ... I never tell the truth. I am so very wicked.'

All the Devils are Here - David Seabrook.

Tonight the tennis courts were unlit as she passed them. Out on the surrounding lawns the conifers sparkled in the moonlight. At the end of the driveway Marmara House hardened from a loose, black mound to something oblong and angular. Her suitcase began to tug at her shoulder. She advanced beyond the hedge animals and the memorial rockery that lined up with a grotto in the woods. Her feet hurt but she quickened her pace. The only light in the house was at the window of the master bedroom. There was a smudge, a smear standing there. It grew in length as she approached. Her coattails billowed behind her and she began to almost like the feel of the grit trapped in her sandals. Nearly there now, she was nearly at the front door. She had a little hope left when finally the portico and the pillars and the gables of Marmara reared up and its chimneys and fortifications tottered and whitened above her.

   In the window his outline shunted sideways. Then, a second later, the light up there went out. This wasn't a coincidence, like the strange happenstance involving the cold cream and Dumb April's birthday supper. It wasn't like the clock in the library mysteriously telling the wrong time when more time was needed. Chance had served no ace here, as it had the night the floodlights at the tennis courts failed just as someone called out her name. This, now, was the worst thing he'd ever said, and he'd not even used any words.

Even now she half-expected the light in the hallway to illuminate the little semi-circular window above the front door before the front door opened wide. She realized that she was waiting, tentatively, as if she had knocked; or it was last week again and she had knocked already and couldn't hold on to herself, anticipating the slow, assured way he always slipped her coat from her shoulders. In the vestibule he would take off the coat to admire the dress she was wearing for him even now. He had bought her the dress somewhere abroad, in Paris or maybe Rome, in the shop of the lady who invented the divided tennis skirt. The dress clung to Rose's waist and her bust and coated her legs, lapped at her feet. It was the fashionable new colour: shocking pink. Shocking pink for Shocking Rose. It must be kept out of sight at home, this colour. It was, however, very much permissible and even encouraged at Marmara, and on one occasion had even witnessed an outing to the pictures and a lovely stroll on the beach. Now it felt like it needed a clean, grubby from so many evenings when the clocks mistold the time and lights went off and on and off and on. The light was not coming on again, at least not on this side of the house, or this side of the cliff. The note would not now keep safely in her pocket.

So he couldn't miss it, she abandoned her suitcase at the front door. She had no need of it now, and as she walked around the house she thought that maybe he'd like something to remember her by. When she reached the top of The Steps she could already hear the slow slosh of the waves. Beyond the headland, a web of stars held the moon in place. A glimmering pathway of white light shone on the surface of the sea. It seemed to flow across the beach from where it trickled down The Hengist Steps and began as a glint in the bootprint embedded in the first concrete stair. Rose knew that many other people, many other girls had come this way before. Tonight, she had a premonition that many would follow her.

In the Shanghai Lantern she'd written the note and the note was in an envelope that she took from her pocket and tucked into the front of the shocking pink dress. She no longer needed the coat to hide the dress, now that it had been found and she need no longer shout down the stories about her and had taken the bus and walked from the Lantern in the middle of town and then along the private roads to Marmara. It was a relief to stoop and unbuckle the clasps of her sandals and then wrap them up in the coat and toss the whole bundle over the rail and wait for the sound. She and April used to drop the fattest pine-cones over the side and count until the beer bottles down there clanked.

No smash or rattle. Her bundle must have snagged. The wind rushed in the long grasses and the trees along the cliff. The trail across the sea glittered. It led to France and France, she knew, was red. She flinched as she placed her bare foot in the bootprint. Once it had been ten-times her size, when Mum had taken her up to see Dad, and Dad was painting or papering a room inside Marmara, when the house was still empty, after Lord Soft Sword, as Jeremy called him, passed away. When the Osbourne-Parks appeared and their little girl April was just the same age and Rose was allowed to come up to Marmara to keep April company, and then, when they were older, play tennis on the floodlit court, a rubber shoe bought for her by Mister Osbourne-Parks filled up half the bootprint at the top of The Steps. The Osbourne-Parks moved away and took Dumb April and the tennis coach with them. She didn't even write from Cairo. Dumb April, that is, not Miss Havers, the tennis coach whose letter said, *You really are very promising. I am willing to have a chat with your father.* But there were things that could not be explained to Miss Havers, and while Marmara had slumbered ownerless Rose crept up here at night and for hours patted a ball against the ground for want of a game. One night she thumped the ball too hard and it bounced so high that she feared it might never come down again. And then the floodlights clicked off. He appeared, strolling over from the generator shed, and called out her name. When he reached her and she stared into the qualities in his face the ball smacked on the surface behind them. Now, at the top of The Steps, she tried to draw her coat in tight and pick up her case. They were gone. She reminded herself, and started to make her way down.

Viking Beach was no more deserted than usual. It belonged to Marmara and Marmara belonged to Jeremy now. The breeze snatched her hair and the hem of the dress, pulling it in the direction of the lighthouse at the periphery of the bay. Momentum took her swiftly across the narrow strip of sand before the ridges of shingle, but she slowed to a sort of stagger as she made her way to the sea's edge. When the foam nipped her feet and shuddered her to a standstill she grabbed hold of the dress and screwed it to her hip. She was shivering and decided, suddenly, not to take it off. Her chin bobbed up and down all of its own as she turned to look back at The Steps and the cliff and Marmara. No window lights. Jeremy would be strong after all. He loved to talk of strength and she'd loved to listen, hadn't she.

It was funny, though, that all the whispers and daft talk about Jeremy Trask in the town had not concerned itself with his strength. They said that he didn't have the decency to admit that he ran that new office by the War Memorial. That he had written what was in those pamphlets there. That someone had done their business in his hero's head and forgotten to flush. And Johnny Rooper couldn't afford his own ale and needed the clean shirts. That's why he marched around with another dozen or so undesirables every Saturday. Rose had thought that none of this had anything to do with Jeremy, who wasn't born in Tangiers or Russia or Romania. He hadn't sucked the blood from his mother's breast. What a rotten thing to say. It was lies. He sold gymnasium apparatus all around the world. He called her Rose and said she could play tennis whenever she liked.

She had come back for the court, but soon was following him into Marmara, bounding along the corridors and landings and the carpets of scarlet and gold patterns. She had sat at the grand walnut dining table by the cocktail bar as he played records on the radiogram or operetta tunes on the pianola, his gaze aloof from the keys as she sipped too quickly the gin and the tonic and the bubbles that rushed up to cling to the ice cubes. Soon there was a dress in a wide white box. When she emerged in costume, the clock in the library told the wrong time.

And of course, it couldn't be true love unless it was proper, whatever he might say, and to make it proper she made him take her to the pictures. They had missed Wimbledon and even she couldn't make him wait a year. He didn't hold her hand in the queue for the tickets but she was by his side and wearing the shocking pink dress. The Hopgoods noticed her in the foyer. So did Philip Drew, Joan Prior who taught physical education and Johnny Rooper's cousin Bert who owned The Norseman's Head on Coronation Row, and Dicky Foster with his runny nose, who knew her family and probably blabbed first, and Nigel Neville and Hector and Miss Privet and the one-armed Barnes who owned the Hengist and Horsa Tea Rooms along the cliff. Rose could see it in their eyes. They marvelled at the dress, what she could do to herself out of school, now that her schooldays were coming to an end.

He insisted the usherette lead them to the front row and a middle seat. When they were settled he placed his hand on Rose's thigh and a warm feeling lifted up her spine. On the newsreel before the film, Hitler was giving a speech in front of a sunburst with a swastika at its heart. He was having a bit of a shout and waving his arms and holding his fists to his chin and when he paused he stared out with black glass eyes at some strange far-off place. And then soldiers jerked their legs across the screen like little clockwork things, and everyone around, the Hopgoods and Philip Drew and Miss Prior laughed like Dad always laughed. Rose laughed. The whole cinema was laughing. She took a sideways glance at Jeremy. Swabs of light from the screen flickered across his face. At first she thought he was sneering, then smirking, but she realized there was no expression there.

The film was called *The Spy in Black* and was set during Dad's war. It started with handsome German submarine sailors, who didn't look like enemies, and a captain dispatched on a secret mission. Meanwhile, a pretty schoolmistress, Anne Burnett was kidnapped on the way to a Scottish island. Good Anne was replaced by bad Fräulein Tiel, who looked like Miss Havers and said things like 'Silk stockings is my cue to go to bed' and 'You and me are only parts of a machine of destruction'. Together on the island, the Submarine Captain and Fräulein Tiel plot to sink fifteen capital ships

in league with a traitor called Ashington who had a cut-glass voice, like
Jeremy. A reverend looked like Mr Osbourne-Parks and a special constable
looked like Dad and a vicar's plain and cheery wife a bit like Mum and the
peasant maid like Dumb April and all the sea dogs and sailors were like the
Roopers and Dicky, Nigel Neville, Hector and the one-armed Barnes. The
Submarine Captain falls in love with Fräulein Tiel, but she's in love with
Ashington. And Ashington is not Ashington and the Fräulein is not the
Fräulein, and it was all double-crosses and betrayals until everyone was sunk
by his own side and lost at sea.

On the drive home to Marmara, in the rear of his car – it was the first
time she realized that Johnny Rooper was merely his chauffeur – she asked
Jeremy if he'd enjoyed the film. He said, softly, holding her hand but
peering at the moon that seemed to speed along the tops of the hedgerows,
that it was a terrible tragedy, that war. It must never happen again. There
were bigger enemies, the empire of disease, monsters that crawled from a
pyramid of skulls.

No one would be allowed to keep their money outside of the country, he
said as they picked their way down The Hengist Steps. The first blast of the
trumpet against interest slavery and cosmopolitan usury. On Viking Beach
he said that he was thinking of changing the name of the house. Marmara
was one of Soft Sword's foibles and sounded like a Turkish baths. It should
be called Hengist House. He'd been doing some reading about old Hengist.
What a chap! Our local hero. At Stonehenge his men had drawn their knives
and dealt calmly with their Celtic foes. England was born. England must be
strong again, he said, back at Marmara, after he'd lifted her onto the cocktail
bar. He cradled her shoe in his hand and his little moustache twitched as
he spoke.

'We only want England to be strong, Rose. Imagine how strong we would
have to be if we'd been humiliated like that in nineteen.' He slipped off
her shoe and then found the other, removed it too and arranged the pair
neatly on the bar. 'If we'd been forced to admit it was all our doing.' He
held her feet and with his fingertips pulled at the heels of her stockings.
'And the king slung out and replaced by the Bolshevik rabble. Our coalfields
and factories looted.' When the stockings had come away he took her by
the hand and eased her off the counter. 'And our colonies parcelled out,
and Scotland and Wales and Ireland and Cornwall made a new ring of
enemies to keep us weak.' She raised her arms and made herself giggle as
the shocking pink dress slid over her head. 'And no army, or navy, or air
force,' said Jeremy, 'and no union allowed with our friends abroad.' She was
uncovered. His hands pinned her arms to her sides. 'And made to pay in
cash and kind forever.' The soft press of his kiss was not like the scratch of
his fingernails as they clawed into her waist and her behind. 'And meanwhile
the bacillus spreads and spreads until nothing remains but a ball of dirt.' He
undressed and arranged her flat on the carpet. His chest hair now pressed

down on her skin. 'What do you think, Rose?'

'I'm not Rose,' she whispered in his ear.

She shut her eyes and waited and held on to him and it was hot and wet and hurt but she was now his Rose.

'Who is this Rose?' he'd declared a month ago as he emerged from the generator shed, and she had muttered and blushed and confessed her name as if she'd done something worse than trespassing. 'I prefer Rose,' he said. 'You are a perfect Rose. Rose Thou Art.' When the tennis ball plopped onto the court behind them, he stared up at the sky. 'Look, Rose Thou Art, it's made of velvet up there.'

That was a month ago. It was August now. The night sky looked like black tin. She did take off the dress and found herself standing in her underthings. Back up at Marmara, no Jeremy appeared in the window in a lightning flash. She didn't want to be Rose any more. She wanted to be Mavis. The name her mum and dad had given her. Mavis. Plays a bit of tennis. Makes sure the clock is wound. Never loses track of time. Mavis Hardcastle. It was a nice name, reliable and decent, whatever Jeremy said.

A smooth, bright stone shone in the foam at the sea's edge. She scooped it up and used it to weigh down the envelope that she'd already wrapped in the dress and left on the beach. She turned back to the moon and started to wade into the sea. A pressure on her legs sent a spike of tingles into her stomach. The smell of brine and wind and rot. The tin sky and the sea. Out there, she imagined France as glowing red. Jeremy said that France was teeming with reds. When the water reached her thighs she could no longer open her mouth to yelp with each swell. When it covered her middle, she heard voices behind her. Men on the beach. 'Missy.' 'Miss.' Their voices harsher, more urgent. A dog barked and splashed. But Mavis was striding, strong now, the water up to her elbows and lifting her up and engulfing her neck and her shoulders, striding away from the voices, towards the reds on the horizon, the dashing crimsons and wonderful rubies.

The Syllabus of Errors

Don't swear, don't say anything sick and don't give a lecture about the Nazis. In the Cantina Reggio, at a table with a clear view on the doorway, Ludo reiterated his rules for successful dating. She was late. He wasn't, despite the distance he had travelled. The coffee-coloured boy throttled the plastic whale again. Another volley of squeaks pulsed around the seating area. At the most central of the tables, three men, a woman and a baby girl, a group Ludo had already dubbed the Young Pioneers blatantly encouraged the boy to keep pumping the whale. This time the two twentysomethings in the corner stopped their performance.

The girl in the corner, a willowy brunette in a pink dress and matching scarf had been on her own since Ludo arrived. She'd been reading *The Organist of Zagreb*, the same book that he'd bought at Liverpool Street Station this morning. When her male friend, a buzz-headed quarterpounder had appeared she'd put *The Organist* away and produced another, thinner volume. They had started to sway over its pages. Sometimes she caressed the strands of her hair as she spoke. Sometimes he waved his fist when he answered. The Young Pioneers had been crowing and babbling and honking the whale so loudly that it took Ludo a while to realize that Pink Dress and Buzz were rehearsing the parts of a play.

Trying to ignore the whale, Ludo picked up his copy of *The Organist* from where it rested spine-up next to the menu rack. He'd managed to skim-read thirty-six pages on the train. Set during the Yugoslav Civil War, it was about an organist from Zagreb and how he stands up and says that war and racism are bad. It bored Ludo. He already knew that war and racism are bad. Everyone knows that war and racism are bad and therefore should not need cheap and predictable novels to tell them this. Recently Ludo had immersed himself in Hitler studies again, still pretty categorical on the subject of war and racism being bad. In his holdall, hidden under his washbag and clean underwear, concealed by a newspaper in case she should notice them, was his new book about Hitler's library. It was a biography that cunningly used as a structure Hitler's reading at key career moments. Ludo wished he'd thought of that. He could have written a book about Hitler's library. He'd probably read all the books in Hitler's library anyway.

His Nazi refresher course had reminded him of Claire. It was a sub-clause of the rules that he wouldn't mention this today. Instead he would joke about things that didn't exist during their time together, like voicemail, Facebook and chi-chi, culturally indeterminate café-bars like the Cantina Reggio. The squeaker squeaked, again. In the corner Pink Dress pressed her long fingers over her eyes. Beyond the bar, with its cocktail shakers and wire bowl of lemons and limes, a rubbish band was beginning to set up.

Ludo was looking forward to reminiscing with Claire about their school ski trip to Austria. What could be more fun than resurrecting Jagger the Red, the geography teacher with the ginormous flares and the ginger beard that looked like the end of an uprooted tree? Or having a laugh about *Bonjour* and *Ça Va*, those French language magazines with adverts for pen pals who *J'aime le Deep Purple*, and articles about *Les Rues de San Francisco* and *Vive Kojak*? The rubbish band could, he feared interrupt or maybe even overpower the conversation.

Across the room Pink Dress rubbed her chin into her shoulder, her eyes full of sparkle. She leant away from Buzz Quarterpounder and delivered an extended monologue. Ludo could picture her lying in a bath, pretending to be Ophelia. Up that mountain in Austria, Claire had told him that her mother once had guests and boasted that her daughter used to lie in the bath pretending to be Ophelia when Claire didn't even know who Ophelia was.

She was twenty-two minutes late now. He checked the door and noticed again the sign above the piano behind the Young Pioneers' table. The Cantina Reggio had a zero-tolerance policy to racist and homophobic behaviour. Anyone indulging in abuse would be slung out and banned.

At the table next to the door, a girl with dour hippy parents took a big ball of swamp-coloured wool from a jute bag and started to plump it with her fingers. Ludo had already heard her tell a gushing anecdote about coffee, cigarettes and 'bohemian gestures' that her parents ignored. The father continually gazed out of the window as if something was going on in the flint wall opposite. He had a bushy white beard and hair like a dandelion clock. The mother's skirt reminded Ludo of a picnic blanket that used to lurk in the boot of his dad's Ford Escort. The squeaker went off again, three irregularly spaced blasts. The boy then hurled the whale on the floor, scampered around the Young Pioneers' table and over to The Girl with the Ball of Wool. He grabbed hold of the wool and tried to tug it away. The girl withdrew it into the front of her olive-green pinafore dress and looked dazedly at Mother Blanket. Meanwhile, Old Man Blanket kept his vigil over the wall. Mother Blanket pushed out a smile and said something. The boy began to scream, flailing at his temples with the backs of his wrists and stamping his heels on the floorboards. The boy's father, the one with the spiked-up, jet-black hair and prominent eyebrow stud walked over and, without acknowledging Ball of Wool and Mother Blanket, let alone Old Man Blanket, guided the boy back to the table. He sat the boy down and then spun the revolving pizza stand around with his fingertip.

'Look, Titus, a Lazy Susan, that's what it's called. A Lazy Susan. Who do you think of when Daddy says Lazy Susan?'

The petite black woman beside him in half-moon spectacles and a silky, bright orange shirt pressed her hands to her cheek and closed her eyes.

'Ooh Suze,' said the blonde Pioneer in the golden waistcoat. 'You bad mother, you filthy stop-out.' The other, extremely thin Pioneer with the shoulder length, frizzy hair picked up the little girl from the seat next to him – she was, Ludo assumed, about eighteen months old – and dangled her over the piano keys. Her small bare feet made a clang and a racket.

'Ottoline, Ottoline, Ottoline,' he sang. 'Oh why art thou such a prodig-ine?'

Everyone else in the Cantina Reggio jolted. The bar staff hesitated. At the other end of the room, the rock and roll stars stopped fiddling with their equipment.

Titus pointed to the piano.

'Daddy. Is that jazz?'

Ludo felt his face tighten. He wished the Cantina Reggio had a zero-tolerance policy to loud and obtrusive behaviour as well as war-and-racism-are-bad. The Young Pioneers quietened down and hushed long enough for Pink Dress and Buzz to return to their drama and the bar staff to their wiping and pouring and the band to their preparations. The flyer caught Ludo's attention again.

The singer's name was Barry RaceHate. His flyer read: *Harassing people for their race, faith or disability, or because they are gay or trans-gendered IS A CRIME. Barry RaceHate: amazing gypsy jazzateer with potently political lyrics.*

Viva Barry RaceHate, thought Ludo. The Weimar Republic would have survived and dictatorship, total war and the Holocaust not happened if only more gypsy jazzateers had blown in the wind in Depression Germany. The storm troopers would have swapped their knuckle-dusters for wind chimes and dance camp if more troubadours like Barry RaceHate had braved the beer halls. The fascists in here, the Blankets, Pioneers and Pink Dresses needed re-educating through the medium of gypsy jazz. And what on earth was gypsy jazz? Ludo's dad used to rant about the gypos' free-form approach to planning permission and road tax. Maybe gypsy jazz was by-law infringement set to the swirl of fiddles. Claire might know. She'd dragged him here. He could send her a text and ask. You couldn't send texts last time round. Back then, if you lost touch with someone you did so forever. He had joined the social networking craze about three hundred and fifty years after everyone else. Since his initial approach had elicited a reply from Claire Vickers-was-Thornley, divorced and interested in a 'relationship', he had sensed again the atmosphere of a high-up world and the blue haze of the mountain.

The first time he remembered noticing Claire Vickers was on the coach as it trundled through Belgium en route to Austria. She was on the other side of the aisle with Lisa Lightman and he was on his own, reading the first of his biographies of Hitler, the one thought suitable for only the brightest of the O-Level history geeks. Both the girls had their feet up and Walkman headphones around their necks. Lisa wore moon boots of a nasty, sunset orange colour but Claire Vickers these cute white pixie boots that he wanted to touch and then take off. He'd seen her before at school but had never wanted to interfere with her footwear. Now they were sixteen, though, and she'd lost the shaggy perm and had a shorter, fringed hairstyle that made her look elfin and sophisticated. She'd changed into a miniature version of the women you saw in adverts for liqueurs in Sunday magazines. When they arrived in the mountains he'd felt a terrible sorrow when they were placed in different chalets. He found himself hovering at breakfast, trying to sit at her table. From a distance he watched her on the slopes, looked out for her in the queues for the lifts and the cable car. In the evenings her hair shone and she wore black leggings, often with a long, tight cable-knit sweater, that made her legs look like they belonged to a superheroine, like Shadowcat or The Black Widow. Foxton had found him moping on his bunk one afternoon and Ludo was shocked and embarrassed when Foxton asked if he was suffering from something called 'heartache'. Claire wasn't with them the night they all got drunk on schnapps in the bar of the Hotel Bloedel and he lost his white scarf in a field of snow and never found it again and Foxton barked up all that gateaux in his bed and everyone had rolled him around in it and made this sort of Abstract Expressionist splurge in the sheets. She was there when they were taken up the mountain at night. That's when it happened. It was twenty-three years ago.

She paused in the doorway and noticed him straightaway. Her stride accelerated slightly as she approached. It was her, Claire. She wore a short-sleeved black cotton dress, one that seemed immaculately ironed, with buttons up its front and side-pockets. Her hair now was longer, down to her shoulders, but still sleek. He couldn't see her eyes behind her massive Jackie O-style sunglasses. He reiterated the rules as her cheek brushed his jawbone.

'My God, Ludo, you've not changed, you look exactly the same.'

'Oh c'mon, I've weathered a bit, surely.'

'No, no,' she said. 'It's Ludo Cluedo.'

'It's still not my fault my parents named me after a board game.' He'd said this on the mountain. She'd laughed then, too.

'Could have been worse,' she said, 'they could have called you Kerplunk.' This had been her reply in Austria as well.

'What did you expect? That I'd fought in a war and lost an eye?'

Her grin vanished. When they sat down, a hot feeling flushed through his chest.

'Useful meeting?' she said, not looking up from the drinks menu.

'OK,' said Ludo. 'Might be writing another textbook, that's all. Inter-war European politics.'

She tutted. 'I knew you'd do something clever, Clever Cluedo.'

When he offered to buy her a drink she asked for a rhubarb and ginger infusion, a Reggio speciality and her favourite 'combo'. He repeated the rules to himself and somehow worried that if he left the table she'd check his bag and find *Hitler's Library* under the clean pants and the washbag. On the way to the bar Titus ran into his knees but Ludo hardly noticed. The blue hazy feeling was back, the woozy sensation that had made it seem that he was on the brink of something before, up on the mountain, when they came in from the viewing platform and everyone milled around. When they were led out, she was ahead of him in the pack and then she stopped. The others filed past. She turned to him and said, 'Luke, have you seen my gloves?'

'Ludo,' he'd said, 'it's Ludo, it's not my fault my parents named me after a board game.'

She laughed. 'Could have been worse …'

At the bar he ordered Claire's combo from a girl in a Yoruba head-tie and a fascinating latticework of tattoos. He waited, absorbed by the hiss of a coffee machine and the squeal of an ice-crusher. He glanced back. Claire smiled at him. The blue feeling was causing him to shiver, like it had before. In the station at the top of the mountain they had carried their search into the cloakroom. He saw the gloves under a bench straightaway. Even though she was flustered, to give the others more of a head start he pretended that he couldn't find them at first, a minor subterfuge, like the ghost meeting today. When they had emerged from the station the snowy track seemed to melt into the lights that glittered ahead, hints of the resort and others further away. A rim of other mountains whose outlines jerked and peaked like line-graphs surrounded their mountain and a blue light rose mistily behind the crests and the ridges. She took his hand to stabilize herself as they picked their way down. She explained about Ophelia. They had a laugh about *Bonjour* and *Ça Va*. She stopped and said she might wet herself after he said that French school kids read English language magazines called

Wotcha and *Fuck Off.* Near the end of the track, by the deserted ski lift, she turned to him.

Viva Claire.

In the Cantina Reggio, twenty-three years later, her combo arrived. Crouching in a semicircle of amps and kit Ludo noticed a white Rasta in mirrored sunglasses, camouflage jacket and a red and white Intifada style scarf tuning an acoustic guitar. That's got to be Barry RaceHate. Look at him. The posturing knob.

Stop it. Don't swear, say anything sick or Nazi. These were the things he did when he was nervous. These were the things he did when he was bored. He carried the drinks over and sat back down.

'Go home much?' said Claire.

'Never,' said Ludo. 'I didn't think I'd see you again. It's good to see you. Great, in fact.'

'I've read this.' She brushed *The Organist* with the back of her hand.

'Last time we saw each other,' he said, 'you could actually still go to Yugoslavia, and Woolworths.'

'I loved it.'

'Woolworths?'

'The book. It made me cry.'

She glanced away, over to the central table where Titus had just whacked Ottoline around the head with the whale and turned her into a high-pitched banshee. The Pioneers organized a peace treaty, and given how loudly they had to address their children its terms would be bullet-pointed in everyone else's memory as clearly as the articles of the Treaty of Versailles were embedded in Ludo's. Buzz Quarterpounder was now holding both of Pink Dress's forearms and she was fluttering her eyelashes. Mother Blanket was handing Ball of Wool a small violin case while the Old Man still fixated on the lost world of the wall.

'Manic thrills,' said Claire, and then she started to tell him, all about how she ended up here, how she'd got frustrated and wanted to be creative, so got into interior design and took a course and raised a loan and bought a tile shop. It was called *Earthsea* and sold striking and expensive tiles from Mexico and Peru. She might have to start looking for a new job soon, the way things were.

'Well, I did come for a man,' she said. 'There's always a man involved.'

'Can't you diversify?' said Ludo. 'Maybe sell patio furniture as well?'

He then told his side of the twenty-three year story, but all the while he was thinking about how it would have played if, when they had come down from the mountain, when they had paused by the ski lift and she'd turned to him – and he was sure now that she was about to take off her gloves, that she was about to shuffle nearer to him, about to close her eyes and part her lips – what if then the torch beams had failed to find them and Jagger the

Red not called out their names. How would it have played? He might not have gone to university and instead stayed at home and occupied himself in the same sort of work that she had before she unleashed her creativity. He wouldn't have studied for his Masters in Comparative History and written his dissertation on the flight from democracy in Spain and the dissolution of the Weimar Republic contrasted with France's resistance to dictatorship until 1940; or undertaken his doctorate and written and published in *The Bulletin of the Institute of Totalitarian Studies* his seminal, rapturously-received and epoch-defining essays *Brief Parenthesis: Primo de Rivera and the Spanish Constitution*, and *The Iron Surgery: Primo de Rivera and Franco Foreshadowed*. Then again, she might have supported him in all this and he might not have abandoned his doctorate. Life might not have become so fraught in Madrid, when he'd started to sense a dark emanation radiating from his piles of books and documents, something toxic in the archives, its black lick in the street names and city squares. He might not have come to believe that he'd spent his youth studying the wrong syllabus, the outdated subjects, the dead languages, folk dance and rhetoric when he would have been better advised to take the easy, useful, modern ones taught by women with nice smiles and short skirts. He might not now have to write textbooks for a living as well as crib sheets for revision websites. He might not have to spend his time taking complicated events and developments and boiling them down to pat answers and platitudes.

His glass was empty. Two of his faces swam in the lenses of the Jackie Os. The squeaker squeaked across the way and then, suddenly roused, Old Man Blanket ushered Ball of Wool across the room. She held a violin in one hand and its bow in the other. Two sentences, one above the other, were printed in big black letters on the chest of the Old Man's sweatshirt:

THERE ARE 10 TYPES OF PEOPLE IN THE WORLD
THOSE WHO UNDERSTAND BINARY
AND THOSE WHO DO NOT.

'Oh what a spanner,' said Ludo.

Unruffled, the Old Man lumbered on towards the band but the girl gave Ludo a look so pained and outraged that he might as well have shot her father in a forest and blamed it on the Nazis.

'Shh,' said Claire. 'She heard that.'

Across the way Waistcoat and Frizzy Pioneer had arranged Ottoline on her back next to the Lazy Susan and were changing her nappy. There was a smell. Susan and Eyebrow-Stud Pioneer were trying to distract a frenzied Titus with the whale. Ludo wished Claire would take off the Jackie Os. He felt a pressure across his shoulders, almost fear when she leaned in close to him.

'See those people over there,' she whispered. 'They're, like, gay dads. That little girl has two dads. Will that mess you up later? Is that right? I just don't know.'

Ludo pointed his finger at the zero-tolerance notice. 'You can't say that in here. They'll have you out.'

'I could be wrong, but . . .'

'You can make a logical case,' said Ludo, 'for saying that parenthood is a heterosexual preserve, except that homosexuals have always borne children, the oft-stated case of Oscar Wilde, for example, and heterosexuals aren't universally making a very good job of child-rearing either.'

He felt like a string had been pulled in his back. Someone else had argued this line with him before, except he or she had been more longwinded and passionate and he'd simply parroted a version of their version.

'Oh,' said Claire. 'I was just saying . . .'

'Anyway, there are those who understand binary and those who do not. Shall we get out of here?'

He wanted to leave before the rubbish band came on. He and Claire could drift around the market place and discuss the architecture as the sun dipped and the air cooled. They could have a drink in a proper pub. He could pick out a decent restaurant for later and another café for breakfast tomorrow. She was inhibited in here, he could tell.

'Maybe in a bit,' she said. She didn't take off her sunglasses. She still hadn't finished her drink. Behind him, fiddle strings whined. The Blankets had all vacated their table now. The Young Pioneers crossed the room with their children and joined the audience gathering around Barry RaceHate. Only Pink Dress and Buzz and Ludo and Claire, the couples, remained at the front of the Cantina Reggio.

'Do you remember *Ça Va?*' said Ludo. 'You know, "J'aime le Deep Purple"?'

Claire frowned.

'*Wotcha* and *Fuck Off?*'

'Ludo!'

'Don't you remember? We had a right laugh about it on that ski trip. When we walked down that mountain?'

'Oh God, it was so cold I nearly wet myself.'

'No, no, that was because of me inventing *Wotcha* and *Fuck Off?*'

'It was all that glühwein they made us drink.'

'Don't you remember? You told me about Ophelia?'

'I remember you translating that graffiti on that cabin that said, "No remorse, this time the world", and Mr Priskin telling you to shut up.'

He winced. 'That was later.'

She craned around him to see what was going on at the other end of the bar. A smattering of applause broke out, followed by strumming and the groan of the fiddle.

'I want to sing a song,' declared a voice, presumably Barry RaceHate's.

'I want to sing it for Iraq, I want to sing it for Darfur. I want to sing it for Palestine and Gaza and the whole wide world. I want you to sing it with me.'

Before he could fully get into the swing, feedback blared like the sound of a ship leaving port. He announced that he needed a minute. Gasps of disappointment came from the crowd.

'This isn't going to be a manic pop thrill, is it?' said Ludo. 'Gypsy jazz is made-up bollocks.'

'No, it's like flamenco,' said Claire.

'Flamenco, but even worse?'

'Give it a chance. You might like it.'

'I mean, look at this bloke,' said Ludo. 'How patronizing can you get? Barry RaceHate. Barry Thought Police more like. It's not exactly Apartheid South Africa round here. He wouldn't know what racism was if it kicked him in the nuts.'

'Ludo ... Please.'

'Do you think he's ever met a real fascist? I've met fascists. I interviewed fascists in Spain. Do you think he's even been to a concentration camp? I've been to the camps. I've seen the piles of shoes. He *needs* racism. He subconsciously loves it. He wouldn't be anyone without it.'

'For crying out loud,' said Claire. She spun her Jackie Os onto the table. Before Ludo had a chance to see her eyes, the girl in the Yoruba head-tie appeared at the table.

'I'm sorry,' she said to Claire. 'I'm going to have to ask him to leave.'

'Why?' said Ludo. 'I've not said anything racist, or slagged off the gays.'

'You're annoying the other customers.'

In the opposing corner, Pink Dress had moved her chair and now sat with her back to the room and her head resting on Buzz Quarterpounder's shoulder. Claire stood up. She turned her back, flapped her hand at her ear and strode towards the door. Yoruba Head-Tie's face was stern and pinchy. Ludo knew when someone had made up their mind. As he collected his bag and slipped *The Organist* in with his clean pants and *Hitler's Library* he felt a sense of pride at being asked to leave the Cantina Reggio. At least now they wouldn't have to suffer Barry RaceHate. At least now they would be on their own.

She was standing by the kerbside, her back to him, smoking a cigarette. He fell in beside her and dropped his bag. Across the street, at either end of the flint wall two multigenerational gangs were squaring up, grizzled inky men in vests and baseball caps and women like bloated replicas of the men. The massive women jerked their pushchairs as if they were revving them up for a demolition derby while their children ran ahead and gestured. A beer can sailed from the left side division to the battalion on the right and landed with an explosion of fizz between them.

'That's an advert for eugenics,' said Ludo. 'Do you know that the Nazis called people like that Useless-Eaters?'

131

'It's not funny,' said Claire.

'It is a bit. Go somewhere else?'

'I can't. I have to stay here.'

'But they chucked me out.'

Over the road, a charismatic speaker emerged from the masses to lead his people. A summit was held in No-Man's Land, the solemnity of the occasion marked by the removal of baseball caps. A Munich Agreement was reached. Someone gobbed at the kerb to symbolize peace in our time. Both armies demobilized and returned to their homelands. Claire flicked her cigarette into a drain.

'We'll keep in touch, OK.' She gave him a gentle hug and briefly pressed her cheek to his cheek. 'Good luck with the book.'

'But I really like you.' He tried to raise his hands so he could take off her sunglasses and see into her eyes this time. 'I like you. I do. I remembered you.'

The blue hazy feeling rose through his shins and up to his knees and his waist.

'You ought to know,' she said, 'that Barry and me, we were . . . He was posted in Bosnia. When he came back he couldn't ... He saw things.'

At first he felt a surge of something like anger – after all, her page had said she was Claire Vickers-was-Thornley, divorced and looking for a relationship, not Claire Vickers-was-RaceHate – but it evaporated as the blue feeling flooded from him. Her face seemed to hold two expressions: wide, frightened eyes above a resolute and defiant mouth. His hands were now suspended at her shoulders. She must have sensed that he was about to touch her – he only wanted to comfort her; he only wanted, again, to understand – because she tried to conceal a shiver as a shrug.

'I ought to go,' she said.

'Why didn't you tell me?' he said.

'You wouldn't understand.'

She turned tail and strode back towards the Cantina Reggio. He grabbed hold of his bag. Its contents slumped against his hip as he chased after her. She disappeared through the doorway before he could catch her. Pink Dress and Buzz, blushing and giggling, fell out onto the step and barred his way. They started to kiss. He had to manoeuvre them sideways to peer inside. They were all in there, all the people. The music could be clearly heard now. There was something Levantine and plaintive detectable in the strings and guitar. From this distance the band was blurred by the audience and he couldn't see Claire, only her sunglasses at a diagonal angle on the table they had quit. He should go to her and listen and help. He should go to Barry Thornley and listen and help him make sense of the past. That's what Ludo had set out to do. Once it had been his purpose, when he was younger than Pink Dress and Buzz, when he noticed Claire Vickers on the coach and stole glances at her over his copy of *A Study in Tyranny*. The music in the Cantina Reggio grew louder. They were stamping their feet. He shouldered the door and swallowed hard. He would reach the bottom this time. He would think harder.

Abyssinia

Pulsing eggs floated in the striplights. The shrieking came from inside the eggs. He swung his legs over the edge of a trolley and laughed. The trolley was curtained off. He was naked beneath a crisp green gown, his clothes piled on an orange plastic chair. On top of his sweater lay his glasses. One arm was bent at a hundred and eighty degrees to the lenses, an arrangement that reminded him of the work of a Scottish sculptor he'd once seen in Brussels. He could picture the gallery but not the name on the banner. He knew he had written a review of that exhibition, though, one admired by at least three colleagues. You don't get any points for doing that nowadays.

Before he'd surfaced here, he remembered, he was laid out on a patch of gravel. The trunks of black trees merged into a starless night. Strangers whispered above him. He'd been anxious about his glasses. He had found them now. Joy throbbed in his veins. A grey yolk twitched at the heart of each egg. What had they devised up there? Why were they shrieking? They had shrieked in his dreams.

The curtains around the trolley did not meet. Girls swayed in the gap. Girls in matching T-shirts stamped with unreadable slogans. Girls with plastic balls chained to their ankles. It was not the brood in the striplights who shrieked. The girls were shrieking, out there, in some sort of waiting room or holding area.

It was possible that he knew the girls. This could make things worse or even more joyous. A slender brunette was standing with her hands pressed together in front of her face, reminding him of the pose of a Victorian statue he'd once walked seven miles to see in a cemetery near Birmingham. He still couldn't read the words on her T-shirt. Another girl appeared and hugged the brunette. On his feet now, he felt clear-headed, no after-effects. He was invincible, a colossus. He must know what was written on those T-shirts. When the larval creatures in the tubes arrived the wording on the shirts could be used as an icebreaker. He found his glasses and carefully worked the arm into its rightful position. As he dithered about whether to first get dressed or sort out the matter of the slogans something rolled over him.

Roland Coburn's party.

On the floor.

Ranting.

The parquet slick.

Red wine.

Mussolini holding her hand.

Fuck.

A tango-orange man with a cuboid head flapped through the curtains.

Him again.

'Awight, mate, back for more, you glutton for punishment, you chippy rascal?'

Doctor Baz dropped a shoulder and jabbed his finger and thumb. His voice was easily the worst thing that had happened during the last twenty-four hours, even worse than Roland's party or the conspiracy against nature gestating on the ceiling. He decided not to listen to Doctor Baz and wondered when doctors became so chummy. There was no doubt a manual – *Chumminess for Medical Professionals* – and role-play and tick box exercises, and a 'narrative therapy' course where medical professionals try to empathize with lovelorn characters in Dostoevsky novels. He would end up teaching those courses. He would then have impact.

'So, Doctor Mellis,' said Doctor Baz, 'you were found getting some zeds on the old frog and toad. And this time you wet yourself.'

Mellis didn't say anything.

'You're a lucky chappie. You hit your bonce on a lion-headed pilaster and wound up in someone's front garden. You're fortunate they came home. It's minus four tonight, very chilly around the willy.'

'These hippy shoes,' said Mellis. 'Inadequate grip.'

'Get real, matey, you're supposed to be a smart geezer. This is the fourth time we've met like this. How much did you drink?'

'You know I can't drink anymore,' said Mellis. During their last encounter Doctor Baz had given him a card. It led to the Reverend Blither's recovery group, where that other charlatan droned on about taking this day and that day one at a time. The others there knew, though. The others understood.

'Chop chop,' said Doctor Baz. 'How much you chuck down your gullet?'

Mellis conjured a figure. He halved it and when he offered it for approval Doctor Baz gasped like he'd rested his hand on a hotplate.

'That's far, far too much, especially at your age.'

'What's in the tubes, you box-ticking monster?'

'I'm keeping you in under observation. You've had a blow to the old nut. Complications are a possibility.'

Mellis put his hand to his head. Three barbs poked out from a strip of gauze over his left eye. He was sure they had not been there when he'd woken up.

'There's things growing up there,' said Mellis. 'And *they* know something, those girls.'

'Lie down, maestro,' said Doctor Baz. 'I'll be back in a few hours.'

The girls were shrieking. The curtain flapped.

'Ladies,' Doctor Baz exclaimed as if launching himself at the audience of the Hammersmith Apollo.

The shrieking stopped.

Mellis lay back on the trolley. The yolks were definitely spreading; each nucleus was darker now. Doctor Baz must be growing a legion of insectoid fascist super soldiers. He was certain of it. Blood swirled in his ears.

Mussolini had been holding her hand.

He must get dressed and discharge himself. Doctor Baz couldn't tell the difference between a head injury and a hangover, and Mellis didn't even have a hangover, not even the ghost of one. He could still save her.

Beyond the curtains, out in the waiting area he finally managed to decipher the slogans on the hen-night girls' T-shirts. 'Karen 4 Dave' was lined across each chest and arranged vertically down the backs:

> dream
> your
> little
> dreams
> for
> us

He must have taken a wrong turn out of A&E. He wandered past the doors of hospital departments that he didn't recognize – Histopathy and Cytology, Prosthodontics – laboratories where Doctor Baz was using taxpayers' money to genetically-engineer fascist super soldiers. Doctor Baz had grown the Reverend Blither in there as well, splicing the genes of a nanny goat and a higher form of moss (a fact he would conceal from the Blither's group so as not to disillusion them). Confronting Doctor Baz about the things in the tubes now seemed like an artistic statement, a blow to the gut of popular credulity. Doctor Baz was the saddest twat he'd ever met. In Doctor Baz's house hung that painting of the waiter serving idiots on a beach. He owned the complete boxed set of *Lost* and had watched all the extras (twice!). He'd read all the Stieg Larsson 'thrillers' and went to 'boutique festivals' in the summer and clapped haggard middle-of-the-road has-beens and shoutybollocks performance poets toss comedians and he played the mandolin for an hour before bed and drank probiotic yoghurts and owned a composter that he revered like a Hindu shrine and attended ecological barbeques in his special yoga sandals and his wife had never articulated a vaguely engaging thought of her own but she was all for the smoking ban because she and Dr Moreau could now nip into The Gatling Gun Arms after badminton on Sundays and stand at the bar in their nice, matching Slazenger tank tops and sip a bitter lemon without reeking like ashtrays afterwards.

Mellis found himself squatting in a deserted stretch of white light, tearful and saturated as he waited for all of this mess to spurt through his pores.

A pressure flowed from his right hip to his left temple as he finally found the main entrance and stepped out into a carpark. Frost glittered on the roofs of cars. A stationary ambulance flashed amber streaks across the tarmac. As he walked across the carpark he slipped his hands into his coat pockets, drawing his arms closer to his frame against the cold. He found two objects there. The smaller was a neat little box with glossy sides and bevelled edges. There were seven left and a disposable lighter was tucked into the packet. He sparked up. The plates of his skull pulsated. He hadn't smoked for eight months. She'd made him stop. No, she'd made a deal with him: if he stopped, she would apply. It wasn't the same. It was. The things he'd done for her.

He couldn't remember when he'd cracked last night. He did remember arriving at The Prince of Lübeck after the meeting. The meeting had been in the morning. He must have decided on the pub well before lunchtime. 'Hello stranger,' said Max the Bar. The party was in the evening. He was supposed to be giving both the pub and the party a very wide berth.

As he stepped over a low wooden fence into a field he took out Item Number Two, the Discman. He didn't have an iPod. iPods were for children. Doctor Baz had an iPod. Doctor Baz did not have any albums by Nick Cave. Doctor Baz had lots of Bluegrass. He loved slave music. When Mellis plugged the headphones into his ears Nick started to sing *Dig Lazarus Dig*. Mellis had history with Nick. Twenty-five years. All the way back to *From Her to Eternity* and *Release the Bats*. He'd released some bats himself last night. Baz and Blither might not approve but Nick would understand. Nick would write a song about this, if he hadn't already done so.

Frost had stiffened the grass. Mellis' shins became wetter as he crossed the field. The crotch of his jeans felt dry. Doctor Baz had lied about that as well, or maybe the Karen 4 Dave girls had dry-cleaned his trousers while he slept. He didn't have a clue where he was. He trudged up a ridge. The moon was full, its surface pocked and scarred. At the top of the ridge, the lights of the city spread out ahead of him. *Dig Lazarus Dig* shut off. The dead battery tone pipped. Nick was cancelled.

A dome of blue light rose from behind the distant steeples and towers of the town. If he carried on over this ridge he would find a road, he was sure, and if he could find a road he could walk through the town to their house. He lit another cigarette, alive with joy as he started to stagger down the bank.

His watch said it was a quarter past four in the morning when he came up from a sunken building site of frozen puddles and solidified tyre tracks. He climbed over a crash barrier and caught his breath on what he assumed was the ring road. Out-of-town superstores loomed, blocks of glass like the fantasies of Weimar architects. He was standing on the middle of the road. He lit his third cigarette, turned full circle and laughed at the night. This was what smoking was like. He'd almost forgotten. Losing it had been like losing a friend. He'd assumed he was no longer capable of joy. This was joy. Mountaintop joy. Cresting joy. Revolutionary fervour.

The hiss of a car grew louder until he could hear its chassis rattle. He scampered across the road, almost sliding over when his innards cramped. His guts settled as he started to walk alongside a multi-storey carpark. He was smoking but still felt like he'd lost a friend. The last time he'd been like this had been a few weeks ago, at home, in the interval between Christmas and New Year. It had started then, this feeling.

During each day of the holiday his parents' house had seemed increasingly strange and unfamiliar. Mum and Dad and the uncles and aunts opened bottle of wine after bottle of wine. He'd managed to abstain, telling them not that Doctor Baz had exiled him to Blither's de-joying seminar but that he was still delicate after a bout of food poisoning. His mother complained a hundred times that it was a shame that the children had stayed in France again this year and that he at least ought to ring them. He told her to mind her own business. Speaking to Bethany and Thomas would, he knew, compel him to drink like it was the last night of the Colony Room.

One afternoon they all nestled down to watch a Michael McIntyre DVD that must be hilarious because *The Sun*, that authority on comedic truth and comedic pain gave it five out of five stars. To survive McIntyre he'd need to soak his liver. He excused himself and wandered the riverside, the one he used to walk along to school listening to things like *Your Funeral, My Trial* by Nick on his Walkman. Mist hung over the water where the river widened out in the park. Leafless trees were steaming black stumps. A muzzled rottweiler that belonged in a George Grosz drawing pulled a man in a sheepskin out of the mist. It was merely an ugly dog, Mellis thought. However ugly the dog, it was better not to read too much into things now.

In the high street the breeze swayed a lattice of unlit Christmas lights above the road. The shops were shut-up and a weird brown gloss slicked the pavements. Even though he didn't have any he found himself reaching in his coat for a cigarette. He was outside what had been in turn the *Coo-ee* newsagents in the seventies; *Hollywood Beyond*, the video shop for video nasties; some sort of bling toilet seat emporium called *Bogz*, and then *Pantry 69*, a now defunct hangout for the heroes of new wealth. He stared into a window smeared with whitewash and swear words. All would lift if he smoked a cigarette. Smoking would exorcise this feeling that a friend had died. It didn't feel like that. It felt like a friend had deserted him. No, betrayed him; betrayed him to the Stasi, then died on him. Died in an unsafe room he'd sublet to her on the cheap. It was that bad.

He sat down on a bench outside the *Porto Bello* tanning salon that used to be the post office. On this bench he'd been sixteen and halfway home. The horse chestnut trees wafted a thick resin smell around the *Hollywood Beyond*-era shops and he'd sat here in the shade with Amanda Tipper. Between them they invented a fantastic city of ballrooms and grand hotels called Marmara Spa that could be placed on top of this borehole of doom. He remembered the night after he'd finished his exams and getting drunk in The Golden Hind with Ludo and Grant. After closing time none of them were able to walk any further than this bench. They sat here, taking the piss and sharing cigarettes, the lowbrow ones as well, Rothmans and JPS. He'd loved The Golden Hind, even though the beer furred your tongue and sometimes the bar was crammed with Young Rotarians and the sort of girls who hang around with Young Rotarians. He loved its brass-framed mirrors and suit of armour in the snug and its one bricked-up window on the first floor that Ludo said was a reminder of the time of the window tax. He'd go there now, have a drink, just one, or two, only beer, and stare in those mirrors. A still-single Amanda Tipper might be perched on a barstool in her tartan mini-skirt and ribbed tights and they could knock back the gin legally and excavate the ruins of Marmara Spa. Or Ludo and Grant might still be arguing some mental academic point - Dickens vs. James, Lenin vs. Trotsky, The Bunnymen vs. The Smiths – and he could confide in them that he was dreading the start of the new semester. The Hind would probably be empty. The day after Boxing Day. He could still have a drink, though. He was cured.

Yes, he was cured and deserved a swift half. This was his reasoning as he negotiated the side streets, anticipating that first swig in The Golden Hind and perplexed that you could live in a place for the first eighteen years of your life and on your return never see a soul who you recognize.

When he turned the corner he couldn't see the galleon pub sign. The Golden Hind had been converted into executive apartments, *The Hind Quarters*. He was outraged, then relieved. The reasoning stopped and he remembered all the things Blither had said about temptation and control and emotional ownership. But Amanda and The Golden Hind: it was over twenty years ago. No one wants to wake up one day to find he's become the man who can say, 'It was over twenty years ago'. He started to walk back. Someone had died. Someone was dead to him.

He was now standing in a cobbled street, in front of a redbrick arch, craning to look up at a square tower. Its flagpole halved the moon. This was the art college, where he was Head of Visual Culture. It wasn't an art college any more. It was a university. This meant no art, by government diktat, and instead lots of box-ticking and creative partnerships with philistine business gimps. He'd been here yesterday. After the meeting he'd fled through this arch in a panic. As he stared up at the tower – a fine example of Victorian Neo-Gothic – he became more aware of a harsh chafing around his inner thighs.

He hadn't felt great when he'd come to work yesterday, the first day of the new semester. Since the Christmas vacation the feeling that Caitlin was dead had not faded. Every night, unable to sleep, he'd worried about his job in Visual Culture and his impact and outcomes. He became enmeshed in great circular arguments with his ex-wife Sally-Anne about her perpetual sodding unreasonable demand to be happy and fulfilled during every minute of every day and how she'd taken Bethany and Thomas to live in St. Malo with France's answer to Doctor Baz and, *quelle surprise*, she was still miserable. When he could leave Sally-Anne alone he continued to worry about the national debt and the melting of the Greenland Pump, the war dead of Helmand, the extinction of the golden frog, the twenty-two million people who would be displaced or drowned when Beijing flooded in a hundred years time and the way British politicians flourish their hands when they talk. And then he would worry about whether he'd ever write anything substantial again and about all the booze, fat and nicotine he'd put into his system over the years to keep himself joyful. After circuiting this gang of nightmares for hours he would find himself fantasizing about a warm nip of Glenfiddich and the metallic taste of Guinness. He worried about these things, night after night until he came back to worrying about Caitlin Palarme.

Fine powdery snow started to fall from a sky like black glass. The tower seemed to sway against the moon. He wondered if the insectoid fascist super soldiers had now hatched and whether Doctor Baz was defending the Karen 4 Dave girls by swiping the flaming neck of his mandolin across an oncoming phalanx of pincers and proboscises. The tower was merely stacked clods of baked mud, no more sophisticated than a Neolithic menhir. He should never have brought Caitlin here.

It would have been so much better all round if he'd seen Caitlin yesterday morning and not Eleanor Spratley, the last of his postgraduate students now that his sector of the Graduate School was all but disbanded. He wasn't looking forward to Eleanor as he sat there waiting in his office. His eyes were sore and a cold jelly sensation had pooled in the pit of his stomach. He'd worried all night about the meeting with Tony Easterman of Human Resources that would follow an hour of listening to Eleanor waffle. He'd fretted too about Roland Coburn's retirement party tonight even though Roland had sternly told him that it was defeatist to keep avoiding them. His torso contracted when Eleanor launched herself into his room without knocking and swung her red and yellow gypsy skirt and her lunettes on a string and the saddlebag-style case she used to heft around half the books from the library. She tossed a paper sack of pastries onto his desk.

'I've got the ache, Ben,' she said, massaging her left shoulder and turning to peer out of his window. 'If it's this shoulder I know it's going to rain. If it's the other, it'll snow.'

'It's sleeting,' said Mellis.

'Do you get that?'

'Weather divination via the medium of muscle stress? Not in my shoulders.'

'Have an apricot and almond croissant,' she said. 'They're yummy.' She sat down and started to unpack piles of notes and sketches from her saddlebag. 'I've got something that I just must show you. It came to me in a great *swoop* last weekend, it was like ... punctum!' She flashed her hands at her cheeks like a magician after a trick. 'We were over in Chipping Norton and the girls, you must meet my girls sometime, took me off to ...'

Eleanor Spratley, a few years his senior, divorced and squandering a chunk of her settlement on a pointless Masters in Visual Bollocks. She was here to discuss her dissertation on the role of horses in Italian Futurist painting. She'd chosen the subject because she liked horses. Italian Futurism was Mellis' speciality. She'd desperately wanted Mellis to supervise her. He'd lost the will to even talk about Italian Futurism, though, and hadn't written anything for years, not even a review. His last contribution had come by way of an accident. While staying in a Tuscan villa with Sally-Anne and the kids, decorators revamping the lobby discovered a Fascist-era propaganda mural of particular stiltedness beneath the cheesy post-war picnic scene that concealed it. Beneath this, restorers went on to find a far more interesting fresco called *Vortice*. Art Detective Benjamin Mellis managed to attribute *Vortice* to a lesser-known Italian painter called Dario Inchesa. Inchesa's role in the murder of a prominent Italian socialist in the twenties formed a chapter in Mellis'' short book, *Vortex and Destiny* (admired by at least three colleagues). For a time the story of Inchesa obsessed Mellis. As a young man Inchesa had developed his craft and sensibilities but was drawn to Fascism for the art and became an accessory and a dupe. Thinking about Inchesa would often remind Mellis of when he used to drink in The Golden Hind and actually mean it when he argued that art would save the world.

Eleanor was droning on and on about the recapitulation of a Donatello bronze horseman in a painting by Boccioni. Even though the room was cold she'd hoiked up her skirt so he could see her shins and knees. He couldn't engage with Eleanor's lower body and spurious recapitulations when he had this long-arranged meeting with Easterman to negotiate and then Roland Coburn's retirement party. He'd stayed dry at parties before. He could stay dry at this one. Eleanor handed him a sheet of art paper.

'This, you see, Ben, is what I came up with after I saw the black mare in Chipping.'

A map of the world was tacked to the sheet, a double-page spread from a pre-World War II atlas. Between Canada and Mexico, Eleanor had filled the outline of America with the image of a black, fire-snorting horse. Florida was its front and California its hind legs. Alaska was its tail and Lake Michigan one of its eyes. Across the Atlantic, Great Britain had been whited-out, giving it the appearance of a *Casper*-style ghost. It didn't work. The horse was too compressed to fit the shape and looked more like a rhino drawn by a four-year old who had never seen a rhino.

'I don't see the connection with your thrust,' he said.

'You see, Ben, it struck me in Chipping, punctum, that America is a demon and Britain a ghost.'

'You're waxing theological again. It doesn't stand up to scrutiny.' He looked at his watch: ten minutes to go. She leaned back into her chair and smoothed down her skirt, something she usually did when he'd made her feel stupid.

'Don't you ever think, Ben, who would win in a fight between a ghost and a demon?'

'No,' he said, 'and I don't see the relevance to our thesis.'

'Okey-dokey,' she said. 'Back to the drawing board.'

'Keep focused on what you're supposed to be doing. I'll see you next week.'

'Ben,' she said, standing up now. 'Can I offer you a home-cooked meal this week sometime? I mean ... I don't know. I just feel we'd get more ... done if we didn't have to sit in here.'

'That would be nice,' he said. 'I'll check my diary and email you.'

He wouldn't. Eleanor was a well-known red wine fiend. He couldn't be around red wine fiends. She was smiling warmly at him, as if his dismissal of the demon/ghost nonsense hadn't happened.

'Fantastic,' she said. 'Apologies in advance. The place is a state. The builders are in. I'll make sure the girls are out.'

The room seemed doubly quiet after she left; more than quiet, it felt empty even though he was still here. He must keep clear of red wine fiends, and Guinness fiends, whisky and gin fiends, lager monsters and cider beasts and anyone who drank shots or cocktails; in fact, he must avoid all of his friends, and everyone in the world, apart from the Reverend Blither's AA sufferers. For the first time in ages, though, he actually fancied some red

145

wine fiendishness, just not with Eleanor Spratley. He'd be alright, he told himself, if he conceded to Joy that he was allowed to drink, and as much as he bloody well liked, but only in The Golden Hind.

Halfway down the staircase he found himself thinking about Eleanor's picture. Who would win in a fight between a demon and a ghost? Who cares? Who would win in a fight between *your* demons and *your* ghosts? Now, that was an altogether more enervating proposition. It was time to see Easterman.

In a room dominated by a circular black table, Easterman's massive bald head whispered to its chief hatchetwoman, the brown-blazered, snub-nosed Erma Flint. Mellis found himself staring into Easterman's eyes. He held that stare until Easterman's own crawled all over him.

'Ben,' said Easterman. 'You're early. So good you could come. Wonderful to see you. Get this all sorted for you, shall we?'

Mellis interpreted this as: *mate in three.*

He sat down. Erma wrote something on her notepad.

'How are you?' said Easterman. 'It's been a long time. Been over in Italy at all? That gorgeous food, eh? Nice old buildings. We have wondered about how you're getting along.'

Kept off the sauce?

'Yes ... fine,' said Mellis.

Easterman glanced at Erma. She wrote on her notepad.

'Now, you know why we've called this meeting, because we spoke last year about your redeployment ...'

career ending

'And you could have brought your line-manager with you ...'

I haven't got one

' ... or your union rep ...'

you wouldn't have turned up

' ... and we did ask you to supply us with your CV so that we can assess what you can do for us ...'

what else you can rob from me

'... but you haven't passed anything through. Is that right, Erma?'

'Yes Tony, that's correct.'

Easterman's shirt was of a military green colour that seemed to tinge the underside of his chin and his cheeks. Mellis wondered if she liked this, if it turned her on. Erma wrote something else on her notepad.

'You already have my CV and employment record, Erma ...'

you want me gone ...

'There are other opportunities here, Ben, as you know, and the team wants to keep its talent ...'

yes, please, Senor Tony, although I am an art historian I can teach Games Design to bedroom-haunting Hagar the Horrible types, or Fashion Tips to airheads in pink tutus.

146

Easterman knitted his fingers together and tilted his head like he was coaxing a child out of a strop.

'You, like us, the people people, have got to start to think like a business, Ben. These are new times with new ideas.'

have you read my book on Dario Inchesa?

Mellis sighed, waiting for Easterman to mention 'the followship of blue-sky' or 'low-hanging box-ticks' or something. He wondered how on earth people like Easterman had gained control. There was no *putsch* or *coup*, no seizure of power, no March on Rome. It had been a process of gradual infiltration, salami tactics. One day you were a lecturer: teaching, writing and supervising research. The next Forza Easterman arrived and you were part of a self-fellating managerial system and statistical exercise. And Easterman knew nothing about anything, let alone how an art school should operate. He had a degree in Business Administration and a Masters in Human Resource Management. He'd been a Human Resources manager for several wasteful and dubious quangos. He was Quangoman, a corporate statesman. Quangomen were now a thread of steel, a revolutionary vanguard. Mellis could write the history of this take-over, the history of the new times and the new ideas. He would call it *Tail Wags Dog*, or *Ten Years That Shook the World*. It would be admired by at least three ex-colleagues.

'I think it's clear what I do,' said Mellis.

'The problem I'm trying to solve for you, Ben, is that as Visual Culture has proved itself unable to contribute sufficiently to the core business of the University College, and we're in the teeth of a recession ...'

caused by people like you ...

' ... it is hard to see what ...'

' ... necessary strategic reorganization ...'

' ... low-hanging blue sky ...'

' ... partnerships with industry ...'

'... teeth of a recession ...'

' ... generous offer ...'

Mellis let the details of the offer glaze over him. He wondered if Easterman had experienced his own Amanda Tipper moment at sixteen but dreamed instead of shutting down all the shops and turning them into useless ones like *Bogz*. Or if after Personnel Manager and Director of Human Resources, Easterman's next title would be *Duce*. He did, conspicuously, resemble Mussolini – the overbearing chin, the froglike mouth, the oblong skull. Young Easterman, the Easterman who worked in Personnel no doubt emitted commendable warmth towards the people whose employment he merely administered. Then there came the HR Revolution and he, along with most of his generation, became radicalized. He was now in the process of wiping out all internal opposition, something that started with the assassination of Roland Coburn and would culminate in his *squadristi* taking out the Principal and the amalgamation of the entire university into HR.

There would be a balcony scene at the end of year show. Then the Battle for Synergy, the Battle for Branding and the Battle for Business Links. The *Duce* would unveil a mammoth public works scheme of expensive admin buildings that no one needed. A dashing new corporate logo would strike fear into the hearts of other higher education establishments. He would annex the tiny Gallery of Ethiopian Art and turn it into a shit croissant shop. Massive bald head further swollen by a full-blown personality cult, he'd be photographed astride the Black Mare of Chipping lofting a rolled-up business plan, jaw like a shovel's blade, nodding imperiously before his army of yes-men and people people. Then he'd enter an ill-fated alliance with the far more extreme, private university down the road, slide into failing-institution status and be overrun by more ruthless and organized entrepreneurs. He'd end up being shot by his business advisers and strung up by his feet from the Texaco garage, his mistress dangling beside him. By then she wouldn't be his mistress. She'd be his wife.

They were all standing up now. The consent forms had been signed and were fanned out on the table. Easterman had his hand out for the shake. If he raised his arms a few more degrees he'd be giving an Olympian salute.

'I hope we'll see you tonight, Ben. You know we'd love to.'

Caitlin hanging from her heels in a garage forecourt. There was still time. History could be rerouted. Mellis was now outside the darkened front of the Prince of Lübeck after exactly the same walk from the college he'd taken yesterday. The stools were upturned on the bar, the chairs nested on the tables. The Blither wouldn't approve of him staring into a pub at five-thirty on a winter's morning. Bollocks to Blither. No sense of mission. Sometimes you have to make sacrifices. This is what Inchesa had failed to do. Mellis would stop this happening. Eventually his children would understand. Even Sally-Anne would be proud of him. He lit a cigarette. There were three left. A night-lamp illuminated the array of bottles behind the bar. Very beautiful. The tawny browns of the whiskys, the purity of vodka, the emerald glow of the gin. He used to drink here all the time. A few after work with Roland, or with Chloe and Che, his part-time tutors, sometimes a couple with a guest lecturer or the strange girl from the print shop who looked at him as if a golden nightingale was singing in his heart. After Sally-Anne left it became a session every night. Then a mini joy-spree at lunchtime or, if they were not teaching in the afternoon, what Roland called a 'symposium', the Greek for beer meeting, from *sympinein*, to drink together. This was when the blackouts were irregular, when his drinking was still admired by at least three colleagues.

'Hello Stranger,' said Max the Bar when Mellis had flapped into the pub yesterday and ordered a Guinness. As the Guinness settled Mellis almost changed his order to tomato juice. The stern words of the Reverend Blither came back to him: *you can't have one drink, be alert, be in control.* Then he remembered the contrary advice he'd received from reading the biographies of the great American drunk writers like Fitzgerald, Yates and Cheever: cut the spirits, stick to beer. Beer wasn't drinking. Fitzgerald one, Blither nil. Demon one, ghost nil.

The first gulp seemed to fill him out into a shape more familiar and comfortable. He told Max a white lie that he'd been teaching in Italy for a year and skim-read the papers Erma had given him. At the end of this semester he was kaput, *finito*, out on his ear. He was forty-two, a specialist in esoteric nonsense, bereft of ideas and now facing the goose chase of finding a new position in the teeth of a recession caused by people like Easterman.

He ordered another pint. When it came he hunched over the glass and gripped it with both hands. Who would win in a fight between your ghosts and your demons? He swilled the Guinness around his cheeks. Demon, obviously. A demon strikes when you least expect it. You can be fine, ambling along, and next thing you're shouting in someone's face, you wake up in hospital, you're confessing to a stranger your most humiliating rejections and childish fears. A demon lurks deep in the blackout called you. And there had been a lot of blackouts, going back to The Golden Hind, a parallel history that shadowed his achievements, the detail of the incidents as obscure to him as the vanished countries on Eleanor Spratley's map. That time in the Hind, just after all-day licensing came in, when he was suddenly telling everyone that they bored him to death was his Bechuanaland. Siam was where, after listening to her bleat about money for four days he had come to his senses in the middle of a busy restaurant terrace swearing his head off at Sally-Anne. Ceylon was after she took the children away and he pulverized the kitchen crockery and kicked to death the vegetable patch and the bird table. Yugoslavia was when he surfaced in Roland's house not knowing what he had said or what he had done and his trousers were splattered with something that looked like toothpaste but smelt like paraffin. The time, though, the worst time, the blackest, most wince-worthy and shivery time of all came after Caitlin told him – barrelling around the lounge to *Murder Ballads*; the memory of the pub like frames from a scratchy film from the 1910s; the text messages that he didn't remember sending – and then being smashed awake in A&E and Doctor Baz looming over him. That was his heart of darkness, his Belgian Congo. You can't guard against your demon. There are no premonitions, no diplomatic stand-offs or warning shots. Demon aces ghost every time.

When Mellis ordered another pint, Max raised his eyebrows and seemed sullen as he poured. The Lübeck was filling up for lunch. Mellis was no longer alone at the bar. The Guinness left its metal tang on his tongue. A ghost. What about the ghost? A ghost is different. A ghost enters you on a summer's day and again there's the resiny smell of horse chestnuts and not kissing Amanda Tipper when she clearly wanted you to kiss her and how that taunts and teases even after twenty years. A ghost is the rows of spirit bottles behind the bar of a classic English boozer, the honey-browns, the crystal whites, the gemstone greens and all their promise of adventure and romance. First dates with Sally-Anne in The Chaffinch off Borough Market when he'd still been at Goldsmiths. In the archive all day, a phone call from a publisher, a commission to write a chapter and the liquid colours there to greet you when you swagger into a bar on the Via Imola. The Hind with Ludo and Grant and talking about everything that you're going to do and could still do and that art will save the world. A ghost was Inchesa and what if he'd not stood by when Mussolini's boys went about their stamping, or if he'd testified against them at the trial. A ghost was *The Archive of Water*.

Next to him a man in a pinstriped suit was now sipping a glass of red wine and peering over half-moon glasses at the *Telegraph* crossword. In the old days Mellis may well have small-talked this bloke but chitchat was impossible in new times with new ideas. He might be found out, his position in the resistance compromised. He slid his empty glass across the bar a bit too forcefully. Max intercepted it before it hit the edge. Mellis was out of cash and had to use his card for his next drink and this meant buying a double scotch or he'd be under the five-pound minimum charge. Outside it was still sleeting. Bundled-up penguin-people tottered along the pavements. There was a clutch of lads around the triv machine and girls in woolly hats and scarves sprawled across one of the larger tables. If anyone was talking, though, he couldn't hear the voices. His head felt mothballed. The drinks arrived and he decided at first not to touch the whisky. Its smell made him queasy and memories shot through him of the toilet bowl and the kidney dish. He stared at his pint and the pint was like one of the tubes in *The Archive of Water* only filled with black milk. The day he saw *The Archive* had been one of the best days, one of the most joyful days since Sally-Anne left.

Over a year ago now, the autumn before last, during reading week he'd taken a trip down to Cornwall. He stayed in a hotel and slept late during the windy mornings, prowled galleries in the afternoons and in the evenings, after a walk along the beach, ate in seafood restaurants, a book held up in his left hand as he twirled spaghetti around a fork with his right. During these days he felt that he could see the sky for the first time in years. Looking back, he must have been ready. He was ready for her that afternoon he found himself in a space where curving white walls snaked towards a window overlooking the harbour.

The exhibition was called *The Archive of Water*, an installation composed of standing glass tubes filled with fluid. She wasn't the first girl that he noticed. A distorted, orange-jacketed little troll, about eight-years old was poised to spring from behind one of the tubes. The water refracted her smile into a grinning blur. He moved closer to the tube and stared through the glass at her face. She reminded him of his own daughter, Bethany. He

150

made a mental note to remember to buy something before he returned home and send it to France. It was only when the girl didn't flinch that it struck Mellis that maybe he shouldn't be looking at her at all.

He took a step back. Under-lighting beamed through each of the tubes. Some of the waters were staggeringly pure, some almost murky. From behind one tube a blonde woman's reflected form rippled across the surface sheen of others. He paid her no attention at first. Fearing that she was the troll's mother, he moved off.

The artist's name was Ralf Poppe, a German Mellis had not encountered before who had filled the tubes with meltwater from Greenlandic glaciers. It was the sort of high-concept, logistical art that often underwhelmed Mellis (to him, the shark in the tank had been no more than a stuffed trout above a pub door). He'd never quite lost his enthusiasm for the verve and emotion of the art of the early twentieth century. *The Promise of the Street. Technology as Manifesto. Impulse, Innovation, Joy.* These were the titles of essays he'd written. But there was an endearing simplicity and sadness to Poppe's work. These ancient waters had been compacted ice for hundreds of thousands of years at least. They had been heated, transformed. There was no vanishing point. The vanishing point was elsewhere. Like memory. Like remembering.

Rapt, he found himself drawn to one particular tube. There were no bubbles, so no air and he wondered how on earth you extracted the air from the water. A yellow balloon thing floated in front of him. The yellow balloon shrank and kinked before expanding into a squarish polygon that blipped into the room. He peered around the tube. Another tube was drawing the blonde woman's attention. As she circled it she held her hand to her throat; her eyes were moist and glittery. He froze. Some old, refreshed feeling tingled his ribs. He knew, knew that she saw what he saw. She would feel too what he felt.

Now there was the vexed issue of how to strike up a conversation. If he didn't it would nag him for at least the rest of his holiday. She might even join Amanda Tipper on the ghost shelf. Maybe he could simply shamble over with a pun about breaking the ice. *No need to break the ice, the ice has already thawed, ha!*

Oh God, no. That was the sort of line someone like Easterman would use. If you're going to use cheese, at least grill it first and splash Tabasco on it.

Instead, he could sidle around the room, pretending to be profoundly affected, then approach, lean on her tube and say, 'Beautiful, aren't they?'

No, that was cheese left over from a dinner party that no one enjoyed.

How about: sidle, make eye contact, say: *I'm an art historian. Can I explain the significance over dinner?*

He was maturing from cheese to sleaze as he pigeon-stepped towards her. She was looking up at where her tube reached the ceiling. Her hands slipped from her waist to under the band of her short, black suede skirt. He might die of grief if he didn't talk to her now. *Fancy a cocktail, girlie!*

That line probably wouldn't work, but even if it did he wasn't allowed to drink. It was so much easier when he'd been drinking. That's the English way. Tank up and lunge. He found himself trying to think of anyone he'd ever successfully chatted up sober. The only girl he could remember was Ruthie 'Wide-Boy' Razzle when he was sixteen, and even then she'd drunk a paddling pool of Malibu and cherryade and afterwards was sick on his kangaroo skin trainers.

He was now looking into the same water as the blonde woman, only from the other side of the tube. It then struck him that at first he'd paid her no attention because she might be Troll Girl's mother. Troll Girl had remained stuck behind her tube. He found himself wondering how she'd managed to stay still for so long. Bethany and Tom would have started and dropped a hundred activities by now. The maybe-mother in the black skirt was coming around the tube towards him, looking up but with her hands knitted behind her back. He chickened out and walked away from her around the tube. Troll Girl suddenly jumped from behind her tube and landed in a claws-up, Godzilla-like pose. Then, the worst thing that could happen happened.

A tall man in a dark suit strode into the room.

A tall, spruce man in a tailored black suit and a white shirt, with a lean, angular face that deserved to be in a Giacometti drawing, and two-day stubble that made him look suave rather than swarthy (if Mellis ever neglected to shave he grew a hangdog Richard Nixon mask).

The sorry reality of the situation would be revealed. Yes, he was right that the woman on the other side of the tube was Troll Girl's mother and here was rich, successful good-looking Daddy come to collect them. Most likely now was that Rich Successful Daddy Man would strike up a conversation. Mellis would have to go to dinner with all three of them, something that no doubt would involve his ego being repeatedly hit for six into the long grass. Rich Successful Daddy Man would turn out to be a more eminent art historian, with a senior lectureship at a great institution, the writer of books the general public bought in their droves and the presenter of his own documentary TV series (something that Mellis had always wanted, even though Roland was probably right when he said that if Mellis ever appeared on the box he'd be the Keith Floyd of the Fine Arts). All the thoughts of connection Mellis had suffered because of the mother now made him feel stupid. No, worse than stupid: drab, divorced and not even allowed to drink it all away.

Troll Girl ran up to the man and grabbed his thumb.

'C'mon Thisbe,' he said. 'Mummy's waiting and you know what happens when Mummy is kept waiting.'

'The omelette,' said the girl.

'That's right. The omelette. And without the red onions.'

He led her out of the room. The woman on the other side of the tube had now rounded the tube and was eyeball-to-eyeball with Mellis.

'Beautiful, aren't they?' she said.

The initial conversation he would hardly remember afterwards. They sauntered around the tubes discussing the waters as like memory and the vanishing point being elsewhere. Her glittery eyes transfixed him, as did the gauzelike peach-coloured scarf wrapped loosely around her neck. At the window they stared out at a line of night rising above the horizon's seam. She talked of being surprised by the exhibition and wondered if Poppe's work counted as sculpture. Meanwhile Mellis tried not to interject with some comment about how he could never have a conversation like this with his ex-wife. After something he said staggered her with laughter she held out a hand for the shake.

'I'm Caitlin,' she said.

He noticed no ring on the significant finger.

In the gallery's café he bought her a cappuccino and they sat at a table next to a glass case of fossils encapsulated in plastic. As she used a stirrer to draw an ammonite shape in the froth he was hoping against hope that she didn't do something boring, something incompatible with his occupation, that she wasn't someone who would find his inclinations impenetrable or weird, that she wasn't in HR or PR or marketing.

'They're beautiful, too,' she said, tip-tapping her scarlet nails on the glass of the display case. 'Seems like it's a day for old things.'

'Well, old is kind of operative for fossils. I hope it's not a day for confrontations with the past, the return of the repressed, grave goods et cetera.' Realizing that he was using his tutorial voice he sharpishly took a swig of coffee and almost scorched his tongue.

'So you're an archaeologist?' she said.

'Yeah, always digging. It's not lucrative. You'll be fossilized yourself before you get another coffee out of me.'

She laughed. 'Poor but happy. I've got a friend who says that. "I'd rather be like you. Poor but happy." Do you have friends like that?'

'My friends are either poor but unhappy, or rich but stupid. So, what makes you poor but unhappy?'

'Apart from men?'

'Seriously or unseriously?'

'I didn't say I was unhappy.'

She told him that she illustrated children's books. She had worked on seven so far, picture books for the under-fives. She'd started out wanting to be a painter but everyone has to earn a living. It's hard to make a living from a hobby. This was good, though, a relief. He could shade into her if she saw even a little of what he saw.

Soon they were sitting face to face in a cramped and crowded Chinese

153

restaurant, the Kowloon Star, eating off a polished Formica table the lanterns above gave a flaming orange shine. Over wonton soup she told him about how she worked, about responding to simple texts with bright warm images. He didn't mention that his son liked pictures like that; he didn't want to alert her to his children, not yet anyway. He did, after she asked him about his last archaeological dig, come clean that he was Head of Visual Culture at an art school soon to be a university and that he'd written two books on the world of Italian Futurist painting that were admired by at least three colleagues. She laughed with him, another relief, as he hadn't wanted to keep up the Indiana Jones deception for too long. He hadn't really deceived her in any case. She'd deceived herself, for him. She wanted, too, he suspected, for him not to be in HR or PR or marketing. Everyone needs a rapport, a meeting of minds. He was no longer searching for words or worried about what he might say if a black hole opened. No bottle of beer warmed in his palm; the iced water was enough and her eyes and the way she held her chopsticks between finger and thumb like she was using a pastel crayon. He liked her extended, expressive finishing school vowels and clipped Ts and Cs. She talked about how the best part of her day was usually just after dawn, when the quality of light in her makeshift studio in her north London flat was perfect for drawing and colouring. She talked about how she'd needed this break. It might be her last for a while. She mentioned no boyfriend or husband. She mentioned no kids. Women with kids talk about little else but their kids. Like him, Caitlin seemed to be on her own and focused on her art.

Outside, afterwards, they walked along the seafront, looking for somewhere to buy ice cream. Caitlin paused, suddenly, and gripped the railing and staring up at the night sky.

'Knickers to ice cream, Ben. Why don't we go for a drink?'

Later, in his hotel room, composed and not bloated, he found himself pacing the floor like a jailbird in solitary. He was glad that he'd not given in to a drink and said goodnight on the seafront. But part of him wished that he had followed her into one of the side-street pubs. Sure, they had swapped mobile numbers. She'd agreed to meet him the next afternoon, but she had been, then, at that moment at the railing, suggestible to the tank-up and lunge. He could tell. He knew it now. It wasn't just that he feared the black hole and finding himself teary and running on about his wife and his kids that the howling hellbat wouldn't let him see. He didn't want to start off by admitting past problems. He didn't need a counsellor or another mother. He needed a collaborator, a soul mate. One day soon he would tell her this. He would get another chance, he was sure.

In bed, he tried not to plot out an evening where they had become tactile and indiscreet and he'd called for a fourth bottle and was sucked into a black hole or whined about that prick in France. Instead he designed a drink-free version where, after a mature and civilized evening they had ended up here, loosely wrapped in the covers, side by side, still talking as they studied the pattern of the shadows on the ceiling.

Later still, in the Prince of Lübeck yesterday afternoon, during his sixth pint and second scotch, midway between the bar and the cigarette machine, anger was building behind his certainty that all would have been sane and correct if he had tanked-up and lunged. At least then she would have known and stayed or known enough to stay away.

The next day in Cornwall, when he did meet her on the beach and walked along the ragged line of the shingle, as he skimmed flat stones and collected razor shells, she became another morose and less carefree Caitlin. She admitted that her work had dried up. She was running out of money. The authors she worked for were not getting new commissions or advances. There were newer, younger illustrators and she'd become expensive to hire. She didn't know what she was going to do. She sat down on a bench on a pier and tried her best not to cry.

'I'll have a drink … I mean, a think,' he said, fighting the desire to put his arm around her shoulder. 'I might be able to help you out there. You might have to, you know, get on your bike.'

In the Lübeck yesterday evening he found his thoughts spiralling around and around the months that followed the walk on the beach. During the weeks that passed before he saw her again a jittery, almost sickish feeling came over him. It was part shivers, part soaring rush, something that he had not experienced since he was a teenager, when he'd a met a girl and had to walk to a phone box to arrange a date, and during the walk all sorts of situations and longed-for sensations would play rough in his mind. This feeling would peak if Caitlin called him, or sent him a text or a witty, self-deprecating e-mail.

That Saturday in London where they went to see the Rodchenko photographs and wandered along the Embankment beneath the hanging lights, his hand drawn to holding her hand, he told her that there was a vacant position at the university where he taught, a lectureship in illustration. He could put in a word. At Liverpool Street Station, a little deflated that she hadn't asked him back to hers, they struck a deal. She would apply, if he gave up smoking.

'What I'll do,' he said, 'is suss out the HR commissar. Mention your name. Get you in the running.'

She hugged him. He watched her walk away towards the escalator. Soon afterwards he met up with Tony Easterman of Human Resources and sat in his white office and told him all about this wonderful illustrator, Caitlin

155

Palarme, who had bags of experience and ideas and who would fit in so well and had lots to offer. Her application was accepted. She passed the interview. She got the job and moved up. Six frustrating weeks later she sat Mellis down in his own front room and told him, sheepishly, her eyes wide and scaredy-cat, that she'd been seeing Tony Easterman outside of work. On the sofa, speechless, merely nodding, Mellis' jittery feeling compressed to a single point in his gut. Before she left she told him that it would be a real shame if he used this as an excuse to go back on the bottle.

At this point, having never mentioned his drinking to Caitlin, or drunk in her company, or drunk on his own or with others for eighteen months he realized that Easterman had been telling tales. *Beware Mellis, he's a pisshead and a psycho. His wife ran away. She took his kids. Inside, he's scrap. There's nothing going on in that head of his that's of use to another human being, let alone an ambitious young hottie like you. Cocktail girlie?*

In the Lübeck, yesterday night, Mellis was so full of drink that he could only see through a shuddering slit in a cloud of black fuzz. Cordial relationships with his legs had broken down. UN negotiators were needed to get his brain and mouth working in concert again. He couldn't remember if Max the Bar refused to serve him in the end, or if eventually he couldn't remember his PIN so couldn't get any more cashback. All he knew was that at some juncture he'd decided that all the things that he'd never said to Caitlin needed to be said, tonight. Then: ranting on the floor at Roland's, the parquet slick with red. Mussolini holding her hand. Eggs pulsating in the striplights. Discharging himself and the yomp across the carpark and the building site. Now, outside the empty pub, he realized that he should have picked up something short and blunt at that building site. He was about to enter the last of the countries on the black hole map: Abyssinia.

In the market square a thin layer of snow lay on the cobbles and the roofs of the stalls. Snow swished around he glow of the streetlights and collected in the joints and the angles of the trees. Mellis lit his second-to-last cigarette even though it would make his mouth even drier. He carried on, checking the bins as he went for anything weighty that he could use when he found their house. He was trying to weigh up other things, too.

Caitlin: bright, funny, creative, free-spirited, brave and as beautiful as Amanda Tipper.

Easterman: smug, smarmy, boring, boorish, insectoid fascist super soldier, Mussolini waxwork and impersonator.

Himself: intelligent, honest, loyal, a *bon viveur*, visionary dreamer and romantic only locked in combat with ghosts and demons because of her.

How could she have chosen Smug-Smarm over Visionary Dream? He didn't know. He'd not asked her. If he had asked her it would have been last night at Roland's. Maybe, in retrospect, the opportune moment wasn't after the floor had dragged him down and while Mussolini was holding her hand. He should have asked her when she first admitted her arrangement with Easterman but he'd lost it and told her to leave. Roland had said later that her choice didn't signify anything. It was no cosmic judgement. There are no answers in the bottom of the glass, either. Stop torturing yourself. If she regrets it, she regrets it. One man's love story is another woman's aberration.

Mellis knew, though, that he must concentrate on the aberrations. What are we without aberrations? What do we learn about ourselves without aberrations? Whose aberration was the more profound? All that had passed was an aberration. Inchesa should have realized that Mussolini was an aberration. Mellis knew in his soul that *Il Duce* was aberrant.

Entering the oldest part of town, in its narrow lanes, the cold closed in on him. His pace slowed until he stopped outside the Cantina Reggio, where he'd taken her to dinner on the day that she arrived in town. His thoughts drifted into a slipstream. He saw Caitlin and himself emerging laughing and sober from the Reggio and instead of retiring to her B&B she came back to his flat. There was another version here, too: that he had still crashed his wagon last night and was heading back to her now, to be contrite and sheepish, looked-after and forgiven. Then again, if she'd come back with him that night and stayed he doubted very much that a black hole would have swallowed him yesterday. He would not now be trekking across the Abyssinian wastes.

He glimpsed a life where the sunrays through the slats would ease them gently awake. He would get ready for work, assembling his books and his notes and leave her at her desk in the back bedroom he'd converted into a studio. Her paints and her brushes and sketchbooks and laptop. He would feel her close by even when he was talking to people like Eleanor Spratley or in meetings with administrators and managers. He would always be longing to return home. They would talk about their day. She would show him her pictures. He would talk about his research, that he was now making progress with the definitive critical study of Italian Futurist painting that he wanted to write before he died. A hot meal, candles and Satie on the stereo while they ate. A DVD and then bed. Over and over. Forever.

In the window he noticed in his reflection that a crest of snow like the peak of a military cap had formed above his forehead. He was a soldier, yes, a partisan, the resistance. He was invincible, a colossus.

The blood then thrummed at his temples. Nausea clawed his stomach. A terrible fatigue pressed down on him. A wave that had been building for hours behind him was catching up, bearing down. He realized that the life that he'd imagined for himself, a life of warm mornings and intimate evenings was Easterman's present, his everyday, his joy, his success. More than this, worse, was the thought that once, during the Chaffinch-Goldsmiths phase a life of warmth and intimacy was how he had seen his future with

Sally-Anne. The wave ripped through him. Mellis was holding on though, grabbing at anything that would secure him. He might be sick from drinking the seawater, he might fall to his knees in a doorway, but he would not be battered off-course. Not him. Never. The wave passed. He had not let himself be carried along by it. He was left standing in front of a deserted restaurant, in subzero temperatures, piss stains on his jeans, a plaster above his eye and his coat splattered with snow. Elsewhere, the medieval bell of the cathedral clock struck six times, each clang reverberating across the roofs and the shop fronts and sending tremors through the bones of Benjamin Mellis.

His grey reflection in the window prevented him from moving. That figure in the glass, he knew, with its featureless face and wonky spectacles was embroiled in the oldest and most mysterious story of all. A boy strikes out, following some girl or light or icon or whispered promise, and whatever he does, whatever he finds, whatever he overcomes, whatever the frontiers that he crosses, he never comes back.

Mellis lit the last of his cigarettes and tossed the crushed packet over his shoulder. He was leaning back on a skip full of builder's rubble and heard a soft thud as the packet lodged in a crack or crevice behind him. In there, a rusted rod like a spike from the backbone of a deep-sea fish thrust from a mound of breezeblocks and timber. He'd noticed it on his approach. The walk from the Cantina had been the most difficult part. His legs ached; the soles of his feet burned and the cold had tightened around his ribcage. He'd almost turned back several times. It had been worth it, though. He was here now. A few lights had appeared in the surrounding houses but none so far in the house ahead.

It was still dark.

It was still snowing.

He clutched the lapels of his coat to his neck. The house was a grand, three-story affair with a dauntingly high gable. The front door was set behind a porch built to look like a Romanesque arch. It was typical of the houses in this part of town, a neighbourhood of professors, business consultants and local government types that had always been beyond his price-range. Sally-Anne had wanted them to buy a house here. Considering that he now ceded a generous portion of his salary to Sally-Anne he found it a bit rich that she described his present address as the twat flat. She would never live in a twat flat. She refused to be poor. Caitlin, too, was no longer poor-but-happy living in a twat flat. She was now vicariously rich.

Ahead, in the uppermost window of the grand house, a light came on with a suddenness that tingled the gash above his eye.

Dawn would soon break. Mellis suspected that across The Channel, Thomas and Bethany had been awake for an hour at least and had probably disturbed Sally-Anne and Docteur Bazir before their alarm. The thought

158

made him smile. Roland might be up now too, hung-over and angry about the fracas and the red wine stain on the parquet but still phoning the twat flat before phoning the hospitals. Mellis wondered if at the hospital the insectoid fascist super soldiers had hatched and if the Karen 4 Dave girls were teaching them how to do the conga along the white corridors. By now the real Doctor Baz would be strumming his mandolin, winding down after his million-year shift. Easterman would be out of bed. He might be in the shower, or polishing his shoes, or squeezing oranges or grinding coffee. Caitlin might be shuffling barefoot all the way down the stairs from the top of the house, maybe disgruntled about the draughts in the old house, the time it took to warm up in the mornings. In the kitchen she would hug him from behind as he placed bagels in the bagel toaster. The percolator would gurgle. Steam would mottle the windowpanes. She would pour granola into a bowl and douse it with milk. Maybe they would then sit together on a pine bench that matched a pine table, she in her dressing gown and he already in his action slacks and shirt with epaulettes. There might be a post-mortem, about last night, about what should be said or done. There might be guilt or bewilderment. They might even feel a greater connection to each other now. There could be such a thing between them. If it were more than that, no one else would ever know.

Mellis wanted another cigarette. There were to be no more cigarettes. He glanced over his shoulder at the rubble. His hands were more or less frozen into fists as he limped his way up the drive towards the house.

The porch had a dank, almost church-like smell. Mellis found himself sniggering to himself, picturing his daughter standing on a stool, yodelling at the top of her voice to get some reaction out of Sally-Anne. His son might well be spilling his breakfast, probably a fry-up of shrews and thrushes all over Docteur Bazir's dogtooth-checked flares. It was unlikely, though, despite being French, that Docteur Bazir wore flares. It was not 1982. Even the French had caught up a bit and would now be wearing the sort of clothes Anglo-Americans wore in 2003. In 1982, long after flares became fashion death in England, Jagger the Red, Mellis' old geography teacher still owned a collection of flarewear so heart-stoppingly uncool that they now ought to be exhibited in the V&A. During a class on the Bemba people of southern Zambia and their slash and burn agricultural methods Mellis was caught holding up a shatterproof ruler to measure the width of a fetching ash-blue pair of bellbottoms that twitched back and forth below the length of the blackboard like two windsocks in an epileptic fit competition. Jagger went mental and harangued him in front of the whole class. 'They'll be in fashion again soon, Mellis, and you'll be wearing them, you'll see, there's nothing different or original about you, Mellis, you need to get your mind set on something more constructive.'

'Like the future history of the flared trouser, Sir?'

After school in detention Mellis was forced to write an essay about responsibility, respect and fitting-in that Jagger, wearing perhaps the smuggest smile any man has ever worn, tore to shreds without even reading. Mellis knew that Jagger was going to do this, that's why he'd not answered the question and written instead a promise to himself that he would never be anyone as joyless and toadish as Jagger. He would always be original and he would always be different. He was fourteen-years old then. During the late-eighties Flarewear Revival Mellis had to concede, as he did now, that Jagger did have all the answers and knew everything that there was to know about the absurdity of post-teenage life and the return of the repressed.

Mellis gave himself half a minute to properly calm down, hoping that on top of everything else he wouldn't seem like a gibbering flarewear-obsessive. This in itself made him laugh. He had to abort an attempt to knock. When he did knock, he closed his eyes while he waited for the latch to click.

When he opened his eyes a pale-faced blonde in a white towelling dressing gown squinted at him. She gave him the once over. She tried to slam the door. He'd put his foot in the gap though, and when she didn't try to slam it harder or retreat into the house, he said, 'I am terribly sorry, I know it's early ...'

'Go away.'

'Is your mum in?'

'The drive's already tarmaced.'

'You must be Anouk?' said Mellis. The girl was about eighteen. He tried to peer around her into the hallway. 'Or is it Aztec? Patchacuti? It's something Pre-Columbian, isn't it?'

'Inca,' she said, 'it's Inca ... look, oh pissing hell ... Mum!'

Hurried footsteps thudded down the stairs. Eleanor Spratley in an eye-wateringly lime green kimono, her hair a mass of night-tangles, poked her head over Inca's shoulder.

'Golly gosh, Ben, what on earth are you doing?'

'You said dinner.'

'But it's seven o'clock.'

'The hour for aperitifs, I believe.'

'It's seven *a.m.*, you div,' said Inca.

'Get inside, you'll freeze to death.'

Eleanor grabbed hold of his arm and pulled him into the hallway. On his knees, on a laminate floor, he was then fighting off as gently as possible two women trying to stop him spiralling down to wherever he was headed. Next he felt that his back was pressed to a wall. The wall was turning at speed like one of the cages of the fairground contraptions that as a child he'd never been allowed to go on. They fall to pieces. You'll spin off and die in the wreckage. Grey smears. Red flashes.

Somehow he was resting on his elbows, staring at the cracks in a tabletop.

When he looked up, the shelving and the earthenware containers and the blue and white china plates and the aga and the stainless steel fridge all assembled themselves as if a celebrity had clicked her fingers in an advert for fitted kitchens. Inca was now wearing jeans and a loose, thick woollen jumper with snowflake patterns. She edged along the work surface, rustling paper packets and clinking mugs.

'I suppose you'll want brown sugar and warmed milk,' she said.

'I'm not diabetic,' said Mellis.

'In your coffee?'

'What are you going to do when you've left school, Inca?'

'Make coffee, obviously,' she said. 'I left last year. Mum's putting her face on.' She placed a mug of coffee on the table in front of him. Leaning back on the fridge, she held her mug with both hands. As she blew across the surface of her coffee he could see in her face that she disliked him. She may well have heard all these gushing things about Doctor Ben, how he was so inspiring and supportive and patient and kind and spoke Italian and shit like that. He could tell that she suspected that her mother was again straying into something unwise and pathetic. And here he was, that lovely man oozing whisky-sweats and smartarse gibberish. He closed his eyes so that he would not see that look in her face.

Inca, you lost civilization, you don't know the half of it.

He felt another presence in the room. Something, probably a mug scraped on a work surface.

'Is he still asleep?' Eleanor whispered.

'I think he's dead,' said Inca.

'Shush, honey, he might have been run-over.'

'Yeah, by a distillery lorry.'

'Cheers,' said Mellis, opening his eyes. 'I'll leave you ladies in peace.'

'Don't be silly, Ben,' said Eleanor, 'you stay here, and you, Miss Judge and Judy, go and get ready for work.'

Inca sulked out of the kitchen. Eleanor sat down opposite him.

'Ben, are you OK? Is there someone I can call?'

'I came to tell you something,' he said. 'I was thinking about what you said yesterday. I've been thinking about it all night.'

'I didn't say anything *that* controversial, did I?'

'Listen. Ghost or demon?' It took him a while to get going, to speak lucidly and not scramble everything together. He told her that she probably knew he had a problem and that he'd been stupid and had made things worse. He told her about the job and Caitlin and waking up in A&E and how he came to be intruding at seven in the morning and for this he was profoundly sorry.

'Listen to me, Ben, listen.' She reached across the table and grabbed both his hands. 'Bad things happen, marriages fail, work goes down the plughole, we do sillybilly things …'

161

He was no longer listening to her. He knew now that a ghost comes back for you. A ghost, if you're lucky enough to have one, returns to you the glimpse of a frontier you saw ahead long ago, a Great Wall in the distance, misted, forbidden. A ghost is a summer's afternoon, the smell of chestnut trees, side-by-side and speaking of all the things that you are going to do and all the things that you want to learn and understand and impart. A ghost will return you here, whatever your catastrophe. The promontory is where it will always stand, just beyond the edge of the map. The climb will be arduous. There will be double-backs and landslides and lost days sitting out the winters but ahead there always stands the city beyond the city.

The sun had risen above the houses. Through the window, the snow in the kitchen garden glittered. Mellis did not interrupt Eleanor to explain that he was going into reverse. Or that he was haunted. He didn't tell her about any resolution or amends he knew he must make, or any other matters that now demanded his attention. He didn't talk about writing his last book or the little dreams he must dream, or a memory he had of his nerves the first time he entered a seminar room with no other ambition than that the kids would leave in an hour thinking about things they had never considered before.

Instead he said: 'Eleanor, tell me about the horses.'

I Remember Nothing

When Mr Paul Fischer of number 76 Yewlands died, an article in *The Sentinel*, the local paper I used to deliver after school presented strong circumstantial evidence that he had, in fact, been Martin Bormann. Until forensic scientists proved that rather than manage our sub-post office for forty years Bormann had been buried under the Lehrter Bahnhof in West Berlin, I lived with the guilt that I had delivered a low-quality free newspaper to Hitler's feared private secretary.

The Fischer/Bormann Scandal was not unusual in the little Surrey town that I now call Banberg. Back then *The Sentinel's* resident Simon Wiesenthal also exposed a Mr Harry Glass of 28 Buff Avenue as Hartwig Glassman, a guard at the *Flughelenlager* Concentration Camp. Nothing was ever proved, though extradition proceedings reached an advanced stage in the case of Mr Teddy Hummel, accused by the same troublemaker at *The Sentinel* of being a willing participant in the 1942 Józefów Massacre.

I never saw or met any of these men on my round. All I remember of 76 Yewlands is that the crazy paving looked like the patterns on the skin of an adder. In Buff Avenue, the swathes of pampas grass would hiss in the breeze. Glass' house, I think, was the one with the rotting pink porch and the dog inside which always howled. I have no idea where Hummel lived, behind which mock-Tudor facade or pebble-dashed bungalow he hid his secrets, if he had secrets, if he was who they said he was.

It was always quiet back then, especially after school, when the shops began to close for the evening and the pubs hadn't yet opened. When I was fifteen, one afternoon a week I trudged the streets carrying a fluorescent orange sack stamped with *The Sentinel's* logo. I would start at the edge of the Common and look back for luck at the turrets of the disused mental hospital that peeped over the tops of the fir trees. Marching up and down the gravel drives of the Victorian villas that bordered the Common it was easy to imagine that you were in a science fiction novel. The human race had mysteriously vanished, except for one resourceful and charismatic boy. In the overgrown garden of a thirties semi on Upton Lane I remember the feeling of trepidation when the gate cracked shut behind me and I faced a house with windows so thick with dirt that a walled-up cube of darkness seemed to glimmer through puncture marks in its casing. If I saw a Range Rover parked in a driveway, its roof encrusted with bird droppings, possibly in the shade of a leylandii hedge, maybe somewhere like Stoneleigh Drive, I would picture its owner staring out to sea from a cliff-top café. Nothing would remain to suggest that he'd been there beyond a pocketful of change abandoned in a saucer. I had already realized that in Banberg everyone has something to hide.

Years later, long after I'd left, a Banberg resident was arrested for shoplifting in the nearby town some call Slutsk. He turned out to be a Serb wanted for war crimes in Croatia. Allegedly, he'd captained a militia that tortured civilians during a raid on a village in the self-proclaimed breakaway Serb Republic of Krajina. Neighbours reported him to be 'remarkably quiet and polite.' A Croatian government statement said, 'We are grateful for his capture, although it is true that we did not have [Banberg] on our radar as a possible hideout.'

This last statement struck me as profoundly naive. Banberg was the first place I would have looked. They don't call it Little Paraguay for nothing.

Sometimes I like to joke that when I was growing-up in the self-proclaimed breakaway Republic of Banberg (a puppet state that in the mid-eighties flourished briefly in territory between the southern rim of Greater London and Old Surrey) we English were second-class citizens. We had to sit behind the Germans at school and because of them were deprived of certain recreational facilities and study options. My lack of sporting prowess and my near-ignorance of the sciences can be attributed to these disciplines being considered 'German preserves'.

At the time, though, my problem was not the *diktat* of an imposed Teutonic hierarchy. My problem, at the start of my fourth year, was Peter Morrison, the new Scottish kid who in two terms had already carved out a reputation as something of an enforcer. My crime: posh voice and being a spaz on a level even lower than the obvious greasers and bookworms. I know now that due to the Highland Clearances and something to do with the imperialism of the Queen's English, bullying me was a heroic act of post-colonial resistance. I would later come to feel sorry for him; at least I'm wise enough to know that I have to say this now. I must tick this box or appear unsympathetic, still at heart a Banberger. The day I first met Mr E was the day Morrison ambushed me after school on Senlac Road.

I blame the Walkman. It was a grey plastic thing the size of a half a brick, a free gift when I'd opened my first bank account that I could squeeze into my blazer's side-pocket. The orange foam headphones no doubt helped Morrison sight me from a distance. I was walking beside a high wall. The overhanging branches of apple trees swayed in time to a track from *Ignite the Seven Cannons*. I didn't have a hope of hearing him come up behind me.

When my chest hit the grass verge a harsh click snapped in my ear. My first panicked thought was not that I might have dashed a hole in my trousers again but that the Walkman had broken. I'd also dropped my school bag. It was standing bolt upright in the gutter. As I reached out for it something pressed down on my ankle.

'Alright there, Bridesheid Revisited. Gizzus a listen.'

From my low-down angle his cheekbones seemed even sharper than usual. His face tightened further as he forced his basketball boot down on my ankle.

'Is that electric jazz-funk you're listening to, Bridesheid?'

Mums with pushchairs and girls from the grammar school ambled past us. Dog-walking pensioners strolled on the other side of Senlac Road, probably veterans of Anzio and Tobruk (maybe not these battles actually; this was Little Paraguay after all). None of them seemed to notice a lanky monster about to break my leg in two.

'C'mon, Brides, gizzus the funk.'

I didn't have the funk. The funk – all that Shakatak and Shalamar stuff – was music for boys who already had girlfriends. He knew that I didn't have the funk. I knew that this wasn't about the funk. Earlier, in the first history class of the new term, Mr Priskin, after the Kenneth Williams impressions had died down – the Jazz Funkateers had recognized that his *right* ear was newly pierced – taught us all about the political upheavals that beset the early years of the Weimar Republic. With what seemed like great sadness he'd explained the failure of the left-wing Spartakist Rising and with great relish the defeat by general strike of the nationalist Kapp Putsch. He described with weary contempt the Freikorps as irregular paramilitaries no better than hired thugs and racist skinheads. He seemed to scowl at Morrison; and I for some reason, for no reason, sniggered. Afterwards in double Geography, Morrison stared me out while everyone else was trying to distract Mr Jagger with questions about solar flares and the political flare-up caused by the sinking of Greenpeace's Rainbow Warrior in Auckland Harbour.

'Don't be scared, Brides,' said Morrison. 'No worries if it's only Electro.'

'It's Electro,' I spluttered.

'Good stuff, Brides. You're a good man, really you are. Here.'

The pressure lifted from my ankle. He held out his hand, which seemed to be offering to pull me up, but instead it flashed into my pocket to grab the Walkman. When I struggled to my feet he was exploring its panels and buttons with his fingers like he'd never seen one before. He flipped the catch and grimaced, as if inside I'd hidden a picture of Mr Priskin. I had a reputation as Priskin's pet that no one, not even the other grease-worms like Mellis and Woods much admired.

'Hey, this is not electric jazz-funk, Brides,' he said. 'Absolutely hunacceptable.'

He threw the Walkman high in the air. The headphones and their lead trailed after it like a kite's tail until the whole contraption dipped. From somewhere behind the apple trees came a thud and a tinkling of plastic. Morrison then picked my school bag from the gutter and sent it over the wall in a similar arcing trajectory.

'Run along and do your homework, Bridesheid. I'll collect it in the morn.'

I watched, sweating murder as he loped off down Senlac Road.

Heaving myself onto the top of the wall took three quite painful and humiliating attempts but there was no way I could go home with a grazed cheek and no school bag or really expensive free Walkman. With one leg hanging down on either side I paused to make sure that I wasn't about to drop into a pit of slavering attack-dogs

(Little Paraguay, remember). Away from the trees a lawn sloped gently down towards a house. A patio and wicker chairs were set out in front of french doors. Beyond the trees, where the slope began, there stood an old man in a white shirt. My school bag lay at his feet. The pages of my French textbook and other papers rippled on the grass. He was holding a piece of paper in his hand, a map Mr Priskin had given out earlier. The old man looked over to where I was perched on his wall. He must have realized that he was being watched. This is how I came to meet Mr E.

I was afraid, even though I knew that he might well be more scared of me than I was of him. He didn't move. He didn't speak. He maintained a rigid, composed stance, the paper now rolled in his fist.

'Can I come down and get my stuff?' I called out.

He merely nodded. My ankle throbbed as my shoes hit the dirt. I approached him with what I remember now as a crab-like, hunched walk, my only thought being to regather my things and get out as quickly as possible. I kept my eyes fixed to the ground and scanned for the Walkman. The back panel had detached. The cassette lay close to an herbaceous border. I picked up the parts onehandedly and rammed them under my armpit. Half-crouched, I started to scrabble around for the papers and books in a hopping toad-like way.

'I don't think you intended to throw your own possessions over my wall, young man,' he said. There was an accent, though not a strong or harsh one.

'I'm sorry,' I said. 'Really sorry. Sorry to bother you.'

'You know who did this?'

'I'm sorry, really sorry, I've said sorry.'

'Hey, calm yourself. You shouldn't let others push you around.'

I stuffed the last of the papers into my bag and took my first clear look at him. He was much taller than me, taller even than Morrison. A halo of pale sunlight flamed around his hair. He had a lot of hair for a man of his age, much more than any of my elderly relatives, and his suntan made his skin seem as thick as the brown paper we used to wrap our textbooks.

'Quite an ordeal, eh?' he said.

He was still holding the map, Mr Priskin's map, *Europe in 1919*, a duplicate machine job with the old pre-war borders in red and the post-Treaty of Versailles frontiers in indigo-blue. That map had already showed me wonderful countries that would never exist again, like Latvia and Estonia, and obscure and exotic nations like Czechoslovakia, Hungary and Yugoslavia (all shaded with left-slanting blue stripes). I'd already memorised the territorial trades and annexations: South Tyrol to Italy; Eupen-Malmedy to Belgium; Memelland to Lithuania. To me, sitting in that class earlier, at the front and itching to ask a question, the map described a charged, alluring continent. I wanted to be on the ground there, to witness and record. I wanted to belong in that Europe. I wanted to own it.

For a moment it didn't look like the man with the white hair was going to give me back the map, so I wasn't even going to own that. He held it up to me with his thumb over the top left-hand corner, somewhere East or West Prussia-ish.

'There,' he said. 'That's where I started.'

For as far back as I can remember, long before I met my great history project, Mr E, I'd known that I lived in the most boring and uneventful of times. I should have lived in the past or far in the future. I'd been drawn to long-ago, distant periods until Mr Priskin's map showed me that the Twentieth Century could be just as tumultuous as Ancient Greece and Imperial Rome, the Dark Ages, the Middle Ages of crusades and battles and kings and their intrigues. In my bedroom I used to turn the pages of the historical atlas for hours, fascinated by how countries had expanded or disappeared, or changed their names, kingdom to empire, province to republic. Nations had colours: France, blue, Russia, red, Italy, orange. Populations were colours. Islands and colonies were colours. Years were events, as if there had been no quiet, no everyday, as if all of a year like 1415 or 1789 was one drawn-out, high-stakes scene. Priskin's map was a world of contest and flux, of troop movements and subterfuge, of secessionist parties and nationalist cults, a chessboard for fantasists and visionaries. Things could happen that couldn't happen here. Anything could happen.

So when Mr E pointed on a map to somewhere East or West Prussia-ish it was to an immediately more exciting place than the little Surrey town that I now call Banberg. It doesn't surprise me at all that within ten minutes I was standing in his spare, white-walled kitchen while he made tea in a brown pot and told me that I might call him Eric. This struck me as odd. It meant that

I might call him something else. I could call him anything.

Eric was a mathematics professor long retired from what he called, 'active service'. He told me that he'd been born in a town called Allenstein but had lived in England for years. England is a funny old place, he said. He had just gotten used to the 'system of twelve' when it was abolished and replaced with something more rational. It was a long time before I realized that he was talking about pre-decimal currency. He'd shown me Allenstein on the map. It was in East Prussia, close to the border with Poland. He told me that an astronomer called Copernicus once lived there. He seemed very proud of this and went on about it for ages until when we were outside he turned his attention to the politics of the map.

'There are important things,' he said, 'that this map is not explaining to you. This map is not showing you that all these places were full of Germans. That was the cause of all the trouble that came afterwards.'

My idea of what came afterwards was admittedly hazy and informed primarily by *The Guns of Navarone* and *Von Ryan's Express*. From my relatives, who often talked as if the Second World War was still going on I'd learned that everyone in the cinema used to laugh at Hitler's ranting. He'd dropped doodlebugs on Banberg and Slutsk and in the end Churchill beat his mad arse into the ground.

'These maps were arbitrary,' said Mr E. 'I mean they are fictions. Germany lost the war, the first war, and afterwards they wanted to keep it weak. Never again, eh? But, you look here . . .' He swept over Poland with a pencil. 'All these places were still full of Germans. You go to the Baltic, to Riga, Germans. You go here . . .' He outlined a claw-shape crushing the tadpole head of Czechoslovakia. '. . . Sudeten Germans. You go here . . .' Romania. '. . . Banat Germans. Only in books do things start with exact dates. But this is not mathematics, yes? You can't start here.'

'Short term, medium term, long term,' I said, parroting Mr Priskin.

'That's right. So what you must realize, going back, far back before the war, before even Germany itself is that Germans always wanted to go East, see. From medieval times. Sometimes, yes, by war, the Teutonic Knights reached as far as Novgorod . . .' He made a pencil-swoosh towards the far north. '. . . but sometimes peacefully. If you wanted good, solid citizens you asked for Germans. The Empress Catherine asked for Germans and that's why you had Germans in the south of Russia. The Empress Maria Theresa had an empty province after the Turks decline, and she filled it with Germans and this became the Banat.'

The names of places and people I'd never heard of caused my head to swim with questions and a desire for facts and backgrounds. Part of me was desperate to get home to use the historical atlas and its encyclopaedia. I was no longer seeing the countries as colours. Blobs of other colours had infiltrated the blocks. Bits of Germany – dark green in the atlas – now floated in the light brown of Poland like the wax in a lava lamp. I was also aware that I was already late home and was going to be in a lot of trouble.

'There's no peace here, that's what I am saying to you,' said Mr E. 'All these Germans, especially the Germans in Poland, they had it hard, they were persecuted, attacked by Poles. I remember it.'

It was when he said this – *I remember it* – that I realized that I had here a witness to history itself. He could tell me everything. I could write better essays. I could get higher grades. I could get higher grades than A++ if I knew what it was like at the time. I could have stayed there all night, listening, asking, but I had to go. I reached out for the map to put it in my bag but found myself staring into his smile. He smiled like we had just concluded a secret arrangement. I'm not sure if it was this that delayed me, or it was because another question occurred to me.

'Didn't you have, like, the Freikorps to protect the borders?' I said. 'That's what Mr Priskin said.' When Mr E didn't answer, I continued. 'He said they were hired thugs and racist skinheads.'

'Priskin is a Hungarian name,' said Mr E. 'They had their own problems with Bolsheviks there. When you have Bolsheviks, you get a backlash. It's easy afterwards to judge. When you didn't see it. If you want to understand Hitler, you have to look at what the Reds did in Munich. Ours was an age of forces. Fight force with force you don't know where it will end. Fight force with guile leads to a happier outcome. Think about that in your predicament.'

I turned back to note the door number when I was halfway up the front path in what was another dim, overshadowed garden. As I emerged into Hadley Road I realized that I'd been delivering *The Sentinel* to Mr E for months. I recognized the holly hedge that surrounded his garden. The first of the autumn spiders were hanging their webs between the spikes on the leaves.

'If you want to understand Hitler, you have to look at what the Reds did in Munich.' I declared this in single history two days later. I declared it even though I knew it would provoke the shrill 'eeyew' the Jazz Funkateers made whenever I spoke. I declared it even though I could sense Morrison's stare heating the back of my head. I declared it even though Mr Priskin had just spent ten minutes telling us that to understand Hitler you have to realize that he was what is called a mountebank, and he was a blackmailer, a gangster, the puppet of big business interests and an irrational crazy person 'a bit like the present Prime Minister'. Mr Priskin offset comments like this last one by using an exaggerated, sniggery voice. He must have known that he wasn't supposed to say this. Loose talk could get you in a lot of trouble in the breakaway republic.

He stopped chalking a list of events in the early history of the Nazi Party on the board. One of the youngest of our teachers, Mr Priskin stood out by always wearing a grey shirt, drainpipe trousers and thin red leather tie. When he wasn't on strike he would arrive at school in a battered 2CV with CND and 'Nuclear Power? No Thanks' stickers on the side. These were statements, I suspect, aimed at the rest of the staff, or the *Großer Generalstab* as they were known at our school. Mr Priskin often gave a lift to Miss Slingsby, the austere German mistress with the short hair and black pencil skirts who had once been a semi-professional basketball player before her exile to Little Paraguay. In the school magazine both had listed the music of Joy Division and Gang of Four as outside interests. I was already becoming the historian of secret alliances.

'And what exactly do you know of what the Reds did in Munich?' said Mr Priskin, pointing his nub of chalk in my direction. Since my meeting with Mr E, I had been doing some extra reading in the public library.

'I mean, Sir, Hitler was in Munich after the war and after the war there was the Munich Soviet, right ...'

'Eeyew,' said the Jazz Funkateers.

'That's right,' said Mr Priskin, nodding and smiling to encourage me. I didn't need any encouragement. This was the only way I could talk back then.

'It was known as the *Räterepublik* ...'

'Eeyew.'

'Quiet, children! Continue.'

'It was a communist government. They killed a lot of people, like the Thule Society ...'

'Huh huh, tool society.'

'See me after class, Morrison.'

'... and they declared war on Switzerland and lots of people died and Hitler saw all this and that's why he became radical, radical enough to want to defend people from the Reds.'

'Eeyew.'

Mr Priskin wasn't really looking at me but at the back of the class.

'Well, it's true that lots of people who later voted for Hitler did so because they feared Communism, this is true, but if you read *Mein Kampf*, have you read *Mein Kampf*?'

'I'd love to, Sir.'

'Eeyeeeeeew.'

'Quiet! ... Don't. It's turgid and mad. If you want to understand Communism, read Marx's *Manifesto*. It's short and snappy. You can read it while the bath is running.' I tried this once. You can't. 'But, if you read *Mein Kampf*, you'll see that Hitler's decision to enter politics came *before* the Munich Soviet, while he was in hospital in 1918.'

'Couldn't that be just what he said afterwards?'

I was actually right here. It's unlikely that Hitler's decision to enter politics came at the Pasewalk hospital, where recovering from the effects of gas

172

he heard the news of the armistice and according to myth realized that the fate of the nation now rested on his Austrian shoulders. It most probably happened later, after the fall of the *Raterepublik*, when Hitler realized his gift for rousing oratory. The Pasewalk story is a fabrication designed by Hitler to clothe himself in a messianic legend. Mr Priskin didn't know this. It was only O-Level, after all.

'Sir,' said a Jazz Funkateer. 'If Hitler was on the far right, did that mean he had his right ear pierced?'

'Don't be stupid. What you want to get your head round here …' Mr Priskin was now talking directly to me, as if there was no jazz in the class. I must say that I liked this.

'… is that during the Munich Soviet, most of the deaths were caused by the *Freikorps*, the illegal army I mentioned before. When the *Freikorps* overthrew the republic thousands of people were killed. It's difficult to know how the Soviet would have fared without an assault by the forces of the right.'

'But when you have Bolsheviks, you get a backlash. It's easy afterwards to judge. When you didn't see it.'

Mr Priskin frowned. 'That's the thing about history. *You* didn't see it.'

The bell went. We were told to read part of the not-very-detailed textbook for next time. Mr Priskin reminded Morrison to come to the front, which prevented me from sidling up to ask if Priskin really was a Hungarian name. Maybe he was descended from Béla Kun, the leader of the Hungarian Soviet Republic and orchestrator of the Red Terror who I'd looked up in the library as well. As I dithered about whether to brave this out and wait for Mr Priskin to deal with Morrison I was bombarded by quite a long salvo of 'eeyew eeyew eeyew' from the exiting Jazz Funkateers. Even though he was getting a bollocking Morrison still scowled in my direction. I'd already done his French homework for him the day before so I should have been safe. I tried to coattail Mellis and Woods but they were having some intense private discussion, like a Blue Team on *Blockbusters* debating an answer. They were always dismissive towards me, their handwriting neater and their maps and diagrams more precise. Even though they were both posher than I was they somehow got away with it. They were not going to acknowledge me today either, so I walked as quickly as I could to the school library where I knew I could hide out for the lunch break.

The next time I undertook a reconnaissance mission in the Republic of Banberg – my *Sentinel* round – I spared Mr E's house as I strafed Hadley Road with low-quality newspapers and returned later to deliver his copy in person. It took him quite a long time to come to the door, leaving me standing in the shade of the holly hedges, counting spiders. Eventually the door creaked open. I flashed the rolled-up edition, sword-style.

'Your *Sentinel*, Sir.'

'Ah, it's you. And entering by the front entrance today I see.'

Soon I was drinking tea again, this time sat on the world's least comfortable sofa in a front room crammed with books and LPs.

'So,' said Mr E, 'have you managed to survive this week without being catapulted over a wall?'

'I did actually climb over the wall,' I said. This seemed an important, face-saving distinction.

'And school is good, yes?'

'We've been learning about Hitler,' I said.

He frowned, his gaze shifting from me towards a point where the corners of the walls met the ceiling. I blush thinking about this now. An elderly German might not want to talk about this subject (and not only a denizen of Little Paraguay). He might have been Jewish for all I knew.

'You don't want to worry yourself about him,' he said. 'How is your mathematics? I expect by the time you are my age you will have plotted our course to Neptune.'

'I don't like maths,' I said. 'It's boring. I only like history. The thing about history is that we don't see it.'

'You don't see mathematics either. You think it, like a foreign language.'

'But you saw history. Can I ask you something?'

He sat up very straight in his chair and crossed his legs tightly before nodding. My account of Mr Priskin refuting that Bolsheviks in Munich explained Hitler might have been hard to follow. Mr E seemed to glaze over and look through me to the holly hedges in the garden.

'I suppose mine is only an opinion,' he said.

'But you said you remembered it.'

'When we heard the news of what went on down there, we were scared, yes, and we had all these unfortunates coming from Russia with their stories, and in Berlin, I was in Berlin then, I saw them, smashing shops and shooting innocent people. But these were strange times, you must understand that.'

Strange was good. I did not want to live in ordinary times.

'Mr Priskin says that Hitler was a mountebank. You know, a gangster and a blackmailer and a tool of big business.'

'It's easy to say that now, I suppose. It was easy to say so at the time. Yes, he looks like a waiter, they said, and yes he shouts off all the time and likes to strut. He plays with the black keys only, they said. The strange times, you must keep coming back to the strangeness of the times. The times allowed a Hitler.'

This was getting ahead of the syllabus. We were only on failure of the Beer Hall Putsch and sentenced to Landsberg Prison to write *Mein Kampf*. I knew that I could store up this information and later use it to keep Mr Priskin talking only to me. I asked Mr E if I could make some notes and took out my navy-blue history exercise book and started to copy what he told me on the back inside cover.

He told me about the defeat that no one believed, and how the soldiers had wanted to push on, knowing that if the politicians at home hadn't knifed them in the back they could still have won. He told me about how they came home and found that the war was still going on in the streets but this time it was the Bolshies who had already ruined Russia coming at them. The treaty was unjust and vengeful, made the people poor and weak and scattered fellow Germans who were persecuted by Poles, the French and communists. Everyone started behaving in a loose, weird way in Berlin. People were allowed to do anything they liked to each other. It was disgusting. Ugly music and ugly painting were all the rage. Then the French invaded and the money died and anyone who was anyone lost all they had or was ripped off by moneylenders and people who owned department stores, and at this time no one was listening to Hitler, just a few who could see where it was going to end. Then it calmed down for a bit. Maybe people would have got used to it, to the republic, to the republic being a part of America, or like America, to Berlin being like Chicago. But then came The Crash and the money died again. Politics stopped, became more corrupt, the Bolshies started the fighting again and then there was only Hitler.

'The voice,' said Mr E. 'That's what you have to remember. Hitler's voice. It's hard when you are not German. When you don't understand German. But to Germans then, that voice could carry you away. That's what you need to remember. They got carried away.'

'Where can I hear this voice?' I said.

'You don't want to hear it. It makes no sense now, believe me. It's not worth hearing. It's better to listen to Beethoven. Would you like to hear some Beethoven?'

I left that time with a new list of things to look up in the library. From the column of events described to me by Mr E I created a web of outward-striking lines that ended in question marks: *Death of Money, Loose Behaviour, The Voice, Carried Away*. These titles reminded me of a track listing on an LP, maybe the sort of LP that Mr Priskin and Miss Slingsby would listen to. I'd read in *Record Mirror* that the first side of *Unknown Pleasures* by Joy Division chronicled the rise of the Nazis (*Disorder* to *New Dawn Fades*). Maybe Mr Priskin parked his 2CV in the grounds of the old mental hospital and they got off with each other to *New Dawn Fades*. Maybe that was what could happen to me if I had all the answers.

I intensified my efforts to find out the answers. The Upper Reading Room of the Banberg Public Library became my after-school club. I would take down a big pile of books and pore over them while around me men were engrossed in scientific journals and car manuals. I had at last entered the silent, serious, masculine world.

Purnell's History of the Twentieth Century was one of my favourites, because there were maps and black and white photographs from old newspapers.

From this I learned that Kurt Eisner, the leader of the Munich Soviet, had a massive beard and that Churchill described Lenin as 'a monster crawling from a pyramid of skulls'. In a book on the painting of Otto Dix that was full of very ugly, disjointed images I found a photograph of a war-wounded soldier. A gunshot had totally destroyed his lower jaw. The book said that such people were made to wear masks. When I couldn't get his face out of my mind I tried to imagine what it would be like to lose my own and wear a mask, and I thought of him wandering the streets of Spartakist Berlin looking for someone he would never find.

Mainly, though, here in the library, as September started to drift into a darker October and rain slicked the windows and sycamore leaves flittered through the low skies over Banberg I would read about Hitler. I felt sorry for Hitler, the young Hitler. He was bullied by his father and unpopular and no one at school thought very much of him. I was fascinated by accounts of his fraught, bohemian existence in Vienna. He'd been an outsider, peering-in through restaurant windows, friendless and unappreciated, dreaming of art and opera and war. Even then I could see how this might happen to a person.

It would be misleading though, to suggest that at this time my thoughts were entirely focused on the early career of Adolf Hitler. On Saturday afternoons I would play *Asteroids* in the clubhouse of the breakaway republic's only golf course. I liked the way the little white chunks fragmented into smaller, drifting pieces, then burst into square dots before they vanished. I'd make a Coke last for hours and eavesdrop on the talk in the bar. Once I overheard a man insist that the way to deal with the Ethiopian famine was not Freddie Mercury prancing like a tart on holiday. When we were running the place they weren't starving, were they? Send a taskforce. Send in the Paras. Turn it back into Abyssinia, and turn Zimbabwe back into Rhodesia while we're at it.

At school, I would forge sick notes so I could sit out games and read in the refectory. Without really noticing it I'd grown-out of fantasy epics about the struggles between good and evil gnome kingdoms and had started to read only novels from the early Twentieth Century: *Under Western Eyes*, *A Farewell to Arms*, *All Quiet on the Western Front*. At this time I also tried to get in with Ludovic Kirk, who seemed to have a similar bent for History but was in another form (Victory Over Kirk Day would come during O-Level mocks where, hitting a year high of ninety-seven out of a hundred I beat his multi-choice score by three). This didn't work either. He was at least as shy and socially rubbish as me but was in his own way as arrogant as Mellis and Woods. Another catastrophic defeat came when I tried to get a part in the school production of *Cabaret*. Graham Longrigg, the sixth form's star actor/director-type said that I was a little short to be a stormtrooper. So I remained on my own and sat on the lower deck of the bus (the

Kindertransport 151, as it was known in Banberg), not talking to the girls from the grammar school in their boots and their scarves and their glasses. In my navy blue exercise book, on the edges of the Nazi History Web, I gave them names like Nikki, Amanda and Claire and wrote down snippets of their conversations. I imagined that somehow I could be transferred to their school for the sake of my general education and wrote about the situations I would find myself in, one girl at a time.

And I delivered *The Sentinel*. I was the herald, the conduit, the drummer boy bringing the news to the people of the breakaway republic: outrage at gypsy invasion; outrage at plans to turn the old asylum into council houses; [Banberg] man accused of war crimes. But one mission a week delineating the borders of Banberg wasn't enough. Soon I was delaying my returns home with a long walk in the after-school dusk. I would skirt the Common until I reached the perimeter fence of the cancer hospital and then head back into the interior, skulking along avenues of mock-Tudor detached houses with their leylandii fortifications, the collar of my black school mac turned up. I would pretend it was 1909 and this was Vienna and I was arriving from some obscure provincial backwater, seeking out those who would recognize my talents and believe in me. This was my routine, my dreamtime until I emerged from the underpass into the precinct one afternoon and Morrison stepped out in front of me. He hadn't done as well in the English Lit test as he'd expected. I was later forced to admit that I'd slipped in the mud. I'd rolled down a bank and banged my face on a tree stump. And they all believed me. They did. It was the sort of thing that always happened to me. They all believed this, apart from Mr E.

'I am still trying to work out how this is possible,' said Mr E, sitting up straight in his chair, his twiglike fingers steepled on his knee. I was trying not to answer by stuffing myself with the macaroons that he'd laid out on the occasional table. It had already grown dark outside and he'd turned down the volume on his rickety three hundred year old stereo. This made it harder to pretend that *The Magic Flute* was so good that I couldn't think about anything else.

'You tripped sideways and rolled down a slope that was a perfect plane, and so steep that you generated such velocity, and then struck a trunk that was perfectly flat and exactly square-on and managed to bruise both sides of the face without the breaking of the nose?'

'Can we listen to *Ride of the Valkyries* again?' I said.

He got up and sauntered over to his bookshelf, retrieving a jotter pad that he flicked my way.

'You are going to have to draw me a diagram so I can analyse this physical feat. We must recreate these conditions. Maybe we can execute this manoeuvre again. Maybe this is something for the circus.'

'I can't draw,' I said. A sweat was beginning to boil behind my ears.

'Be honest,' he said. 'The sorcery is involved here, that once upon a time caused your bag to levitate over my wall, yes?'

I put my head in my hands, leaning forwards so that all I could see were the crumbs on the doily.

'Have you told anyone about this?' he said.

'I can't,' I muttered. 'They won't do anything.'

'Then you must do something for yourself. It's the law for the weak. It will keep recurring until you confront it openly.'

When I looked up this time the smile had contracted and his face was a spiderweb of deep-grooved lines, an expression that seemed designed to shame me into action. Until then I'd thought wearing a mask might be the answer.

'I'm going to kill him,' I said.

He blinked and tipped his head sideways as if suddenly hit by something firm and sharp.

'No, no, no,' he said, 'that is not the way, believe me. If I have learned one thing in my life it is that this is not the way.'

'Is that what you learned from Hitler?' I'd been waiting for this inroad and took the opportunity to slip the navy-blue exercise book from my schoolbag.

'Put that away. Let's not have any talk of Herr Hitler today.'

'Is that because you hated Hitler? When you were there?'

'Listen, you need to learn some cunning here, or you will keep taking the beatings.'

'Mr Priskin said yesterday that Hitler only came to power because the rich and the army bought him.'

'Your Priskin is an idiot. Hitler couldn't be bought. He could only be rented. He was clever. This is what I am saying now. He bided his time. He used others against themselves. He waited until the time was right. He got himself in the right position so he held the strong cards. And do not ever forget that it was terrible then, after the Crash. Everyone poor and starving, the politicians squabbling bourgeois, the President decrepit, the Reds and their hirelings circling like hyenas, tearing off a piece then a piece, stripping the carcass, stealing and marching and firing off their pistols on the trains. If it had been allowed to go on there would only have been dust. That's why we had Hitler and Hitler got things done. I am telling you that at least he got things done. But, no more of this today ...'

Until this point I'd not heard Mr E speak so fast and with such passion. He was speaking faster than I could write it all down in my navy-blue book. I was working backwards in that book now. The front was for Mr Priskin and the end pages were for Mr E. I was looking forward to the time when the two texts met in the middle and I would have to ask for another book.

During the next History class I wondered for a time whether I would achieve even the minor miracle of filling-in the navy-blue exercise book. When Mr Priskin handed back the books – we had all written essays the previous week on the foreign policy of the Weimer Republic, a topic that despite allowing me to display my analytical expertise did not show off my insider knowledge and original research – he paced around the room, flicking the books at the Jazz Funkateers with a comment here and a comment there. He paused alongside Morrison at the back of the class. In the same tone of voice that he used for his asides he commended The National Enemy for the astuteness and erudition of his argument. I was still blushing when, anticipating the return of my own work, Priskin simply told me to see him afterwards. 'Eeyew,' said the Jazz Funkateers.

All through the class my navy-blue book lay on Priskin's desk. We were discussing Hitler's coming to power in 1933. Mr Priskin followed rigidly, what I'd learned from Mr E, was a straightforward Bolshevik interpretation. Hitler was the pawn of big business and reactionary landowners, industrialists and generals, and the whole thing was no more than a predictable conservative stitch-up that had terrible repercussions for the world. Wouldn't it be better if we had not been shown what we know about ourselves now just because conservatives gave power to Hitler?

I was forced to contradict him, insisting that Hitler couldn't be bought. He could only be rented. He was clever. And it was terrible anyway. If the terrible conditions had been allowed to go on there would have been only dust. Hitler got things done. If Hitler were a mere puppet and a mental case, nothing would have got done.

'Isn't it true, Sir, surely, that nothing would have been done if the people didn't *like* Hitler? Hitler turned it around. He made people like him.'

'Eeyew,' said the Jazz Funkateers.

The hands of the clock ticked up to noon. The bell went. Without looking at me, staring at the far-distance beyond the back row Mr Priskin repeated that I needed to see him after class before he set next week's essay. The big question: *Explain how Hitler became chancellor of Germany in 1933.*

When sundry Jazz Funkateers, The Dismissives and Morrison's retinue of Red Front thugs had filtered out of the classroom, I approached Mr Priskin. He was leaning on the desk, the fingers of one hand pressing down on my navy-blue book. A jittery excitement coursed through me, anticipating praise for the majesty and detail of my essay, my domination of the sources and intellectual position well in advance of the syllabus. But Mr Priskin didn't say anything, nor ask me to take a seat. He made me wait as he polished his circular spectacles with the tip of his red tie.

'So,' he said, at last as he picked up my book and flapped it against his hip. 'Going into business, I see. Establishing your own private enterprise zone. This is not Taiwan. There are no tax breaks here for homework factories.'

I was cooking beneath my black blazer and grey V-necked jumper, so much so that I feared I was already starting to smell, not of sweat but guilt and weakness.

Streaks of light caught on the surface of Priskin's glasses. I could not see his eyes clearly enough to read him. For a second I realized that I must tell him about Morrison, tell him that I had no choice, that each time I could either capitulate or would have to kill Peter Morrison.

'Are you doing it for money?' he said. This sent a surge of resentful anger through me. I didn't need money. I delivered *The Sentinel*.

'No,' I said. 'I'm not doing anything.'

'You sure? You need to tell me if you are.'

'I'm not. For God's sake.'

'Well, someone is. It's not beyond the realms of possibility that it's you.'

It crossed my mind that he was more likely to fall victim to a big lie than a small one.

'It's probably Kirk in 4B,' I said. 'He's weak. Can I go now?'

'Look, there is something else I need to talk to you about.' He raised the navy-blue book, took it in both hands and swiftly thumbed through the pages. 'Do you want to tell me anything about this?'

He turned to the back of the book and held up the Nazi History Web. Standing out in slightly stronger pen-strokes was one particular cluster of connections.

LOST —» MONEYLENDERS —» DEPARTMENT STORE OWNERS —» "HOOKED-NOSED MARXIST SCUM" —» DUST ...

The last word spawned a line of dashes that led to the bottom of the facing page and a box drawn in red biro. The box contained a short account of undressing a girl called Nikki in a Paris hotel room that I'd composed in great haste on the *Kindertransport 151* one afternoon while hailstones hammered the roof of the bus. Oh God, he'd read about Nikki. My shirt collar was becoming a noose. I desperately wanted to snatch the book and run all the way home and up the stairs to my room and shut the door and hide under the covers.

'I don't want to cast aspersions here,' said Mr Priskin. 'But there's some stuff here that could be misunderstood. I know you, and I know that this isn't you.'

Well, of course it wasn't me. The boy in the story was undressing a girl in a Paris hotel room.

'You need to be careful,' he said. 'I know you're keen, and I'm all for that. But these people spoke a seductive, emotive language. Don't repeat it. I'm relieved to see that some of these things have quote marks around them. Just keep it out of my book.'

'Your book?'

He folded the navy-blue exercise book shut and handed it back to me.

'I want to see no more of this.'

'Yes, Sir. Can I go now, Sir?'

'Of course.' He turned his back on me and in one seamless movement picked up a board rubber from the desk and started to wipe off the key points about 1933 from the blackboard. I'd just reached the door when he called me back.

'By the way, what happened to your face?'

'Fell out of a tree, Sir. Sir, are you Hungarian?'

'My father was. He came here in 1956. Why?'

'No reason. Bye.'

I knew then that I was going to have to keep a secret notebook and conceal my ideas from Commissar Priskin, the reincarnation of Béla Kun, orchestrator of Red Terror. In my blood I sensed that the writing of the 1933 essay would be the turning point of the war.

On the Friday before Essay Deadline Day (E-D Day) I paid what would turn out to be my last visit to Mr E. I arrived straight from school. I left three hours later. Standing in the dark on Hadley Road then, my back to the holly hedge the spiders had deserted with the onset of the November frosts, I felt my skull buzz with secret knowledge. This time I hadn't needed to coax Mr E. I'd simply reported what Priskin had said about 1933 and he was off. He stalked around the front room, waving his arms and at some points seemed about to burst into tears. When he was spent he sat morosely brooding while I sketched in my new black notebook what was almost a complete essay plan. In Hadley Road that night I had a Pasewalk-style revelation that I was made here, at this time, at this moment only to win this argument and crush those who would undermine me.

I walked to the phone box on Banberg High Street, called home and told my mother that I'd been invited to have dinner with Ludovic Kirk and his family. We we're going to talk about history, I said, and, no, we wouldn't be watching ITV. She seemed relieved that I was actually out and about, not hiding in my room with my maps. I then began to pace the streets of the breakaway republic.

It was like it was now 1926 and I'd arrived for the first time in Berlin, city of M and Sally Bowles, and, according to various books I'd skimmed in the library, city of nets where nothing is caught. I turned the black fin of my collar up and tightened the belt of my trench coat. Opposite the *Cheers* bar I watched angular phantoms swilling beer in the red glow cast by the neon signage. Outside an off-licence on Reigate Road men talked a language I could not understand while inside its strip-lit interior girls younger than me were openly buying vodka and cigarettes. At the end of the road, where 'slappers corner' was aerosoled onto the brick wall I was jeered at by a group of particularly apelike Funkateers. One of them threw something, an apple it turned out. I let it bounce off my shoulder as I kept on walking, striding, full of fire and crackling with electricity along Endersby Lane. Here there were houses behind trees in which only the faintest of lights glimmered and no one knew each other or had conversed with each other on any level for as long as anyone could remember. I would smash all this up. I would galvanize and bring destiny. I would carry them away on dreams to the end of dreaming.

I crossed the Common at a slant until I reached the slip road, the first time I remember feeling unafraid of surrounding trees at night. Soon I'd reached the entrance of the mental hospital. The iron gates had long gone. A letter published by *The Sentinel* and written in colourfully intemperate language had complained that gypsies were being allowed to strip the old asylum of its metal. I walked into the carpark in front of the main building. When the weather was warm this carpark had a reputation as something of a lovers' lane. In the summer Jazz Funkateers would park their Capris and Escorts here. They would listen to electric jazz-funk on dashboard cassette players and lower the seats so they could do whatever their Claires and Nikkis allowed them to do. Tonight, though, there were no cars, only thistles and rippling grasses. I didn't trip on the steps that led up to the main entrance. The chipboard that covered the doors had been kicked-in already. For a moment I felt that trepidation I experienced in front of the black house on Upton Lane. Trepidation was for the weak. I crossed the threshold and entered the damp darkness of the interior.

A few years later I was in *Cheers* and a boiler fitter from Slutsk called Dean told me a story about the old mental hospital in its heyday. He said that one time he and his mates had driven up to the carpark to smoke some well-pukka weed. It was a hot night. The place was rammed. The cars were lined up in rows, their suspensions bobbed up and down to the music of Freeez and Level 42. Slap-basslines competed with each other beneath the moon and the building. All of Banberg's Jazz Funkateers must have been there, lolling in the sweat of that night. Dean swore to me that the weed had nothing to do with it, nor the Budweiser or the sniff, but at some point, up in the asylum's turret, the highest point of a building that had been derelict for twenty years or so, a light flashed on. A smudged figure loomed in a window and even from a distance you could see that the head was unnaturally square.

Now, the mental hospital always had a certain reputation. That story you've all heard of the car that breaks down on a lonely road, an escaped maniac on the loose and the girlfriend hearing a thump on the roof of the car that turns out to be said-maniac banging the boyfriend's severed head: that first occurred here, in Banberg-Little Paraguay, on the road that leads up to the mental hospital. Everyone knew this true story, so when that light came on in that high tower, all the cars stopped quivering. Mass panic erupted. According to Dean, naked men clambered out of the backs of their cars and ran round to the front, gunned their fuel-injected engines and hared off. There was a veritable traffic jam at the exit. Horns blared.

Bumpers sparked along the wings of Beetles and Princesses. Girls called Nikki and Claire screamed. The songs of Freeez and Level 42 would save no one that night. And all the while someone, something was staring out from the turret window.

It wasn't me.

I found myself in the asylum's black entrance hall. Even though I'd assumed that all the electrics had been disconnected I was conscious of the public information film *Building Sites Bite* we'd watched in primary school and the section in which a boy grabs a hanging cable in a condemned house and gets a fatal shock. I didn't touch anything that dangled or swayed as I made my way to the turret. But I can't say that I was unaware of the stories as I explored the old building in the dark, making my way up through vast wards and gaping stairwells, its offices and examination rooms lined with cubicles where anything could lurk. In these chambers and hallways I felt the ghosts of the mad lift behind me in a swarm of whispers. In those days the notoriety of the place spread well beyond the borders of the breakaway republic. Throughout South London [Banberg] meant the mental hospital, which in turn was shorthand for any psychological illness or condition: for spastication, for congenital imbecility, for slow-wittedness, shit-for-brains and moronism. [Banberg]: You'll end up in [Banberg]. Urrrrrrrrrrrrrrrrrrrrrr, [Banberg]. [Banberg]: a catch-all word for flids, mongoloids, Special Olympians, benders, quasis, joeys and all the other cranks, eccentrics and dangerous fantasists that hid-out and lay-low in the breakaway republic. It was not a place you wanted to end up. I knew this, but had made it here. At aged fifteen and on the brink of my greatest achievement I'd found my way into the turret room.

I ascended an almost vertical staircase and emerged into a circular space with a bench running around its circumference and four oblong windows. Wary of the permanently open hatch I paced around the room, pausing in front of each window frame, their glass long-since kicked out. On one side I could see the charcoal-grey expanse of the carpark that merged into the black flatland of the Common and beyond it the grid of the breakaway republic. It was a white and orange network where the glowing boxes of service stations and pubs pulsed along the artery of the High Street. Beyond it the blur of the Old Surrey hinterland rose up like a thundercloud. On the other side the promised land of London stretched ahead of me, a constellation of lights. I knew then that this was where I was going. First I would deal with Banberg, show them, show *him*, march on Banberg, then take Slutsk and march on to London. I would annex the London Protectorate. Everyone would know. Everyone would see, see that I was right, that I had the voice and saw into the future as well as the past. The past and future seemed to stand up before me. A cloak of shivers wrapped itself around my torso and I realized how cold I was now that I'd stopped moving. I stood there staring at the lights of the London Protectorate and with my hand on the black notebook I'd secreted in my trench coat pocket I mentally revisited what Mr E had told me. In my head I planned the 1933 essay that would show the world: Adolf Hitler as the sword unsheathed in the war against dust.

The history class after E-D Day was the first for nearly three terms that I could sit through without sensing Morrison's stare burning into the back of my head. When Mr Priskin distributed the exercise books to the Jazz Funkateers, as previously he withheld my work and told me to see him after class. 'Eeyew,' said the Jazz Funkateers.

This was the last time they said this though. All through the class, as Mr Priskin explained the making of Hitler's dictatorship from the Reichstag Fire to The Night of the Long Knives, I kept my mouth shut. As a result the class stalled on the crucial issue of whether Ernst Röhm, ex-leader of the Munich *Freikorps* and the man responsible for introducing homosexuality to Bolivia had had his right ear pierced or not. After the bell I stayed in my seat and waited while Mellis and Woods occupied Mr Priskin in some earnest discussion. When they'd finally finished, Mr Priskin waved me over.

He forced a smiley face as he appeared to wipe something from his thigh with my navy-blue exercise book.

'How are you today?' he said.

'Fine, thank you.'

'Is that all you've got to say?'

'Yes, Sir.'

'Is that all you've got to say about this?' He held up the book by a corner and let it flop over. Wincing, he cocked his head sideways. This close up I could see that he'd had his hair cut and parted to look like Gary Numan's on the cover of the *Berserker* LP except it wasn't dyed an iceman blue.

'You have surpassed yourself this time,' he said, 'really you have. This … now this.' He let the book fall open to the back where the concluding paragraphs of my 1933 essay nudged the crossed-out remains of the Nazi History Web. 'This is the best essay I've ever seen from a fourth former. Seriously, if it didn't have your style all over it I'd assumed you'd copied it from a book.'

'I didn't copy it, Sir.'

'I'd be impressed if this were a sixth-former's work. You really have put in a lot of thought here.'

'Thank you, Sir.'

He handed me back the book. I'd received a grade of A+++ ✓✓✓

I felt nothing.

Either that or I need to remember nothing of what I felt.

'What impresses me most is that you've already grasped that it's not about answering the question, but addressing as well all the ways the question has been answered. Quite, quite brilliant. Made me think in a few places, too.'

'I've been spending a lot of time in the library, Sir.'

'I can see that. We may well have a bona fide historian in our midst.'

'Can I go now?'

'Sit down, there's something else. You know there's something else, don't you?'

'No, Sir.'

'You do know that the powers that be have closed the homework factory.'

'What homework factory, Sir?'

'You know that Peter Morrison has been expelled from school?'

Ever since Tuesday, the day after E-D Day, when Morrison was hauled out of registration by the deputy head the rumours had circulated. He'd pissed in a Coke can and given it to the kid in 3C with the wet-look perm and the terrible speech impediment. They'd found a bloody flick-knife, a stash of porn mags from Denmark and a cannabis plant growing in his locker. He'd been caught tampering with the brakes on Mr Jagger's Robin Reliant. Maybe all these things were true as well, but on Monday morning I'd feigned as much reluctance as possible when I handed over Version 1 of my 1933 essay ('The Secret Protocols') in the toilets by the science lab. A strange coldness and stillness came over me and stayed all morning and afternoon as I thought about Morrison copying out word for word all the phrases that Mr E had used on the night I made it to the turret, and then handing in those words to the Orchestrator of Red Terror.

'And you don't have anything to say?' said Mr Priskin.

'Why should I, Sir?'

'He'd written some quite nasty stuff ...'

I shrugged.

'... and he swore blue to the headmaster that *you* wrote it.'

'What did you say about that, Sir?'

He grimaced as he took off his glasses and hid them behind his back.

'I said that I knew that it couldn't be you, that you wouldn't be capable of such hateful language. Look, I know he had it coming.'

'He did, Sir.'

'Sometimes the rules can't help. Just don't tell anyone that I said that.'

'I won't, Sir.'

'And, I'm not going to ask, but whoever's been feeding you those ideas, those words, have a think about who they really are.'

'I don't know who he is.'

'You should.'

'He's someone from history.'

'Let me tell you something about history,' said Mr Priskin. 'No one knows anything. There is no truth. People in the past found their times as confusing as we do our own. Too much is lost minute by minute, day-by-day. There's too much to know. There are only questions and versions. Just make sure you always choose the human version, OK? And let's just put this behind us both, Foxton.'

I knew then that I would never make a bona fide historian.

Shortly after this someone wrote anonymously to the Simon Wiesenthal at *The Sentinel.* A series of articles appeared, alleging that a Mr Erich Eisenmenger of 18 Hadley Road, [Banberg] was in fact a Gerd Rügen whose name appeared on wanted lists held by the governments of Israel, the Soviet Union and the Federal Republic of Germany. Born in 1901, in Berlin, Rügen became well known in German nationalist circles and *Freikorps* groups after the end of World War I. During the 1919 Spartakist Uprising he participated in a notorious and bloody incident. The headquarters of a left-wing newspaper was set-alight while striking printers were still trapped inside it. He joined the Nazi Party in 1926 and became a close associate of Josef Goebbels, so said *The Sentinel.* In the late thirties, now using the assumed name Jeremy Trask he ran a pro-fascist public relations bureau on the south coast of England until a scandal involving a local girl caused him to flee shortly before the invasion of Poland. During the war, it's alleged, he was part of a brutal *Einsatzgruppe*, an SS death squad that razed villages and murdered Jews in the Ukraine and the Romanian-occupied Transnistria region. He was assumed killed during the final months of the war but there were no eyewitnesses. Rumours had stirred in the sixties that he may have escaped and entered Britain via Paraguay and Canada under a false identity.

I don't know if any of this is true. I kept away from Hadley Road. I even gave up my *Sentinel* round so I didn't have to go there. Once I passed it, months after the articles in the paper had stopped. The holly hedges made it impossible to see inside. A prominent for-sale sign was strapped to the gatepost. All I do know is that years later, when I looked for evidence of the teaching career and publications record of an Erich Eisenmenger, professor of mathematics from Allenstein, East Prussia no such man seemed to have existed. When I was fifteen my only friend had been the ghost of a ghost.

All this was recorded in the black notebooks that I continued to keep. After Morrison was expelled things improved at school. I became less *eeyew* and most of the Jazz Funkateers left before sixth form. I never did quite make friends with Mellis, Woods and Kirk, though they did seem to tolerate me a little more during our last two years. Mr Priskin remained my history teacher. We never spoke again of Morrison or The Secret Protocols. I don't know how long he stayed in Banberg after my escape. He might still be teaching there for all I know, but I doubt it. All I know is that I got away. And I got away because I was good at Nazi Germany. I'd like to be able to look back at school and say that there were enduring friendships and witty banter and I played cricket and football and was captain of the debating society and experienced the springtime of love with girls called Nikki and Claire in the carpark of the abandoned mental hospital while low quality jazz-funk played on dashboard cassette players, but I didn't. I was just good at Nazi Germany. I hung out with ghosts and was good at Nazi Germany.

The self-proclaimed breakaway Republic of Banberg is no more. It faded into the books, like Allenstein, like the Holy Roman Empire and Prussia, the Weimar Republic and the Third Reich. It disintegrated and reordered itself soon after I left. I don't remember enough. I'm just relieved that it fell, that it's no longer inside me. But sometimes, though, sometimes I sense it, feel it back there behind me as I pass those houses behind trees where the lights are low and people only whisper, when a sheen snakes across a conifer hedge on a dead-still afternoon, as I tighten my coat against the chill breeze.

Ashley Stokes was born in Carshalton, Surrey in 1970 and educated at St Anne's College, Oxford and the University of East Anglia. His fiction has appeared in many journals and anthologies. His first novel, *Touching the Starfish* was published by Unthank Books in 2010. He lives in Norwich.

Of the stories here, *Island Gardens* was originally published in *Beat the Dust*; *Storming the Bastille* appeared in *London Magazine*; *A Short Story about a Short Film* appeared in *Unthology*; *Ultima Thule* appeared in *Fwriction Review* ; *Post-Leading Man* appeared in *Bonfire* and *Marmara* in *Staple*.

Much respect and thank you to: Robin Jones, Ian Nettleton, Jenny Swindells, Hazel Compton, Melissa Mann, Danny Goodman, Wayne Burrows, Lander Hawes, Nick Sweeney, Jane Harris, David Rose, Jo Boxall, Tom Collin, Ingrid Perrin, Charlotte Cox, Lorna Mackinnon, Glenn Stokes and Bryan and Daphne Stokes. I'd also like to say a big thank you to Lindsay Clarke (a long-standing debt of gratitude) and to Glenn Ogden for encouraging me to write in the first place.

Touching the Starfish

- Ashley Stokes -

'Crisp, witty and scalpel-sharp, *Touching the Starfish* doesn't miss a
trick in its arch depiction of the orthodoxies and absurdities of Creative
Writing
Programmes and the many varieties of pond-life to be found therein.
It's deadly accurate too on the often hilarious miseries of the writing life.'
Lindsay Clarke

Ashley Stokes's comic masterpiece stars Nathan Flack, a writer
exiled in a backwater and teaching creative writing to a group of high
maintenance cranks and fantasists. When a very literary ghost by the
name of James O'Mailer starts to haunt Flack, he was to ask himself: is
he sinking into a netherworld of delusion, or is he actually O'Mailer's
instrument?

'The work of an anarchic imagination stuffed with incident and
mordantly humorous observations.'
Eastern Daily Press

'… a book for every creative writing lecturer out there. If you ever
wanted to write about your experiences in this area, then don't. It's been
done. And I can't imagine it being done better than *TTS* manages to do.'
Sarah Dobbs

ISBN 978-0-9564223-0-9

Available from www.unthankbooks.com, The Book Depository,
Amazon, Waterstones.com and all good booksellers.